ULSER

Dear Library Reader,

I hope you enjoy this novel where Ted, Ulser & Dublin are all characters.

R/Reeds.

ULSER

Raphael Jonas (RJ) Deeds

atmosphere press

Contents

Chapter 1	3
Chapter 2	23
Chapter 3	43
Chapter 4	52
Chapter 5	62
Chapter 6	78
Chapter 7	92
Chapter 8	97
Chapter 9	108
Chapter 10	116
Chapter 11	124
Chapter 12	136
Chapter 13	142
Chapter 14	154
Chapter 15	167
Chapter 16	171
Chapter 17	184
Chapter 18	190
Chapter 19	203
Chapter 20	208
Chapter 21	220
Chapter 22	225
Chapter 23	241
Chapter 24	249
Chapter 25	262
Penultimate Chapter	267
Final Chapter	294

CHAPTER 1

He was feeling more alive the more he died inside. The figure in the veteran blue Mazda 626 observed the scene dispassionately. The car was warm and comfortable. The fan blew hot air to prevent the windows fogging up. At intervals, the wipers emitted a quiet click. The worn wiper blades scratched the windscreen as they cleared the rain to give a view.

Ulser lay prostrate on the ground, two silhouetted figures looming over him. The ground pools glistened in a shaft of yellow light. The rain beat down incessantly. The rain hopped off the pavements. Water gurgled down the shores in the nearby gutters. A cat scurried for shelter under a car. The noise of the downpour muffled Ulser's cries of pain. The next kick was delivered full into his ribs, shattering one more bone.

One of the men was heavy, sporting a beer belly—he had drunk for Ireland. His cheap brown leather jacket bore all the hallmarks of Sheriff Street haute couture. His heavy "bovver" boots were National Front standard issue. He had employed his footwear for purposes "Doc Martin" never envisaged. His pockmarked face had a nasty sneer. His shaven head entombed the brain of an amoeba

His mate was lean, with a mean, taut face. He wore a woolly fisherman's cap. His leather jacket was of good quality. He barked instructions to his corpulent collaborator.

The car was parked adjacent the alleyway leading to 'Dolphin Motor Repairs'. The Stone Age neon sign was suffering a lingering death. Only 'Do...Mo...Re' remained lit.

"Do Re Me", he sang quietly. "Save a little for me."

He continued to observe the drama with cold detachment.

The small one fell to one knee and put his face close to Ulser's. His gargoylean, overweight accomplice stood directly over, head bowed and hands on knees, catching his breath. Water flowed along forehead then nose to ground. He seemed as if he was listening intently to the instructions provided by his mate to Ulser.

Ulser hadn't moved in some time. The small one stood up and shook his head. He stared at Ulser's limp body. He turned away, staring blankly into space.

He remained static in that position for at least a minute. He shouted something to the wind before swivelling round. Taking two strides forward, he unleashed a further kick at Ulser, catching him square on the temple. Ulser's head shot back. His hands reached up in agony.

Mr. Heavy took it upon himself to take umbrage on behalf of Mr. Small. He joined the onslaught by lashing into Ulser as well, catching him full in the ribs. Ulser coiled his body into the foetal position.

The key turned in the ignition of the ancient Mazda. The gloved hands on the wheel steered the car from the kerb, lights off. The figure in the car scoured the street for movement. He faced the nose of the car directly at the entrance to the yard. He had waited a long time for this moment. He knew there was no room for error.

The figure in the car turned a knob on the dash and headlight beams lit up the alleyway. Three sodden figures looked back at the white glaring headlights, startled and confused. They shielded their eyes, all three with their mouths open.

He noted how white they looked, as if posing for a photograph, as if Christ had appeared. They seemed caught in a moment. The world was still. The driver felt a sense of greatness. He was invincible, sure and ice cool. He was in total control. He had caught them by surprise and the time had come to bring things to finality.

The wheels spun. The engine roared. The car hurtled forward towards the cowering group. They all, to a man, threw themselves to one side. (Ulser more rolled himself than threw!) The car landed inside the yard, hitting the large entrance gate on its way, smashing it to the wall.

The skinny one flung himself over oil barrels and disappeared backwards into the void beyond. The heavy one tripped over a wheel jack—falling to the ground on his back. Ulser had rolled over twice, ending up against a stack of tyres.

The driver yanked the handbrake, spinning the car a full 180, nose now facing the exit. The wheels threw up a spectacular parabolic arch of silver spray which glistened in the light from the garage entrance. The car screeched to a halt beside Ulser and the passenger door shot open.

Ulser didn't need a second invitation. Like a scuttling rat, he scampered along the ground and hauled himself in. He slammed the door without as much as a glance towards his driver. No words were exchanged. The front wheels spun on the oily wet ground and the car made its exit with the engine snarling.

Ulser eventually turned to observe his saviour. Dressed in a baseball cap, the driver's face was covered completely in a rubber face mask of President Nixon. He certainly presented as a strange sight. He wore black leather gloves and was covered from head to toe in black plastic sacks!

"Who the fuck are you! Charlie Haughey?" Ulser's grasp of politics was minimal. He hadn't even managed the right continent.

The figure barely acknowledged his presence. He was eye-balling the rear-view mirror. Ulser glanced at the one on the passenger door. Both saw Mr. Heavy rising to his feet and reach into his jacket. The pair saw the glint of metal at the same time. Mr. Heavy raised the weapon. The driver had already ducked before glass exploded all around.

"Fucking hell", Ulser declared.

Ulser scrutinised the side mirror again. His attackers were pursuing the fleeing car, realising their prey was heading out of sight. Mr. Small produced *his* weapon. A second shot rang out. Ulser heard the ping of a ricochet on the passenger door.

The Mazda spun into the street, coming close to shortening the life of a startled cyclist in the process. The cyclist had been on his way home from the evening shift. He fell to the ground as his bike mounted the footpath. Nixon did a quick mirror check and saw the cyclist was still moving. The man raised a fist. Enough information!

He floored the pedal once more and the car took off, veering left to right for traction.

It roared at speed along the empty cobbled streets at the back of the Guinness brewery. The familiar smell of hops in the malting house filled the air, a sickly, sweet aroma not unlike silage. The driver loved that scent.

In his youth, that fragrance—combined with that of Keefe the Knackers—suffocated half of south Dublin when the west wind blew! Keefe the Knackers' slaughterhouse was based at the top of the Coombe. It was not uncommon to observe the blood of dead animals flowing into the street from under the double doors. Health Inspector, as of then, was a profession unknown.

'There will be blood spilt tonight!' he thought.

He turned the car into the familiar streets around Pimlico. He loved the soft orange radiance of streetlights on wet red-brick houses. It always gave him a warm feeling.

As a kid, the sight of orange streetlights on South Circular Road from the back of his dad's car meant he was nearing home—home from the monthly visit to his uncle's farm in the midlands. He soon would be in his own warm bed and would be playing football in the street with the lads in the morning.

This was the city he loved—civilisation. The same streets were no longer civilized. He himself was now a barbarian. He looked at the battered soul beside him.

"Let me out here—I'll find my way home—you've done your bit", sneered Ulser.

"You're going where I decide, scumbag", the driver whispered in a Northern accent.

"Who the fuck are you? Stop the bleedin' car!" Ulser

reached for the door handle.

President Nixon reached down under the driver's seat. He pulled a lever. The passenger seat shot forward, pinning Ulser to the dashboard. There was a loud crack as his ribs broke with the force. In the earlier commotion, Ulser failed to notice a massive torsion spring behind his seat. This had been released by the lever.

"Reckon you'll be my passenger a little while longer. The good news is I won't be charging you full fare", the driver hissed. "The bad news is your journey is nearly done."

There was no response from the crushed figure. Ulser had passed out with the force of the impact.

He turned the car down the familiar streets of the Coombe, past Massey the butcher's and 100 yards on, Massey's Funeral Parlour. Even on a night like this, the irony wasn't lost on Nixon.

He stopped at the set of lights at the bottom of the Coombe—where it met Clanbrassil Street. He was stuck behind a beat-up red Toyota with "go fast" stripes. "Toyota Corolla" was emblazoned across the back window—for emphasis—so any driver behind was in no doubt. As a young buck, surely he didn't want to advertise the fact he had such a crap babe magnet?

From their left, two "young wans" stepped up to the Corolla and leaned in the passenger window. They wore skirts akin to napkins and boots to their knees. Each girl looked about 17. One had bleach-blonde hair tied behind. The other girl was brunette—her hair Mohican—shaven to the temples and a centre mane along the top of her head. She had a ponytail hanging at the back. In the pouring rain, neither had a coat on—this was obviously to maintain some type of image. Both looked like wet rag dolls. Nonetheless, they seemed to be succeeding in negotiating a lift from the willing young studs.

The lights changed red to green. The racing Le Mans-bound Corolla in front didn't budge. The hanky-wearing long-legged raconteurs continued their conversation through the passenger window. Nixon cursed under his breath and wound down the window...

-o-o-o-o-o-

...On the right-hand side of the road, a weary office worker—obviously the worse for wear with drink—fell out of Fallon's pub. His top shirt button was undone. The knot of his tie approached his navel. The end of the self-same multi-coloured tie touched his knees. The left side of his collar was turned up. The left leg of his trousers was wet, stained with drink. This had occurred earlier when his hand and mouth failed to synchronise during his 11th pint. The jacket clung valiantly to his left shoulder.

The drunkard struggled manfully to make forward progress. He lurched violently from side to side. He raised his right hand in the air to hail a taxi. He looked at his hand quizzically. He did a few confused calculations and concluded that pulling it down with his left hand was a better idea. This made him more confused. He revisited the original plan and raised his left hand this time high in the air.

"Tack-shee", he bawled—to no one in particular.

Cars slowed down as he lurched along the pavement. He stepped onto the road to a screech of brakes. He used the bonnet of the stopped car to support himself. He attempted a few drunken steps forward before coming to a stop in the middle of the road. He raised his hand in the air again.

"Tack-see", he bawled even louder, managing to sound a mite more coherent.

A car mirror hit him as it passed by.

"You shtoopid bollicksh", he roared after the receding red taillights.

He spotted Nixon's car at the lights ...

-o-o-o-o-o-

...Nixon had his head out the window—he was about to roar at the morons in front when the rear door of the car opened. The inebriated one fell into car with relief, slamming the door behind him.

"Terenure", the drunk bawled for the world to hear.

Startled, Nixon pulled his head back in, bumping it hard on the door sill as he did so.

"What the fuck?" he ventured.

"Terenure—you know, the place with the Collishhe...?"

"I know where the fuck Terenure is—the question is, what the hell are you doing in *my* car?" He nearly forgot to apply his Northern accent in the process.

"Payin' for a lift home", his new friend ventured.

"I'm not giving you a lift home—now rev up and fuck off!", he hissed.

"That's no way to get repeat business and keep cushtomers..." the drunk retorted.

He continued "...an' anyways up, if you take a right

here and head up Clanbrassil Street and keep goin', you'll have me home in jig-time ..."

The pick-up lines had worked. The two slappers were getting into the back seat of the Corolla. The Corolla took off at speed, spinning the wheels and leaving a big fat 11 in the road. This would undoubtably impress all other road users as to their manhood.

The traffic lights were now turning amber.

Nixon heard the screech of wheels and saw that the lights were about to change. Before he had time to negotiate terms with his new unwelcome arrival, he slammed the pedal to the metal, cut across oncoming traffic, and charged up Clanbrassil Street.

"You know it makes it shense ..." commented his passenger as he made himself comfortable in the back seat. "Here, I heard a great gjoke in the pub tonight—wanna hear it?"

Ulser groaned as he started to come around. "Where the fuck are we?"

"Aw—that's a great gjoke—the **Where the fuck are we tribe!!!** —busss tha's not the gshoke I was goin' to tell yez."

The drunk let out a great guffaw, as if he had just been told the funniest joke in the world.

"No, there were these 2 women on the tear one night—tonight's the night—now that's another grayshe joke ...", he mumbled.

"I don't want to hear your effing joke", Nixon shouted, trying to remain calm.

"Who the hell is he?" Ulser cried as he vainly tried to lift his head and look back at the new incumbent in the back seat. He was coming to.

"Jayney mac, you're a bit the worshe for wear—like meself", the passenger said with great emphasis, for the first time noticing the other passenger in the front of the car. "Puttin' the head down, I see?...remember though, only brings it all back up", he proffered.

This is surreal, thought Nixon. How the hell did I manage to end up in a situation like this? What am I goin' to do with the plonker in the back? He was beginning to panic.

'I'm not thinking as clearly as I need to', he thought.

Nixon was concerned about travelling along main streets and being seen. What a collection! His friend slumped over the dashboard, he as President Nixon and an inebriated comedian in the back!

Nixon had been meticulous in planning for this night. He was fairly certain that, on a wet night, it was next nigh to impossible to see through the windscreen from the pavement—at least while the car was moving. He couldn't help but be nervous though. If he has to stop at lights, someone might see what he doesn't want them to see. He'd be better on the back streets.

He passed the 5-storey corporation red-brick flats on his left which were illuminated top to bottom in Santa Claus and Christmas lights. Rudolph straddled the roof. Obviously, there had been a getting together of minds among the residents and they had all invested to create this riot of Americana. All 3 travellers were distracted by the Christmas display, taken with the colours.

Nixon focused back on the road but too late! The pedestrian lights were red 15 yards ahead and he was driving too fast. He hit the brakes but not hard enough. He hit the car in front.

"Bollix!!" he grunted. The door of the car in front began to open.

'I can't afford to allow them see me with this gang', he thought.

"Jaysus...what kind of taxi school did you go to?...did you get one of them cowboy licences?" The drunk roared his disapproval from the back.

Nixon horsed the wheel to his right and cut across oncoming traffic, slipping down Malpas Street by Fast Fit Tyres. This wasn't in the script and it was getting worse by the minute. To add to the mix, the drunk had a thought.

"Here, I was going to tell you this joke I heard."

"F off with your joke."

"No...No. You'll like this one. Here, listen for a moment. These two women are having their first night out in months...this is a great one, I'm telling ya...and they get stoned...absolulley stoned, y' know what I mean, loike ..." He was settling into centre stage.

"Pissed like you ..."

"Yeah, yeah...only worsht ..." and he fell back into the seat, cackling.

The street was narrow, cars parked along one side only, leaving room for only one car to pass. He turned left along the convent wall and into Black Pitts. The roads were narrow and quiet. He knew his way around here—like the back of his hand. This was the universe of his childhood, his centre, his fulcrum. This friendly place seemed to be guiding him, minding him, directing him.

He hopped over the speed ramps, popping his passengers in the air each time. With each bump, the head of his front seat passenger rose and fell with a thud.

Ulser cursed each time.

Rudolph, the red-nosed drunk, bellowed from the back:

"Whas de hurry? De yes wan' me te throw up on yer shoulder?"

Nixon passed Donore Avenue School, his alma mater, and then on past what used to be the White Swan Laundry. White Swan was built over the underground River Poddle. It provided a free source of water for the laundry. Now, a mini Industrial Estate had taken its place.

"Anyway's up, the two women are heading home, and one says to the other...'I'm burstin' for a slash' ..."

"I DO NOT NEED THIS", threatened Nixon.

"No, no...listen...this is good."

Ulser managed a smirk despite being pinned to the dash. The drunk was unnerving Nixon.

"The women are beside a cemetery and decide they got to do somethin' abourr it...so, they hop over the wall."

"You're pissin' me!" Nixon warned.

"No—they're DYING for a piss", explained the drunk.

Nixon couldn't work out whether he was deliberately winding him up or not.

"Anyways up, they're in the cemetery and doing the business ..." He took a long pause for dramatic effect. "...so, they're goin' to clean themselves up afterwards. Mary turns around to Marg'ret and says: 'Maarr-gre', Oi've nuttin' to clean meselve wi', wot'll I do?' 'Ah, sur' use yar knickers, Mary'..."

Nixon was becoming agitated for two reasons
- 1, he'd heard the joke before and

- 2, he couldn't think straight as his passenger nattered on.

"...so, Mary cleaned herself with her knickers. 'Christ, Mary, I wore no knickers goin' ou' 'cos I was 'spectin' a bir of action—whor' am I gonna do?' 'Aw, find a wreath an' use the paper card off of i", says Mary. So Marg're' reached around in the dark, found one and did what Mary said. Now this is the good bit ..." and he started to laugh anticipating the climax.

"Good Jaysus", muttered Nixon under his breath, preparing himself for the final onslaught.

"...the two husbands are out in the pub the next night and one turns to the other: 'C'mere, Lar, did ya see what our two owl wans were up to last night?

"I was getting outa the bed this mornin' and threw back the bedclothes. Ther was my wan, bare-arsed, no knickers. We'll have to keep an eye on these two."

"'You think that's bad, Mick—I was looking for a bit of action this mornin'—know whor I mean? —and I was lying against her back...when I feel this THING stickin' into me. I reached down to see what it was. I pulled out a card...yeah, a paper card—stuck between the cheeks of her arse, it was.

"So, I turn on the light to read i'...I'm curious, like, and open it. Do you know what's written on it, Mick...well, I'll tell ya ...

From all the lads at the Fire Brigade, We'll never forget ya!.."

With that, the drunk convulsed into fits of laughter and fell back in the seat, delighted with his wit and repartee.

Ulser laughed out loud and winced when his ribs

hurt. Nixon's face showed no trace of emotion.

-o-o-o-o-o-

Nixon stopped the car at the South Circular Road/Donore Avenue junction. The long familiar red-brick Victorian terraces faced him; their bay windows familiar to him. The Bed & Breakfast sign opposite was lit. The flashing red lights proclaimed: "B&B—Vacancies". He'd never in his life seen it flash "Full".

The owner of the Halal shop on the other corner was taking a breath of fresh air. He stood at the door of the premises. He seemed to be looking in Nixon's direction.

"Change—lights—please!" pleaded Nixon.

Even though he had checked/double-checked many times and he knew you could not see inside cars at night, he couldn't help feeling uneasy. He believed the shop owner could see this merry threesome.

The lights changed—Nixon stalled the car. He looked down at the ignition to restart. There was a loud bang. He looked up, startled. A young man was staring down the bonnet through the windscreen straight at him.

"Happy Christmas", the reveller roared. He and his two companions laughed and continued on their merry way. Nixon's heart missed a beat.

Nixon crossed the junction. 50 yards up he stopped at the lights on Sally's bridge. This was unnerving him. He was sweating. His hands were damp.

There was quiet in the back seat. The passenger babble had spontaneously combusted and was replaced by loud snoring.

Nixon looked vacantly out the window. The canal

stretched forever in the distance. In his childhood, the banks of the canal were allotments, planted with cabbages and fresh vegetables. Those days seemed so long ago—the innocence of a bygone age.

He headed up Clogher Road, homing in on his final destination. Ulser was groaning.

The ramps on Clogher Road were four blobs, with a gap between each pair. This allowed speeding emergency vehicles to pass through without becoming airborne. Nixon cursed as he manoeuvred the car around the speed ramps.

He turned left at the football ground—down towards the gates of Sundrive Park. The park loomed dark and looked forbidding in front of him. It seemed eerie.

Just then, the heavens opened, and rain pummelled the car.

"Perfect!" he whispered. The clamour of the rain on the roof drowned his words. Droplets hopped off the pavement, creating a mist close to the ground.

He drove slowly to the main gate of the park—firmly locked. He did a U turn—so that the passenger door faced the footpath. He brought the car to a halt alongside the railings of the park.

There was no one around. The rain had gotten even heavier. In his mind, he couldn't have planned it better. This will keep everyone indoors. He reached under his driver's seat and pulled out a hammer, chisel, and pliers. He removed the car key. He took the chisel to the ignition slot and hammered it hard. It disintegrated. He rammed the chisel in hard again. He tried turning the ignition with the chisel. It failed.

He hacked at the plastic around the steering column

until he could see the wires. Within seconds, he had levered the wires free. This was the only part of the plan he hadn't been able to test easily. He knew the likely combinations of wires that would start the car. After 3 different attempts, he got the engine to start. He was keen to cover his tracks. He didn't want anyone to know a key was used.

He put all implements back in his pocket. He then took two sets of handcuffs from under the seat.

Ulser continued to groan, his eyes closed. Nixon got out of the car and opened the back door. The rain streamed down the black sacks that were his suit.

"Insurance time", he whispered.

He reached into the jacket of his uninvited, inebriated guest and removed his wallet. He found the familiar pink driver's license immediately.

1. Sloinne/Surname: Traynor.

2. Reamhainm (neacha)/First Name (s): John Michael

3. Data breithe/date of birth: 15-03-1959
Ait bhreithe/place of birth: Ireland/Eire

4.Udaras eisithe/issued by: Dublin
Data eisiuna/issued on: 28-02-1997

5. Uimhir/Number: 25/0089345   *M 9873456*

7. Signature:

8. Buanseoladh/permanent address: 257 Firhouse Road,

Templeogue, Dublin 14

"Bingo!" said Nixon.

He looked at item no. 6. **grianghrai/photograph.** He

studied the limp figure in front of him.

"Christ, you are an ugly git! Only your mother could love ya!"

Nixon reached under the rubbish bags he was wearing. He found his pocket and placed the wallet in. He walked around the car and opened the passenger door.

Ulser's head was resting on the dash, his head facing away from Nixon. Nixon reached to the floor. He snapped the cuffs on Ulser's ankles without getting a reaction. Rivulets had formed where the path met the road and the road was starting to flood.

He opened the back door. He ratcheted back the spring with a lever near the floor. Gradually, the front seat came away from the dashboard. Ulser's head slid down the dash in slow motion as a gap emerged.

Nixon pulled a gun from the pocket in the back of the passenger's seat. He continued to ratchet back the spring. When he was satisfied it was back far enough, he went to the front passenger door. He placed the pistol against Ulser's temple. Ulser wasn't to know it was a fake.

"Put your hands behind your back or I'll blow your fucking head off", he said in a strong Northern accent.

Ulser acquiesced immediately. He placed his filthy black, oily hands at the small of his back. Nixon, using his free hand, clicked the cuffs first on Ulser's left hand. He then ran his hand along the chain, gripped the other side of the cuffs and clicked it shut on Ulser's right hand.

"Right! —out of the car, shithead", Nixon ordered.

Ulser wriggled and groaned, turning to face his tormentor. Nixon caught him by the left shoulder and pulled him into a standing position.

Ulser was drowned immediately with the rain. His

hair matted to his head. He attempted to walk but stumbled as the cuffs on his ankles took effect. Nixon caught him before he fell completely. He could smell Ulser's tobacco breath with his head on his shoulder.

"Shuffle, fuckhead", hissed Nixon.

Nixon guided his prey from the car to the railings.

"Stand there." Ulser wasn't going anywhere with his feet cuffed.

Nixon closed the doors of the car. His "paying" passenger remained in the land of Nod. He walked to the railings and pulled at one of them. It gave way at the bottom immediately. He pulled the next railing to similar effect. Now there was ample room for a person to step through.

Ulser shuffled his way up to the gap. Nixon stood behind Ulser and unleashed a ferocious kick into the small of his back. Ulser went through the gap at speed, falling heavily into the other side on his shoulder in the grass and muck.

Nixon stepped through after him. He stepped straight into a newly formed puddle, which wet his socks. He opened the cuffs on Ulser's ankles with a key and put them in his pocket.

"Up and do as I say—one false move and you're a dead man. Got it?"

Ulser got it alright and nodded vigorously. Nixon pulled Ulser upright.

"Walk towards the hill in front of you—you scream or make noise and I'll kill you", warned Nixon.

"You working for the 'RA or what? I know I'm behind on payments, but I'll sort it out...." whined Ulser.

"Those pussies?...nah, this is the real deal", Nixon

said, upping the ante.

"INLA...you one of those breakaway groups?"

Nixon could feel the panic in Ulser's voice.

"If I told you, I'd have to kill you—just walk." This hit home with Ulser and he shut up immediately.

The rain was so heavy that it was hard to see the lights on Sundrive Road 200 yards away. The pair worked their way slowly through the trees. The ground hissed with rain. They crossed the path to climb the side of a hill. They slipped and slid on its mucky surface. Nixon held the scruff of Ulser's neck to keep him balanced. Eventually they were standing atop, near the soccer pitches.

Nixon had played many times here as a young boy and as a teenager. Memories of 'Sunboy'—who he believed for many years was a Man United talent scout walking the touchlines in search of the new George Best—came flooding back. He could visualize 'Sunboy'— the Park ranger, a small man who sported a shaven head long before it was fashionable, waving to kids in the park on long summer evenings—a tough character with a genuine interest in kids' welfare.

The rain began to ease, and it was possible to see the outline of the Wicklow Mountains—black against grey— over the roofs of the Corporation houses. To Nixon's left was the imposing spire of Mount Argus Church.

How far from God was he now?

The torrent reduced to a light drizzle in seconds. There was an ungodly silence around them. Nixon could hear Ulser's heavy breathing and see each breath on the cold air.

They walked in silence over an area that was being

resurfaced and reseeded. Each step made an imprint on the ground. 2 sets of footprints were inexorably moving towards the River Styx. Nixon kicked Ulser at the back of the knee and he collapsed to the ground.

"Lie on your back and listen to what I have to say", Nixon said quietly.

Ulser was startled to hear a Dublin accent. The voice was familiar, but he couldn't place it. He stared at Nixon, confused and frightened....

CHAPTER 2

Ted Black turned right off Shelbourne Road towards Shelbourne Park. He passed under the old stone railway bridge. He was driving his newly acquired black Audi Quattro—only collected last week, the company car that went with his new job. A touch of class but it befitted his new status! A few neighbours had already commented on his newly acquired motor and he had been pleased about that.

Ted was both nervous and excited at the prospect of his first day as General Manager of Eirtran, a large wholesale and distribution business based in Ringsend.

He crossed the Ringsend Road at the Shelbourne Dog Stadium. He could see the Eirtran sign peeking from behind a concrete wall 100 yards ahead of him. He turned left into the entrance and was stopped by a red and white horizontal barrier.

A tough looking security man emerged from the security hut. He knew he was security because he had a Garda style cap with 'Security' emblazoned all over it. The gate minder had scruffy stubble and looked like he hadn't shaven in the last few days.

"Yeah", he said as peered in the driver's window. His breath smelt of stale beer. Ted tried to hold his as he responded.

"I'm here to meet Tom Hannigan, the supervisor."

"And you are? ..." Bad Breath demanded. He was already starting to annoy Ted.

"My name is Ted Black." He decided against telling him that he was his new boss.

"Hold on a second."

Bad Breath re-entered the hut and Ted could see him on the phone. Bad Breath stared with total disinterest at the ceiling as he spoke. After about a minute, he finished. The barrier lifted and his new friend leaned out the side window of the hut.

"Go up the yard and park at the end wall. The entrance door is to your left. Ask for Tom at the reception desk when you go in." The window then closed.

'Service with a smile!...It will be!' thought Ted.

Ted parked his car and "bipped" it as he walked away. The car park was newly tarmacadammed and the edges were planted with shrubs, breaking the monotony of the large open space.

Ted was 5'9" and always looked slightly tanned. He had a slight frown, but his soft blue eyes took away the sternness. He wore a good quality, dark Italian suit, set off with a well-pressed, blue Yves Saint Lauren shirt and red tie. He had a full head of straight jet-black hair, pushed back from his forehead. At 45, he scrubbed up well.

He entered reception and saw a window facing him. When he approached, a girl appeared like magic at the hatch. She slid the window back.

"You're looking for Tom. Go up the stairs and he's first on the right—he's expecting you", she commanded without introduction.

She wasn't particularly attractive and spoke with a slight Cork accent. The heavy-rimmed glasses did nothing to improve her appearance either, thought Ted.

He climbed the stairs and was hit by the greyness of his surroundings. The walls were painted off-white and the doors grey. Even the carpet was grey, with a blue fleck. Depressing, he thought. He knocked on the door and heard "come in" on the other side.

When he entered, a tall, tough, broad-shouldered man of about 6'4" strolled towards him, with an extended hand out for greeting.

"I'm Tom Hannigan. I take it you're Ted Black? I heard my new master was in the building—from the Bush Telegraph, you understand! I'm glad to meet you", he ventured with a grin. He had a strong Dublin accent and Ted sensed a bit of the rogue about him.

"Obviously word travels fast—I thought the security guy wouldn't know who I was."

"I'd be surprised at this stage if he doesn't know what you had for breakfast, your shoe size, where you live and the number of sugars you take in your tea! These guys size you up fast, believe me. Welcome to the wacky world of Eirtran." To Ted, Tom seemed a bit too forward and a tad too familiar with someone he hardly knew yet.

"I'll show you your office and then introduce you around, if that's ok?" Ted nodded agreement.

The next 2 hours were spent pressing the flesh— firstly with the Administration staff. After that, he stepped onto the large warehouse floor to meet the supervisors and the Craft and General Staff. He was hit immediately by the sheer size of the massive building.

From his vantage point, the scale was staggering. The building was 30 metres high, 600 metres long and 100 metres wide. To Ted's eyes, vast.

There were rows and rows of high-rise racking. Cherry-picking machines were moving in and out of the aisles, carrying pallets of goods on the forks. A large Matrix sign at the end of the building read:

- The last time an accident occurred in the building (*210 days for the record*),
- Goods Inwards gates A, B, D, F, and H are active
- Goods Out gates 1, 2, 3, 5, 6, and 9 are active and
- The racks are currently in "pick" mode.

Down the centre of the building were separate 'lay-down' areas for goods—one set for those picked from the racks and the others for offloaded items from the Goods Inwards gates. The bays were clearly marked on the floor. Cartons, crates, and pallets of materials were being placed by the cherry-pickers in the appropriate floor positions. Further down the warehouse, smaller forklift machines were placing pallets from the Goods Inwards area onto holding bays. The level of activity—and the number of machines—was impressive.

To his right were a series of large doors—"Goods In" and "Goods Out". Each Door was clearly labelled, and trucks were backed into most of them. The roller-shutter doors were pulled down where no activity was taking place. Each bay had a small hut for paperwork and for access to a PC terminal.

There were large numbers of staff, everyone in yellow helmets and dark blue overalls, actively engaged in the whole process. Ted took in what he saw, and for the first time it gave him a feeling of the scale of the job he had taken on.

-o-o-o-o-o-

Ulser drove the cherry-picker down aisle 3 at level 4. The cab was 6 metres off the ground. He stopped at location 3A-4-07 containing a pallet of brown boxes. He needed four. He reached across to pull them into the bin which was sitting on the cherry picker forks. As he lifted the boxes from the rack, he let out a cry of pain.

"Aw, Jaysus . . ! Me bloody back is gone." He stepped back with his hand against the small of his back. He eased himself into the driver's seat and started up the cherry picker. He drove to the lay-down area, stopping beside one of his workmates, Mossie.

"Moss, I'm after doin' my back in—it's bloody killin' me. I'm going to have to get to a doctor. Is Hannigan about? I'm going to have to report this as an accident."

Mossie nodded in the direction of the high platform at the end of the stores. He didn't seem overly concerned about Ulser's plight, turning his back on him and walking away. Ulser was a bit put out. He lifted the safety bar of the cherry picker and stepped gingerly to the floor. Everyone around was engrossed in their work.

"Jem, give us a hand here", Ulser roared to Jim Hughes, the trade union rep. Jem was a heavy-set man with a large beer belly, the result of many years of late night union negotiations in Dwyers pub in Ringsend. It was clear from his demeanour that he was not keen to be seen by Ulser.

"Jem!" Jim knew he had no choice but to respond.

"What's the problem, Ulser?"

"I've done me back in on the picker and need someone to go with me to the supervisor. I need to be brought to the doctor. You know what Tom Hannigan is like when he deals with me. I want you to be there to make sure there's no hassle."

"What were you doin' when you hurt your back?" Jem had reason to be suspicious of anything Ulser ever said.

"I was leaning over to get those bloody boxes in the racks, stretched a bit and pulled me back. They say they teach us how to lift—but where the hell else can I stand on the picker? You have to bloody well reach. The company is at fault for forcing us to reach like that."

Jem knew exactly where Ulser was coming from. Ulser had a claim up his sleeve and wanted to haul the company over the coals on safety grounds. Jem didn't like Ulser—or trust him either, for that matter. But whether Jem liked it or not, Ulser was one of the lads and he would have to represent him if things got tricky...which, he knew from experience, things definitely would.

"First thing I want to do is get the Accident Report Form signed and witnessed. I need someone to come up to Hannigan's office with me."

He beckoned at Jem as he started to hobble along the marked walkway leading to the offices.

-o-o-o-o-o-

Tom Hannigan was in his element—pointing out the activities in the various areas around the building.

28

However, his eyes were drawn to Ulser limping towards the offices with Jem Hughes in tow. His eyes narrowed. Ted noticed that the garrulous Tom Hannigan had dried up suddenly and followed his eyes towards the approaching pair.

"I think I may have to leave you in a second. It looks like my friend Ulser is in one of his moods."

"Ulser—who's Ulser?...and what's the problem?"

"I'm afraid you're going to have an early introduction to one of Eirtran's best known employees today. I hope you brushed up on our IR and Safety procedures before you came. I'll deal with it first and if I can't solve it, I may need some help later on. Look, Mick Fitzmaurice here is our Administration Supervisor. Mick will introduce you around, show you the workings of the place and give you a look at the transport fleet outside in the yard. If you could just excuse me for a while, I'll see you later." Tom Hannigan left abruptly and headed back to the offices.

-o-o-o-o-o-

Tom Hannigan knew that trouble lay ahead. He placed his helmet on the hat rack, unlocked the filing cabinet, and pulled a large paper file from the top drawer without having to look. He was well accustomed to it. He flicked quickly to the opening page of Martin Cullen's personal file. There lay a resume of Ulser's recent track record. He'd had three accidents in the space of the last 7 years.

- Out for a month in one. He suffered whiplash and back injuries in a crash involving an Eirtran truck when he was travelling as a helper. He

29

returned to work on light duties for a further 3 months. Made a claim for damages and won £20,000 on the steps of the Circuit court.

- Out for 3 months for trauma. Witnessed an accident where a mate of his got crushed against a wall where a forklift backed into him. His mate was severely injured but survived. Was on medication for a year to get over shock. Made a claim for damages and won on steps of court—£35,000 this time in the High Court. Lapses in procedure by the company meant it was going to be difficult to defend the case, despite it being clear that the procedures the company laid down were flagrantly ignored by the fork-lift driver. It transpired, after the case had been settled, that the driver had drink taken.

- Finger got caught under a pallet and a bone was broken. Out again for a few weeks on heavy sedation for pain. Again, sued the company and won £12,000.

Tom Hannigan was in his current job a year and knew Ulser's reputation. He had crossed swords with Ulser more than a few times on the issue of overtime, around his general poor work performance and in relation to his timekeeping. He never had to deal with any of his many accidents. However, he knew, judging by the way Ulser had been limping towards the office, that such a time had now arrived! The fact that the shop steward was in tow was not a good sign.

There was a loud knock on the door. Tom closed the file and pushed it into a drawer in his table. He opened the door to be met by Jem and Ulser.

"There's been an accident on the floor with Martin

and I want to report it officially." Jem was brief.

"What happened? We've had a very good record in this depot over the last year and this may bring it to an end. I'd like to discuss what happened. Did anyone see it?" asked Tom.

"Are you fucking saying I'm trying it on?" demanded Ulser.

"Cool it, Martin. There's no need to get aggressive. Let's talk about this in a civilised manner", said Jem.

Jem tried to conceal his annoyance with Ulser—his accident (if that is what it was) would bring an excellent safety record in the stores to an end. Bonuses would be impacted...and all because of this very dubious character.

"Let's just sit down and talk this one over", said Tom, knowing that Jem wasn't pushed on the issue.

In a tense atmosphere, Ulser went over his story. Tom asked a couple of standard questions and wrote a few notes. At the end, Ulser leaned across the table, narrowed his eyes, and focussed menacingly on Tom.

"I don't see you signing the accident report form?" he said quietly.

"Well, you don't seem to have any witnesses to your accident, do you?" Tom replied evenly.

"Nobody from the floor saw it. You say that you've done your back in but over the years, you've been out regularly with back trouble. Our company Occupational Health doctor has looked at you umpteen times and failed to confirm any of the injuries you claim to have sustained. If no-one has seen it on this occasion, it's hard for me not to conclude that this is just a recurrence of an old injury. You possibly did your back in at home...over the week-end...for all I know." Tom knew he was upping the ante, but he wasn't going to make it easy for Ulser.

"Callin' me a fucking liar? I had a bleedin' accident out there. I did me back in working for this company and you say I didn't." Spittle flew from Ulser's mouth and covered Tom's face.

"Look, my fellow brother is claiming that he injured himself out there and, it seems to me, you're only interested in keeping the stats on safety right, regardless of staff welfare? Our union does not buy into that. I want an investigation into what happened." Jem couldn't resist the worker versus management bit—it was shop steward knee-jerk reaction stuff which took over in such situations, despite his dislike of Ulser.

"Well, if no-one on the ground has seen it and no-one is prepared to back up his story, I'm not prepared to sign any accident form. He has a history of back injury and a sick leave record as long as your arm. I think I'm within my rights to question the legitimacy of this accident." Tom was adamant and was sticking to his guns.

"Are you saying you won't investigate what happened down there? I'm going to get our Safety Rep to do an investigation in any case, and I expect him to be listened to."

"I'm not wasting time on an incident that no-one witnessed."

"Are you therefore saying that accidents only happen when someone else is around? That's bloody ridiculous. Are you honestly saying that if someone was seriously injured in the racks and no-one else saw it, Eirtran would say it wasn't an accident? I don't think the Health and Safety Authority would agree with you on that one...." Jem retorted, pithily.

"If he is as gravely injured as he says he is, someone would have had to find him in the racks because he wouldn't have been able to move! In any case, because of Martin's previous record of back injury, because of the fact that today is Monday—the first day after the weekend—and because Martin has a history of 'Mondayitis', I am questioning the validity of his claim." Tom knew he was stepping over the line, but his back was up.

Ulser reached across the table to catch Tom by the lapels but Jem was up just in time to pull him off.

"You're getting mighty close to assault of a supervisor—a disciplinary matter, Martin, I might remind you. I'd cool down if I were you," Tom said quietly, nose to nose with Ulser.

"Don't push me, you big bollix", retorted Ulser.

"This is getting nowhere. Our brother is being discriminated against and I demand we see the manager over this matter. I'm not happy the way this is being handled, and you're going to hear from the union." Jem knew, even in this heated state, that if he was to prevent World War 3, he would have to call a halt.

"If I don't get satisfaction there, I'll be calling a meeting of the lads to see what further steps we'll take", Jem stated.

"Are you trying to step over procedures, Jem? Let's take it a step at a time. I'll talk to the new manager in a few minutes and be back to you in a while."

"Be back in less than an hour or there'll be a backlash", Jem threatened.

'Bloody procedures', thought Tom. 'They would bust your balls. We spend more time dealing with this kind of crap than running the business. It seems, no matter how ridiculous the claim, workers have all the rights to waste our time pursuing it. No responsibilities for them, mind you. No balance in legislation.

'These left leaning, hippy-dippy, liberal, social justice parliamentarians, nearly all of them former teachers, lawyers, or full-time politicians (by definition, total wastes of space) come up with this stuff without ever having run a business.

'How has society let this happen? Who in God's name signed off on legislation, year after year, which has now become a *wasters' charter* and a noose around every manager's neck? These gits can claim whatever they like, no matter how ridiculous, and we as managers are meant to suck it up like good little boys. Can we ever elect a government who has a scintilla of common sense? Workers' rights, me arse.'

-o-o-o-o-o-

Mick Fitzmaurice was explaining to Ted Black how Eirtran business was a mixture of long-distance bulk haulage i.e. for the large electrical retailers, and door-to-door deliveries to customers. Eirtran was the market leader in Ireland in terms of white goods haulage.

He described the *drop body* concept to Ted Black. They stood in a yard full of high-sided trailers. Each trailer was emblazoned in the Eirtran logo—red background with yellow Roman Script lettering.

The drop bodies were effectively trailers on legs. Each 20-foot truck was paired with two drop bodies. A 20-foot truck, he explained, could back into a loading bay each evening, lower the legs at each corner of the drop body and pull away from underneath. The truck could then back up at another bay and pick up a fully loaded drop body.

Prior to drop body introduction, he explained, the company had rigid body trucks. In that instance, trucks could only be loaded when they were at base. With drop bodies, trucks were on the road 8 hours of the day delivering a full load. Before this, trucks were leaving at 11 a.m. after being loaded and running into constant overtime to complete deliveries. Productivity had improved 50% with drop bodies and costs had reduced 60%. It made picking and loading in the warehouse more streamlined.

As they spoke, a small weedy man with white hair—holding a clipboard—approached. He strode forward, as purposefully as his timid frame would allow, towards the pair who were deep in conversation. Val Somerville coughed to get attention.

"Good morning, gentlemen", he said in a voice reminiscent of a union delegate trying to sound officious.

"I understand, sir", Val said looking at Ted, "that you are the new Warehouse Manager. Could I instigate myself as Val Somerville, the Safety Representative for the staff? I feel it is incumberent on me to conform to you that a highly contemptuous—er...contemporaneous—safety situation has arisen in the warehouse which is causing egregiousness amongst the staff on the floor. I am told that an accident has been inferred this morning to the Supervisor. However, on production of the evidence, the supervisor refused to vilify the potent of the aforementioned Accident Form." This litany was delivered without a hint of embarrassment.

Val puffed out his chest in deference to his oratorial finesse. Ted fought valiantly not to laugh. To make things worse, Mick Fitzmaurice winked and smirked.

"Good to meet you, Val", said Ted, holding out his hand. "I'm not clear what's at issue here. As you can imagine, I've just landed and am getting up to speed. You might explain what the problem is—if you wouldn't mind?"

"Well, sir, our fellow brother, a mister Martin Cullen,"... (...even though Val wasn't a union official, he tried to speak as one—always moving in that direction—it was his life's ambition to be one!)..."was operating one of the cherry pickers in the racks. He had reason to reach out to grapz a box from the racks. Whilst lifting it in said manner, he did erstwhile do an injury to his lower pubic muscles."

"I suspect you mean pelvic, Val", Mick intervened, really trying hard to keep a straight face. Ronnie Barker's mispronunciation sketch flashed through Ted's mind. He was finding it increasingly hard to concentrate on what Val was saying. Ted was also intrigued with the clipboard. Val had not yet looked at it.

"This would be an operational (*he really wanted to say ecumenical—as in Father Ted ...*) matter, Val, and I'm sure that Tom Hannigan can sort it out."

"I'm afraid it's way past that", replied Val gravely. "The shop steward and Mr. Cullen met with said aforementioned and were unable to come to an infusion on the matter. This led the shop steward to inquire if I would become immersed—being, as it were, a safety matter—in the hope that I could interlocute before the matter was excalated."

"By escalated you mean? ..." asked Ted.

"By excalated, I mean the lads will come out in support of their colleague...industrial action, I mean", explained Val.

"Perhaps it might be a good idea that you meet Tom to see what could be done?"

-o-o-o-o-o-

Tom Hannigan hadn't yet got his boss's mobile phone number. He wanted to find Ted Black before someone else did. After asking a few of the lads on the floor, he headed for the yard. He could see Ted Black with Mick. Val had already beaten him to it and was in a huddle in the distance with the other two.

"Fuck—how did that git get ahead of me?" he murmured under his breath. The three heads turned to observe Tom's approach.

"Ted, could I have a word?" Tom asked.

Val looked at Tom with a level of annoyance and bade farewell. He brushed past Tom, heading for the main building.

"Is it to do with this accident involving Martin Cullen? Yer man Val has been going on about it and said something about industrial action?" Ted was all ears.

"Yeah—was trying to find you but I hadn't your mobile number. This is the lad, Ulser, I told you about. He's a slippery operator who claims to have had an accident this morning. Nobody saw it...and with his record, I was slow to sign the accident report form. Cullen claimed I was discriminating against him and demanded to see the manager on the matter. The shop steward said he would be calling a meeting of the lads on the floor if he doesn't meet you in the next hour. Sorry for dropping you in it on your first day...but can't be helped." Ted reckoned it certainly could have been helped and couldn't work out how it had got so far so quickly.

"I'm not that familiar with Eirtran IR (Industrial Relations) procedures...but I'm sure they have to be along the lines of my previous firm. Have you anything to give me as a guideline?" Ted asked. He was fast trying to focus his thoughts. He didn't fancy going into what was bound to be a difficult meeting unprepared.

"Ring the shop steward but tell him I can't see him for a while. I need to read myself into this. Let's go to your office, have a look at Ulser's file and pull out any safety training courses that this Ulser lad has had in the last few years. In addition, I want any detail you have on the content of that safety training", he stated, going into autopilot.

"Get this Ulser lad to meet us in the next 5 minutes, either on his own or with the Safety Rep, near the racks to see where, and how, this incident is supposed to have happened." Tom immediately got on the mobile and made a few quick calls.

Within minutes Ulser and Val, the Safety Rep, were standing with Ted and Tom at the racks. Donned in helmets and site boots, they all got on board Ulser's cherry picker and moved to the location of the incident.

Ted was feeling overwhelmed by the smell of B.O. from Val. They moved in silence, packed like sardines in the cockpit. Conscious that vomiting over the side of a cherry picker from a height of 20 feet on his first day as manager might look a trifle undignified, Ted held his breath for as long as humanly possible without turning purple.

Ted found every possible reason to turn his head away from Val and look at something, in fact, anything remotely interesting in the warehouse. At one point, he launched into a monologue on the value of sprinkler systems in a modern warehouse that lasted 2 minutes—all the while suffering severe neck strain so that he could remain facing the opposite direction to Val.

As a result, he found it exceedingly difficult to concentrate on the issue at hand. How it was possible for everyone else to remain either indifferent, or immune, to the stench of body odour, Ted could not fathom!

Playing the old soldier, Ulser asked Val to recreate the incident because the pain in his own back wouldn't allow him to. He muttered that he was "pissed off" that he hadn't been let go to see the doctor by this juncture, as his back was getting worse.

Ted asked very few questions during Val's demonstration because 1) he was trying not to breathe and 2) he wanted him to hurry up with it so that he could escape the smell.

Ted's penance came to an end when they alighted from the cherry picker. Heading back to Tom's office, there was little conversation. Ted remained in a state of recovery. Tom pulled out Ulser's file and lay it out on a table in front of them.

-o-o-o-o-o-

Jem and Val stood in the locker room facing Ulser.

Jem had Ulser by the lapels.

"If you're screwing with me again in your quest to find another way to hit this company for more compo, I'll have you. I've more important fish to fry than you and your fucking schemes. There's a whole pile of issues we've been winning in the last while. Management think they're getting a great deal from us, and the lads are getting handy money for sweet F.A. If management come sniffing around with an audit, because their noses are out of joint on account of a cunt like you, I'll have you sorted."

Ulser didn't bat an eyelid and looked defiantly back at Jem. He'd been cornered before and this was nothing new. He didn't give a toss about the lads on the job. They were all gobshites in Eirtran, as far as he was concerned. He had no friends here and was loyal to no one but himself. It was just a poxy job. He was his own man, with plenty of little earners on the side outside the company.

For some reason, Ulser's thoughts drifted to his late father at this point. His father had been a complete wanker, drinking all his wages away. They had nothing as kids as a result. Ulser wished they could have left Ballyer for somewhere better, but his Da just drank away any possible savings. The result was that his Ma, after their Da passed on, ended up having to stay there as they couldn't afford to move anywhere else. What a dump it was. The cretin living as a next-door neighbour stabled his horse in the front room, the horse with his head stuck out the window for all to see. The smell of horse shite and the embarrassment stays with you, you know.

'I'll be better than that for me and me sister', he

thought... 'but I can't do that on the crappy wages they pay here in Eirtran ...'

"You calling me a liar?" ventured Ulser. His eyes were blazing.

"In here, if I called you that, they'd think I was going soft." Jem smiled a contemptuous smile.

"You're a scumbag and a thieving bastard, in my most humble opinion." Jem smirked to enrage his defiant companion.

"...but unfortunately, as the shop steward here, I'm like Jesus Christ...I must put my own opinions aside and fight the cause for the lowest of the low. You're in that category, by the way", replied Jem. His face betrayed no emotion.

"An' anyways, I've hurt me back...I take it you're going to defend me up there? If you don't, I'll put a picket on the front gate, and the lads'll have no choice but join me", Ulser hissed, as if nothing had gone before. Jem put his face right into Ulser, noses now touching.

"Don't bank on it, shithead", replied Jem, nearly whispering. "We're all on a nice little earner here and we'll all take pleasure in kicking the living shite out of you if you even dare."

Ulser showed no fear, staring directly into Jem's eyes, never blinking.

"I pay my union dues. You're my union rep—for all the fucking use you are; are you goin' to represent me or not? If not, stuff your effing union—I'll go on my own steam."

Both men were now breathing heavily. The tension was palpable.

"Is this fucking Christmas or wot?" Jem shot back,

looking over at Val as he said it. He smiled at the thought of Ulser not being in his life.

Jem looked him straight in the eye. He had a hand on the wall over each side of Ulser's shoulders, towering over him, looking down.

"Wouldn't it be simply great if you revved up and fucked off? My job as a shop steward would then be my own. I could pick my battles with management and not defend scumbags like you. Could you repeat that offer about your own steam?" Jem asked sarcastically.

"I pay my effing union dues and you're going to represent me", retorted Ulser defiantly.

"Well, give me a basis then ..." Jem ventured, "...'cos right now, I ain't seeing it."

-o-o-o-o-o-

CHAPTER 3

Tom and Ted sat one side of a very shiny desk, with Ulser's large brown personal file to one side of Ted. Each had a blank A4 pad of paper in front of them. Both were immaculately dressed—Ted in the navy-blue suit and red tie and Tom in an off-brown suit, with white shirt and yellow patterned tie.

On the other side of the table sat Ulser, decked out in the traditional blue boiler suit. He scowled at everyone. Jem wore a scruffy white shirt, open necked, under his boiler suit. He sat straight, comfortable in his surroundings. Ulser was to his right, Val to his left, with his head buried in his chest. It was obvious who would do the talking.

Jem leaned in and slid an A4 form across the table—an official Accident Report Form filled out in Ulser's rough handwriting. He started talking without any formal introduction.

"Our brother, Martin, had an accident in the picker this morning. In the course of his duties, he was forced to lift a small, heavy object, in accordance with the picking list, from a pallet sitting in the racks. He experienced severe lower back pain when lifting and reported it immediately to his Supervisor."

He paused and almost imperceptibly winked at Tom.

"It is the view of this union that the design of the picker, the design of the racks and the fact that we don't pick full pallets, but units thereof, means all members of staff are at risk when in the position of reaching out from the pickers to pull items from the pallets. The resultant posture is ergonomically unsafe, putting them at risk of injury. The posture adopted puts pressure on their lower backs and is likely to cause problems."

Val's head remained in his chest but as he listened, he yearned for Jem's mastery of the English language.

Ulser remained unbowed and unmoved. He was of the view that the management were scuppering his plans for a few bob. He was entitled to screw them in order to make up for the low wages they paid him. He had plans for the future and these well-paid executives wouldn't miss a few shillings from the exorbitant profits the company made on the back of his labours.

Tom's feet shuffled under the desk and Ted tapped his pen on the table. A blackbird sung to its heart's content outside the window, the beauty of its song lost to the tension in the room.

"It is the union's contention that management is in breach of its statutory duty to employees if it refuses to sign a Notification of Accident form, as required by the Safety Act."

He looked directly at Tom, who nodded. He took a note as well.

"We certainly do not want to make an issue of this on your first day as manager." This sounded conciliatory to Ted... or was it an attempt to wrong-foot him on his first day?

"However, I have taken the liberty of consulting with national union representatives in Liberty Hall and they regard this as a serious breach of faith if the form remains unsigned. I therefore hope that this matter can be resolved reasonably. By the time we are leaving, the form will be signed!"

Tom leaned forward and looked Jem straight in the eye.

"You are well aware that we are talking about Mr. Martin Cullen here?!" Tom noticed a smile in the eyes of Jem, knowing he had understood his meaning.

"He has had more accidents on his own than the rest of the staff put together. In the last 10 years, he took 5 actions in relation to alleged accidents against this firm—succeeding in 3—taking this firm to the tune of £67,000 in total."

Jem raised his eyes in mock surprise. Tom knew he understood where he was coming from.

"Mr. Cullen's level of safety awareness is a cause for concern and would lead us to wonder whether he is suitable to hold down such a position. In some of his accidents, I would venture to say that perhaps he did not always apply the correct safety procedures as laid down in Safety Training Courses."

Tom talked evenly, with icy detachment. He intended to stand firm on this one. He saw a slight movement forward of Ulser, who was beginning to boil up nicely. Val looked up from his stomach as if to say something—then stopped himself.

"You have made some very rash accusations there, Tom. Are you threatening this man with dismissal because he was unfortunate enough to have an accident in the course of his duties? I am assuming that my hearing was off and hope that I didn't hear a threat to my fellow worker...you might put my mind at rest, or our discussion this afternoon is terminated."

The import of what he was saying wasn't lost on Tom or Ted. However, neither batted an eyelid. Jem knew he had to play for the crowd and Tom understood the play. Jem loved the game, irrespective of the outcome. Tom was similar.

"Even from what you say, it would seem that there were two occasions when you settled on the steps. I would suggest that you did that because it was likely, in the view of Eirtran's legal team, that the court would agree with Mr. Cullen's assertions: in other words, that on those two occasions, the courts were likely to agree that safety procedures were inadequate in this company and you decided to pay up. I would say that in this morning's incident, they may find that it is also the case."

Tom and Ted were picking up from Jem not to draw it out too much more. Jem didn't mind winding up Ulser just a little...but everything he said here would be reported back by Val. He couldn't let it be seen that management was winning, no matter how poor Ulser's case was. Tom and Ted knew Jem had a role and they would have to work with him in future. They understood the warning.

"You are also proffering that Brother Cullen wishes to bring a case against the company. At no point has Brother Cullen inferred that. He just wishes his accident to be recognised as such and to ensure that steps are taken to prevent a similar accident in the future for any of his colleagues. He wants the company to learn from this. Surely management is interested in the safety and welfare of their staff?"

Again, Ted and Tom knew that there was no answer to that and remained silent. Jem knew, as well as Tom, the level of Ulser's disdain for his fellow man...Jem knew himself that this line of argument was total bullshit. Tom realised that Jem was courting the audience and restrained his natural urges, in the hope that Jem would get to the nub of it as soon as possible.

"In any case, if you had reason to believe that Mr. Cullen's adherence to safe ways of working were inadequate, I doubt we will find any evidence of any type of warning on his file", said Jem, nodding to the brown file at the side of the desk.

Tom at this stage was bursting to speak. Ted knew that Jem was directing him not to go down that line...and he was probably right. He took another tack.

"I think that the courts *would be* very interested in Mr. Cullen's record of making claims against this company and would take it fully into account in the event he took another action." Ted lifted his hand to Tom to stop him talking further.

"I think Jem has already made it clear that there is no indication that a claim is being considered. From what I understand you are saying, you just want the form signed—am I right?" Jem nodded in agreement.

Ted's experience kicked in at this point. He, as a manager, had to make a fight of it. If it were too easy, it would seem to the audience that Jem didn't need to do much to win the argument. That would only raise the stakes—and expectations of staff—in the future and indicate a weakness in management negotiation skills.

"Unfortunately, we have a big difficulty here. Mr. Cullen may well be suffering from a back injury. However, neither of us is certain that he picked up that injury this morning in the course of his duties on this premises."

Jem nodded. It wasn't just to indicate to Ted that he understood, but to let Ted know that this was a better line of attack to take his client, Ulser, down a few pegs.

"We are all aware that Mr. Cullen works as a mechanic in his own time. It is well documented on his file. The fact that today is Monday is also particularly important. Whereas this company operates an extremely strict safety policy, we have no guarantee that the same principles of safety are applied in Mr. Cullen's other places of work."

He had Ulser's full attention at this stage. He noticed his neck was starting to redden. His sullenness had turned to aggressiveness.

'This bastard, in his high falutin' company, just in the door, with his swanky car, thinks he can take away the chance of a few bob I badly need?...he has another thing comin'. I have rights at work, and he has no idea of the responsibilities I have to me sister...fuck him!', he thought. 'This is not going away....'

"You see, there were no witnesses to the accident this morning and Tom, due to Mr. Cullen's previous history, is understandably finding it difficult to believe Mr. Cullen's version of events. Tom feels that there is the possibility that if he has sustained an injury, he may well have done so over the weekend in the course of other pursuits. We are not 100% sure it necessarily occurred on this premises", Ted concluded.

Ulser's eyes now widened considerably. Jem could sense the ball of subdued energy coming from beside him and that Ulser was about to explode. The bird singing outside was now silent.

"You big cunt", Ulser fizzed.

"You callin' me a liar? This bloody company is goin' to pay for pissin' me about. I should be at the doctor at this point, instead of arguin' the toss abour i'. Reaching from that effing machine is after doin' my back in and that's the long and the short of it." Jem put a hand on Ulser's shoulder and gave him a look Medusa would have been proud of.

Jem lowered his head imperceptibly...but enough for Ted to recognise that Jem was indicating that he would take care of Ulser and not to worry about the outburst.

"As you can see, Brother Martin is visibly upset and feels very strongly on this one. Notwithstanding your contention, which I believe is verging on victimisation, I would suggest you desist from innuendo and hearsay and deal with the matter in hand...otherwise this union will have to consider more serious action to get this resolved. I am asking that Tom sign the accident form as requested, otherwise this union will see management's commitment to safety as less than total."

"Unfortunately, Jem, we are not dealing with conjecture and innuendo. The file clearly states Mr. Cullen's history in relation to accidents and his work pursuits outside. You, as union shop steward, are all too aware of its contents. We are seriously concerned when accidents are reported to us...but there is a credibility issue here. No one was witness to it."

Ted looked Ulser straight in the eye while addressing

Jem. Jem was happy with the line of argument and was willing to play ball.

"So what you're saying is that an accident is only an accident when it's witnessed?...So if a man falls off a mountain in the Himalayas and no one sees him, he's not dead—is that it?"

Val, still intently surveying the floor, sniggered. Tom couldn't resist a smirk in spite of himself and hoped that Ted hadn't seen it. Ulser certainly did. Ted knew the game was on now. Kick the ball about a bit and give Ulser a run for his money. Jem was clearly in the mood.

"That is ridiculous. His base camp will know he hasn't arrived back and will go to search for him. Of course, it's an accident!" replied Ted, trying to reason the unreasonable.

Both parties engaged in earnest debate around the perilous aspects of mountaineering safety in the mystical land of Nepal—Jem and Ted trying to pick points off each other. It spiralled into farce. Eventually, Ulser had enough.

"For fuck's sake, I didn't come for a cunted geography lesson. I had an accident—sign the bleedin' form." Jem and Ted pulled back from the brink, the dead climber mystery unresolved.

They had played out the game. This was going nowhere but had generated enough heat to satisfy the audience. They could both hit the pause button now and dissipate the hot air.

"I think perhaps that it might be best if we took some time out to consider what you've said. I've taken on board your concerns but need some time to consider it. Could we meet sometime after lunch to discuss again?"

Jem was as glad of the break, as Ted was, and agreed immediately.

There was silence as the three amigos pushed back their chairs in unison, scraping them along the floor as they did so. Ted and Tom didn't look up from the blank A4 pads. When the door closed, Ted could hear the bird outside singing its happy tune again.

'What a madhouse. How has it got to the point where every asshole has rights—but no responsibilities? Our IR systems are nonsense. These guys now have developed an entitlement culture on the back of leftist, namby panby employment legislation which Civil Servants dole out on the back of decisions made by useless politicians—which *we* elect. Do they realise that they leave management with an impossible task?' thought Ted.

CHAPTER 4

Rebecca Black stood on the balcony of the detached red-brick Georgian house, on Torca Road in Dalkey. She held her 4-month old boy, Aaron, over her right shoulder. The warm breeze blew her auburn hair around her face. She was enjoying the view of Dublin Bay. The elegant Dun Laoghaire-Holyhead catamaran ferry was rounding the Howth headland, making its way south to Dun Laoghaire harbour. The remains of a cup of freshly brewed coffee sat on the table, the aroma of the recent brew adding to the warm, homely feel of the scene.

The phone rang in the hall and Rebecca remained in two minds as to whether to answer it or not. To answer would mean pulling away from the tranquil scene, and she was reluctant to do so. The continuing racket from the phone was ruining the moment in any event, so she made for the hallway of dark mahogany floor and panelling. The phone had rung twelve times before she got to pick it up.

"Yes?"

"Rebecca, I know I promised I'd start the new job afresh and be home early, but something has cropped up. It's going to take a bit of time to resolve it. I reckon I'm going to be delayed and home late." Ted knew it was a familiar tale and he hated himself for saying it.

"The whole point of this new job, you said, was that you'd ease up in it and give more time to home. You know you promised we'd go out for a drink tonight after walking the Vico." The disappointment in Rebecca's voice was palpable. He felt a heel for doing this again.

He knew she was feeling isolated at home. They had only moved in a few months ago and as of now, Rebecca didn't yet know any of her neighbours. She therefore hated when Ted was late—it was the only adult conversation she would have in the whole day.

Rebecca was a country girl from Clifden, County Galway. Clifden is about as remote as it gets from Dublin, located as it is on the Atlantic West coast. She sensed the distance between home and Dublin. She missed not having her parents nearby. They were elderly and didn't like to travel to the "big smoke", this despite the fact they now had free travel passes for bus and rail. Her two brothers and her sister all lived abroad. The result was she couldn't maintain the personal relationship with family that she would like and was restricted to occasional phone calls to keep in contact.

She went to College in Galway and studied nursing. After she qualified, she first worked in London. Then she moved to Dublin, where she met Ted, and realised quickly that all her own friends were elsewhere. Her only social interactions became Ted's circle of friends and their partners or with Ted's work colleagues in Dublin. Most of her friends still lived in Galway or England.

Since marrying some years ago, they had two children quickly—first Jason, who was now 2, and then Aaron, who was 4 months. However, Rebecca felt trapped in her new home without family and the fact that she didn't really know the neighbours meant there was no relief from the monotony of the days at home. She really looked forward to Ted getting in from work.

"I promise I'll make it up to you. At least we'll have plenty of time for a drink if we skip the walk. Talk to you later." Ted knew it sounded lame as he hung up.

-o-o-o-o-o-

Ted watched Ulser closely as he put forward the proposal. It was now 6.15 pm in the evening and Ted had spent hours to-ing and fro-ing discretely with Jem to come up with a solution that might work. He was knackered and just wanted to go home. He hoped this was the final throw of the dice.

'Why am I forced to appease this little git? If we weren't forced by this nonsensical legislation to interact on his *so-called* workers' rights, I'd have long ago given him his cards. If he doesn't want to work and prefers to skive, let him live on the bloody dole', Ted fumed in his own mind.

"What I'm suggesting may resolve the impasse. Both sides have their own points of view on this incident. What we, as management, **are** prepared to do is sign the form with a rider on it. We would need to add a comment on the form stating that the signed form is just recording the fact that Mr. Cullen **reported** an accident and not that we necessarily accept that such an accident occurred."

'What a bloody load of nonsense. You'd swear I was writing the Magna Carta, picking my words so as not to offend the sensibilities of this little prick', thought Ted, hoping his disdain wasn't showing in his voice.

"For the moment, the incident will be recorded as an accident in our stats but will be subject to further review. We are also prepared to set up a joint Management/Safety Representative committee to look at the picking process with a view to removing any safety issues that we might observe."

Ted and Jem knew that this was a total whitewash, but it was probably enough to make both sides happy—excluding Ulser, of course, who wanted total capitulation by management. Ulser made a move to open his mouth, but Jem was long enough in the tooth to know when not to rub management's nose in it and jumped in before Ulser could utter a sound. In addition, he was irritated with Ulser that he was going to be late for his regular darts match in his local that evening.

"Obviously, from a union perspective, we feel that the accident warrants investigation to prevent future injuries or accidents to our members. I believe your proposal gets over the immediate issues and is helpful towards the expressed management commitment of a collaborative approach to safety. We, from the perspective of the staff welfare of our members, are keen to see this matter investigated thoroughly. It cements management's continued commitment to safety in Eirtran—which is welcome. I would expect that this proposal will help bring this matter to a speedy conclusion."

In fact, what Jem meant was that he hoped the investigation would disappear up its own arse and would be so protracted that even Ulser would get pissed off waiting for it to make recommendations. Jem had no intention of pushing Ulser's agenda at the expense of upsetting the cushy number his members currently enjoyed in terms of handy overtime.

The investigation, Jem was convinced, would in fact do nothing. He was astute enough to realise that, whilst a committee had been mentioned, no names were proposed. Hopefully, by the time the union and management fought over the make-up of the candidates, something else more pressing would arrive on the I.R scene and shove the accident investigation into oblivion.

Val was such a dopey git that he would relish being involved in a *committee*. To Val's way of thinking, it would give him *street cred* with his colleagues. Jem knew that Val was utterly incompetent and would be the last one to put a fire under anyone in the investigation, least of all any management people. If management were equally judicious in selecting incompetents on their side, the committee might last for decades without ever concluding anything.

Jem reckoned it had been a fruitful day—Ulser usurped and he himself with two hours overtime doing nothing except feathering his nest as a shop steward. In addition, he had avoided upsetting anyone on the management side too much. The only thing that jarred was that his darts appointment was out the window.

Jem pushed back his chair and reached out his hand to Ted.

"Sorry you've had such a busy first day, Ted, but I believe that the outcome, in difficult circumstances, is a reasonable one. I look forward to doing business with you in the future", said Jem.

"Hopefully we won't have many disputes and our

meetings will be collaborative rather than combative. I've certainly had an interesting day."

Ted knew exactly what Jem was saying.

'He's as pissed off with these procedures as I am...at the same time, he's far happier bullshitting as a shop steward than doing any real work on the floor. To boot, I also have to pay him overtime for the privilege of doing nothing. What kind of shite is that?', thought Ted.

'What a pampered workforce we have created which protects the waster. Worker Protection, my arse. A waster's charter, more like.'

Ted looked to Ulser.

"I hope that the accident investigation committee can be assured of your full co-operation?" Ulser looked Ted up and down.

"One thing is for sure...I won't spend my time kissing management arses to get a result—unlike my bleedin' shop steward here...your face is fucking well tanned from brown-nosing management", he roared, eyeballing Jem.

"Fuckin' co-operation, is it? This is an effin' stitch-up and I'll have no part in it. You'll be hearin' from my solicitor."

Jem tried to suppress his delight. This was better than he could have hoped: a committee that couldn't convene because its key witness was AWOL! Happy days! Ulser pissed off...the lads on the floor happy because Ulser was upset. However, Jem feigned horror.

Ulser kicked the chair back and stormed out of the room. In the ensuing pregnant silence, those remaining could hear the clock on Ringsend church chime 6.30pm.

-o-o-o-o-o-

The traffic on Strand Road in Sandymount was

chaotic. The traffic bulletin said that some vehicle had hit the gates at the railway crossing on Merrion Road and crews had arrived to fix it. Ted was still tense after the day's events. He was right beside one of the car parks next to the sea. He pulled off the road for a break. He gazed blankly at the red and white striped stacks of the old Poolbeg power station in the distance, beyond the sands.

He stepped out, taking a deep breath and sucking in the freshness of the sea. There was a light breeze which was soothing on his face.

'What in God's name have I got myself into? This was meant to be a less stressful job than the one I just walked out of. Nine to five, I thought. Bit of travel to the European HQ and loads of supervisory and admin support to run the joint. At least I thought they'd be competent, but Tom seems to abrogate and land everything that gets sticky my way.

'At least in the last job, if there was an issue, it was genuine. No unions—and we had an adult discussion on adult issues. I didn't have to deal with unreasonable demands and our policies were there to solve problems. Here we seem to have grown-up children trying to get one over on the creche minder. We have self-appointed adult babies as shop stewards trying to play pretend adults. I used to vote for the Labour Party because I had this idealistic view that Workers rights would be protected. What I didn't expect was that it seems to be skangers' rights being protected. It seems to tie the hands of the manager behind his back, blindfold him and make him stand on one leg while he tackles these wankers. I should be able to give him the sack for what he's done.

Sure, if all the others see we can't deal with an ingrate like him, they'll down tools as well. What about all the decent workers who just do their job? Since when was legislation there to defend the indefensible? Where's the justice for the vast majority?'

Ted could feel his mind racing and the anger rising.

'Are we, as managers, not entitled to look for fairness, power to deal with complete arseholes who have no desire to work? What will other workmates think when the procedures don't deal with arseholes like Ulser? Sure, they're bound to kick up at some point knowing we're powerless. Society has created this monster...me included. Why am I worrying about this?...well, because I want to run a good show, that's why. The rules seem to only snuff out the flames with kerosene?!'

The same thoughts continued milling around in his head when he realised that, after 15 minutes, he'd walked the full length of the footpath beside the beach.

He stopped, sat on a bench and watched the gulls swooping and cackling. He observed a ship emerging from behind the west pier at Dun Laoghaire, leaving for Holyhead in a developing sea fog. He focussed on it until it disappeared around the back of Howth Head. It helped calm his nerves and slow his mind.

-o-o-o-o-o-

Ted arrived at the front door of his home. His mind was numb. If this was the first day on the job, what would the rest of his tenure be like? He felt drained working on adrenaline all day. He was looking forward to crashing on the sofa and vegetating in front of the television with a beer. When he opened the hall door, Rebecca appeared in front of him, dressed to the nines and ready to go out. She knew by his expression that he had completely forgotten.

"You promised, Ted, that you'd be back on time. The babysitter is here for the last half an hour...."

"I'm sorry, love, I just had a hell of a day...." As he spoke the phone rang. Rebecca ignored his excuse and went to answer the phone.

"At least, whoever is on the line might talk to me if my husband can't find time to do it!" She picked up the receiver.

"Hello...hello...hello, who's there?...hello?" She was met with silence. Then there was a click on the line and the caller hung up.

"Must have been a wrong number...is anyone going to talk to me today? Are we going out or not?", she demanded.

"Of course, we are. Will we go to Finnegan's beside the Railway Station?" The phone started ringing again. This time Ted was closest and lifted the receiver.

"Hello...hello...hello? ..."

He could hear light breathing on the line and traffic humming in the background....

"Is there anyone there? Hello?" Still breathing and traffic hum but nothing else. There was a click on the line as the caller hung up.

"Maybe its some pervert who fancies you...maybe me as well...maybe he fancies us as a twosome? Maybe he has Alzheimer's and wants to talk dirty—but forgets what he wants to say each time he picks up the phone? Maybe he has laryngitis and we just can't hear him talking dirty?"

Rebecca started to laugh despite her fury. Ted was glad to have the icebreaker. He hated when Rebecca was upset. He loved her to bits and cherished the moments she laughed and smiled. The room lit up with her smile.

"Am I forgiven? ..." knowing full well he was.

"C'mon, let's get ossified together and make wild, passionate love when we get home. Are you on?" He pulled her to him, gave her a deep kiss, and she reciprocated.

Life was good again.

CHAPTER 5

Ted sat at the desk listening intently on the phone. He held the earpiece an inch or two from his ear. Tom Hannigan sat on the edge of his desk but could only hear one side of the animated conversation.

"I appreciate that you are upset, Mrs Connolly....No, I assure you that I am not condoning the behaviour of staff, if they did what you allege ..." He lifted his eyes to heaven for Tom's benefit.

"Yes, I appreciate you went to the shop in Finglas...yes, that it is the third time you have had to do so...I know that this is the third attempted delivery...and that this latest delivery of your washing machine has also been unsuccessful."

There was a long litany from the woman on the other side of the phone, which lasted a minute. Tom understood this to be the woman demanding an explanation for the behaviour of Eirtran staff.

"Yes, Mrs Connolly. However, if you would just let me explain. You have to understand that each time we made a delivery, your husband was the only one at home—you do agree that that is what occurred?...On each occasion, your husband threatened my staff—in fact, my staff were in fear of their lives this last time"...(about a minute's pause)...

"He did produce a gun saying he would put the washing machine 'where the sun don't shine', to quote him, if they didn't remove it...yes, I know you say it was an imitation...However, my staff, in fairness, didn't know that at the time and were in fear of their lives when confronted by your husband—my apologies, **Ms** Connolly...your partner...I do apologise...and they felt it prudent to withdraw in the circumstances with the washing machine...why with the washing machine??...well, he did threaten to blow their effin' heads off if they didn't." Tom's chest was starting to heave as he tried not to laugh.

"The first time?...Well, he is quite a large man, as you know, Ms Connolly...No, I most certainly am not suggesting he is overweight and has a beer belly...No, as in a man who works out...as you said yourself, he *is* a champion boxer. When he first appeared in his underwear with the hurley, he did threaten to smash both the appliance and my staff with the self-same implement in equal measure...*they are* instructed by the company not to get involved in altercations...well, it is not very convenient for us either, Ms Connolly, considering the lifts in the flats were broken on each occasion. You are living on the 7th floor!...I *do* appreciate that your kids washing is piling up and it is very inconvenient for you also."

Tom had retired to the leather chair across the room. He was doubled up with laughter, snorting and sniggering, but was losing the battle in his attempt at not being heard by the customer on the phone. Ted was fighting the urge to laugh. He waved his hand furiously at Tom to leave the room—just in case he might actually start laughing himself.

"The first time we arrived?...Well, your husband... sorry, my partner—your partner...my mistake, Ms Connolly...yes, I know, you did tell me already...."

Tears were rolling down Tom's eyes at this point. His face was going red to purple and he was holding the arm of the chair for support.

"Well, his very words were: 'I'm not paying for that effing machine...I don't give a toss whether she ordered it or not—I pay the bills and she can make do with whatever she has.' He took hold of the machine on that occasion, single-handedly lifting it onto the balcony wall and threatened to throw it over the side—down on top of our truck in the yard below, if I recall rightly. I think our lads did very well to convince your partner to desist from such action and were able to negotiate the washing machine safely back to the truck...."

Tom couldn't stand it any longer and exploded into uncontrollable laughter. He ran for the door and staggered out. Ted could hear him down the corridor, gasping for breath between convulsions of laughter.

"No, Ms. Connolly...there must be a crossed line for the last minute...I don't know what that noise was...laughing? Absolutely not! Compensation? I really don't think in the circumstances that compensation is warranted. Every reasonable attempt was made by us to deliver the washing machine...."

-o-o-o-o-o-

Ulser walked out of the doctor's surgery smugly with

a smile of satisfaction. He held a doctor's certificate in his hand stating that he was unfit for heavy work and needed at least two weeks off to recover. He was diagnosed as having a pulled muscle in his lower back. He rang a number on his mobile.

"Tom Hannigan", the voice answered at the other end.

"I know who you are—I fucking rang you. I've a doctor's cert to say I'm off work for a few weeks because of the accident yesterday. Me back is killing me. Don't expect me for work. I'll touch base with you in a fortnight."

Without waiting for a reply, Ulser rang off. Informing the supervisor meant he was abiding by procedure.

He was passing Chasers pub and decided that at 10.00 a.m., it was a fitting time to celebrate with a pint. His mate, Nicko, was serving behind the bar. He and Nicko went back a long way, back to when they were robbin' orchards as little divils of seven or eight years of age.

"Usual, Nicko. How's she hangin'?"

"Same ol', same ol'. Ya know how it is. How's you and the sister gettin' on? How come you're off work so early today? One of yer 'getting it together' days?"

"Wouldn't ya know it. I pulled me back liftin' a bloody engine into place on the weekend. Just need a bit of rest, that's all. I won't even be missed back at that place they call work. That on its own would never pay the bills."

Nicko knew what he meant. He knew that they both always dreamed at getting out of this kip all their lives. Nicko had got his girlfriend pregnant when he was sixteen, so that was the end of that. However, his mate had never given up on the dream, even after his Da left him and his sister nothing after the fire. Ulser was always grafting, trying to squeeze an extra few bob by constantly scheming. He'd get there some day, he thought.

"We've a new manager in the place. Has notions above his station. You can see he thinks he's going to make his mark—at our expense. They're trying to make out I'm not injured and need some rest. He bust my balls yesterday, denying me sick leave for me back."

Nicko thought the world of Ulser and believed his every word.

"But you're entitled to sick leave. You know that."

"Yeah, but this guy's trying to cut down sick leave rates at work. Makes it sticky to get what we're entitled to. Isn't this what the unions fought for? I shouldn't have to fight to get what's rightfully mine."

"Bloody right mate. What are you doing later?"

"You might give us a hand in the garage to get that engine sitting right on the chassis. Few bob in it for ya", Ulser said without a hint of irony.

-o-o-o-o-o-

Rebecca was changing the baby's nappy whilst kneeling on the mat on the floor. Gerry Ryan rattled on about something inconsequential in the background on RTE Radio 2. The dross and noise took the place of adult conversation. She rubbed her nose on Aaron's tummy and the child broke into a giggle. His hands came up to tug her hair and he looked her straight in the eye. She lowered her head into his tummy again and the child laughed heartily again. He held her hair and brought his little feet around her neck. The phone rang to interrupt this tête-à-tête—tête-à-tummy in this case.

Rebecca stood up, looking around for the home mobile. It lay on the table. She answered and listened.

"Hello?...Hello? ..." she said.

She could hear traffic in the background but no answer. She tried again.

"Hello...who are you looking for?"

"You look terrific in pink...." whispered a male voice. The line clicked off.

Rebecca's heart missed a beat and immediately, she felt uncomfortable and alone. Her mind was racing and could sense very real fear. She dialled Ted's landline at work, but it was engaged.

She had to sit down, as her legs had turned to jelly. She felt weak. Her little toddler lay on the floor gurgling, stretching his neck around to see where Mammy was. She felt as if someone had come into her house and robbed something from it. She had to think straight. She dialled Ted's mobile this time, only to receive the usual message.

"The number you have dialled is inaccessible because the phone is either turned off or the person is not available. Please try again later."

In frustration, she texted a message.

'Ted, please ring me as soon as you can. Rebecca'. At this juncture, she really missed her friends and family, and felt utterly alone.

-o-o-o-o-o-

Ted was at his desk, recovering from the onslaught of the customer on the phone. He had written a few words on a sheet of paper in preparation for his first official briefing of the staff at the 10 a.m. tea-break. He had agreed with Tom that deliveries would be delayed that morning so that all staff could meet him for the first time, particularly the drivers and others who wouldn't normally be in the stores. Tom poked his head around the office door.

"Ms. Connolly is now a happy camper, I take it?" Tom grinned as he said it.

"You deliberately offloaded that call onto me, didn't you? You knew what was coming?" Ted growled.

"Well, Ms. Connolly is a regular customer and she did ask for the manager. Who was I to refuse the customer's request?...an' anyways up, have you your speech prepared for our esteemed colleagues, who are now assembled in the canteen waiting with bated breath for your words of wisdom?"

"I've barely my wits about me after that nutcase! I'm going to keep it brief, then sit down for tea with a few of them afterwards. You can look out for me if conversation starts getting anyway heated. I'm likely to be hit with every grievance known to man when they get going."

"Ah, no...they'll at least give you until dinnertime—as you're on honeymoon!", replied Tom. He gave that big grin again.

"We're already a bit late. Do you think you can wing it?" said Tom.

"I've a few rough notes—it'll be enough to get me going. C'mon, lead me to the lion's den!" said Ted, and they left the room.

As he strolled down the corridor, his desk phone had begun to ring again, but he was out of earshot. Rebecca waited on the other end of the line, tears in her eyes.

-o-o-o-o-o-

"...I expect the current stock reconciliation will produce a vast improvement on the 5% variance we had last year. Since then, we invested in a Warehouse Management IT system and associated bar-code readers, on which you are all now trained. This should further reduce error levels on stock "put-away". I expect the level of misallocation of stock this year will be well down as a result ..." Murmurs and smothered laughter among the rank and file.

Ted had always got a buzz from hitting targets and deadlines, to the detriment of maintaining and developing relationships. Not that he didn't care about people—it's just that he got too caught up in meeting the goals sometimes. They felt more tangible somehow.

Ted was talking to the assembled group from the serving area in the cafeteria. Five rows of tables faced him, which seated every known variation on Homo Sapiens. He leaned back—his buttocks supported by the serving counter and his back to the kitchen staff. The kitchen staff were a whole other kettle of fish; a motley crew consisting of a mad 6' 5" Latvian chef, two 4' 3" dwarf Chinese assistants and three women servers who wouldn't have been out of place selling 'Cheeky Charlies' on Moore St.

When Ted was paying for his tea earlier at the till, one of the women said: "Are ye on a diet, luv? Ye'll shrink away ta nothin'. Heaw, take a bun—on the house, luv!" She exploded into a loud, smoky cackle and winked to her fellow witches, who were tending the cauldron behind the counter. They cackled in harmony. Macbeth it wasn't...all hail the leader....

The eyes from the floor were trained on their leader, with his sharp Italian suit and eye-catching pink tie.

"I am initiating a new safety drive in the next few weeks. I was looking at our safety record and our safety performance which is below the industry average. That should concern you as much as me. I do not relish going to anyone's home to tell them that their husband, son, or daughter won't be home from work ever again. I want a safe place of work for us all. Every person, by virtue of taking personal responsibility for their own safety, makes this workplace safer for others. In particular I will be initiating a programme of awareness around slips, trips, and falls to get the ball rolling.

"We are under severe pressure on our unit cost of delivery. With two of our major contracts due for renewal next month, our clients are putting severe pressure on me to reduce our charges. As you know, two new players entered the market from the UK last year and are going in low for much of our business. We must remain competitive. We can only do that by being slicker—doing things faster, more efficiently, and giving an edge in customer satisfaction."

He was now in Winston Churchill mode, trying to rally his charges in the trenches.

"You are the face of Eirtran to the customer. Going forward, every time you are in contact with a customer it is a 'Moment of Truth'...."

Despite his hatred of 'Management Speak', he couldn't prevent himself descending into it.

"Going forward"...'Christ, unless you intended going backwards. I can't believe I said that. When did I start using that horse manure?' he thought to himself.

He was now speaking Harvard Best Practice Consultant 'Bullshitese'. The clichés started to flow. He felt he was losing his audience. Tom, who had initially been standing beside him, had put physical distance between them. Self-consciously, he had shuffled two steps away over the course of Ted's speech. Tom was rocking side-to-side, staring intently at his shoes to inspect how well polished they were.

Ted blathered on for another minute or two. Tom knew full well the lads in the canteen were getting chawed off with the speech. The new manager was eating into valuable personal time, set aside to discuss last night's United match. Ted sensed the restlessness and decided to draw his 'State of the Nation' speech to a close. He had begun to sweat, and his face was starting to redden.

"...so, to conclude, it's a start of a new era for Eirtran and I hope that we can all work together to make our company a success."

There was immediate applause—a measure of relief that the gaffer had finished rather than for the content of the oration. Before the clapping ended, feeding at the zoo resumed and the low hum of the group conversation recommenced. Ted turned to Tom.

"How'd that go down?"

Tom gathered himself to say something appropriate.

"They'd have been keen to see you—the last manager

barely ventured out of his office. It's important that they hear it from the horse's mouth."

Tom hoped that his reply was obtuse enough that Ted could take from it whatever he liked. Ted, from experience, knew not to elaborate any further.

"I want to move around and talk to some of the lads on a one-to-one. I just want you to direct me to the appropriate fall guys and then disappear! Mind you, don't put me in with the Rottweilers first—just a few lads where I can press the flesh."

"Know what you mean, boss. Follow me and I'll introduce a few lads".... He moved very quickly to a corner of the canteen where a faded picture of Kylie Minogue in fish-net tights adorned the wall.

"Lads, this is our new manager, Ted Black. He'd like to meet a few of you, so I said that he better know all the rogues first...." Some laughter from the group and winks from Tom....

"Ted, this is Bruno, who drives the fastest milk cart in the West!!...lightning fast when going through West Dublin—in case they hijack the van! In Neilstown, they can remove hubcaps at thirty miles an hour. At twenty they can steal a fridge from the back of a van. At ten, they take the truck! You've got to be fast! Bruno has the record number of deliveries in a day for door-to-door...63 hits between 8 and 6. Mind you, he went sick for a week afterwards! ..."

A wry smile from Tom and a wistful raising of eyebrows from Bruno....

"...the last bit's not really true. He's our best man on deliveries. Must be the Weetabix he has in the morning."

Bruno was a wiry man in his mid-fifties. He had a

slicked-back full mop of straight, greasy black hair, grey showing at the temples. He had the leathery look of a regular pint man, his complexion a mixture of purple and grey. He looked a hard man who didn't suffer fools.

Beside him sat a stout man that Ted reckoned was in his early sixties. He had been talking animatedly to those around him as Tom and Ted approached. There was a boyish twinkle in his eye but also a fatherly aura about him. With his elbows on the table, Ted couldn't help but notice how big his hands were. He had a broad grin on his face.

"Bruno would be useless without Sachmo here, riding side-saddle! This is Georgie Hartnett, Bruno's trusted aide-de-camp. Georgie is the best singer we have on the shop floor. He can deliver 'What a Wonderful World' better than the great Sachmo himself."

Georgie held out his hand and shook Ted's hand. He seemed genuinely pleased to have been picked out to meet the boss man.

"I wish you every success in your new job, sir. This place needs a strong hand to run it and I'm glad to be making your acquaintance, sir. Here, take a seat ..."

Georgie pulled out the seat back beside him, beckoned and Ted sat down. Ted warmed to Sachmo—there was a genuineness about him.

"Georgie, tell Ted about the time Bruno and yourself came across the oul' fella with the new Escort....It's a good one", said Tom.

"Ah, Jaysus, not again. I've told it a hundred times."

The lads around him all turned to Georgie. There was a big roar.

"C'mon Georgie, it gets bigger and better ever time!"

"All right...all right, I'll tell it." You could see straight away that Georgie was dying to tell the story. His eyes looked Ted straight in the eye.

"A few years ago, meself and Bruno were out on deliveries...somewhere around Rush in North County Dublin. We were going down this country road. We saw this oul' fella with the bonnet up. Staring into the engine, he was, of his brand-new Ford Escort. The Escort was bleedin' lovely. It was obviously his pride and joy...Alloy wheels, black, spoiler on the back when no-one had them....Lovely red stripes down the side...you get the picture. It was obvious the oul' fella hadn't a clue what he was lookin' at. Bruno—he may be Ayrton bleedin' Senna in Neilstown, but he doesn't know his arse from his elbow when it comes to lookin' into engines—decided that we better do the Good Samaritan and help him out. Bruno is to a mechanic what a fish is to a bicycle", he said, looking at Bruno and grinning.

Most of the table, left and right, had their eyes trained on Satchmo. No-one was talking. They were all engrossed in the story.

"Anyways up, down we get from the truck...yer man here ventures up to the oul' fella. The bonnet is up, and Bruno pokes his head in where it don't belong to see what the problem is. 'What's the problem', says Bruno. 'Have no idea', says the oul' fella. 'I only got the car a week ago. She just completely conked out. I'm sittin' here for the last half hour. You're the first to come along.' 'Get in the car there and turn her over', says our friend here."

Bruno, the subject of the story, was grinning and going a bit red at the same time.

"So, the oul' fella turns over the ignition and the car

chugs a bit. Bruno says: 'Hold on a second. I think I can see the problem. There's something leaking...I can't see where its comin' from though.'" Georgie was making faces as if he was under the bonnet himself. He had his head cocked at an angle as if he was looking at the carburettor at that moment in time.

"The only thing leakin', I reckon, was the last bit of Bruno's brain from his earhole!...or was that wax...or is it one and the same?...(long pause and laughter).

"Mind you, for the first time in his life, in all fairness, Bruno seemed to know what he was talking about. I was nearly believin' him—and I know what an idiot he is!" He threw his eyes to heaven and the group guffawed.

"'Turn her over again', he says. Now alls I can see is Bruno's big arse in me face and he rootin' under the bonnet. I don't know what the fuck he's at—beggin' your pardon sir for the vernacular—but *he* doesn't know what the fuck he's at!"

There's a big cheer from the group at the table and he gets a few back-slaps. Bruno, despite the hard man look, seemed to be enjoying the attention.

"What's he do next when he can't see? Sure, it's obvious to a smoker...pulls a lighter out of his arse pocket. Before I realise what he's at, he's only gone and lit the bloody thing and is using it to look under the bonnet ..." (long pause)

"Phoooosh!...flames bleedin' everywhere from under the bonnet of the oul' fella's new car....There's fuckin' pandemonium! Bruno jumps back, his hair on fire, effing and blinding like a fisherwoman...the car has flames jumping five foot in the air from the engine...the oul' fella's jumped out of the car shouting 'Me car...me brand new fucking car!!!'...There's a smell of burning everywhere...Bruno's clothes are on fire...I'm in a panic, so I jumps on Bruno and drags him to the ground—I didn't kiss him nor nothin', mind you. He's not my type!! ..." he said, camping it up with a limp wrist and blowing a kiss in Bruno's direction. Georgie was beginning to warm to his own story at this stage and some of the listeners were starting to convulse.

"Anyways, I pulls off me dunkey jacket to beat down the flames on Bruno's head. All that oil in your hair...no fuckin' wonder it started burnin'...you're a mobile fire hazard with that Brylcream in your hair...or is it just bleedin' greasy, Bruno? The flames were leppin' off him. Anyways up, for the first 20 seconds, I just beat the shite out of Bruno with the coat—cos' I was enjoying it...." Georgie looked at Bruno as he said it with a grin ...another big roar from the crowd.

"...then I thought I'd better put the fire out in his hair after I knocked the shit outa him enough"...laughter all around....

"The oul' fella at this stage is hysterical: 'You effin' dickhead...me beautiful new car...' I have to admit that I did feel sorry for him, y' know, I really did; seats are on fire, the paintwork is curling up, flames are leppin' 15 feet into the air out of it. So 'Brain-dead' here ..." pointing at Bruno..."has another bright idea. He grabs me dunkey jacket to throw on the engine and douse the flames...waste of time and energy of course at this stage...the car's fucking destroyed...but what Braindead here doesn't realise is that I'd bought two canisters of spray paint for me car that morning and they're in the pocket.... Effin' things explode the minute he throws the coat on the engine...one of the canisters takes off like an Exocet, hits the oul' fella on the head and knocks him to the ground. We're talking Sarajevo here!" Most of the group are in knots at this stage. Tears are flowing down Ted's cheeks from laughing.

"Anyway, we have no choice but to ring 999 on the mobile at this stage: it's a war zone...they ask me 'what service do you require'...I says 'how many you got?'..." another explosion of laughter....

"Eventually we had two squad cars, a unit of the fire brigade, and an ambulance on the scene. It's carnage out there! There's traffic jams both sides of us and the cops are directing traffic around the wreckage. At this stage, Bruno and meself are back in the cab...the oul' fella's head is in a big bandage: he's wrapped head to toe in blankets, looking like an Arab Sheikh....Anyways, Bruno turns around to me in the cab and says: 'Ah look, that's nice: the oul' fella's wavin' at us'....'You big dickhead', I says, 'its not wavin' he is'"...he stood up and waved extravagantly to the listening hordes, which at this stage extended across the whole canteen..."'it's this he's doing'"...reaching across the table and threatening Bruno with a clenched fist..."'it's fucking shaking his fist at you he is.'"

The whole canteen let out a one big guffaw in unison and started chanting: "Bruno-oh!...Bruno-oh! ..." as if at a football match. Ted was in stitches at this stage, thoroughly enjoying the moment....

CHAPTER 6

"Micko" Stenson and "Josser" Hughes could hear the roars of laughter back at the canteen. The two of them were making their way to the cherry-pickers, which were parked at the front of the racks. There was no-one else on the shop floor—no supervisor, no staff—just as "Josser" had planned it. No-one noticed them slipping out the side door of the canteen when Georgie was in full swing.

Micko Stenson, 37, cut a small, wiry figure. He had a small shaven head, typical of "Skin-heads" in the 70's. There were a few nicks around his head where the blade wasn't the best. He would be described in Dublin vernacular as a "shaper".

A typical "shaper" struts around as if owning the place. A "shaper" is usually on the stumpy side of small and has notions above his station (and height). As he walks—rather, struts—he typically holds his arms out from his body—as would a body builder. He is convinced his body bares an uncanny resemblance to that of Arnold Schwarzenegger (not) and therefore his arms are incapable of hanging any closer to his sides.

A "shaper" possesses pronounced bowed legs—feet facing slightly out from the ankles. A "shaper" rolls from side-to-side when strutting around self-importantly. A "shaper" is never out of character. He has opinions on everything. A "shaper" rolls his shoulders whilst walking. He sticks his jaw in and out—chicken-like—at irregular intervals for no apparent reason, usually in advance of speaking. He has an annoying habit of uttering "ye know like" at every opportunity, particularly at the start of sentences.

He draws himself to his full miniscule height when providing self-important answers to the major issues in life—whether Liverpool are a shite team or *the Sun* (his preferred reading material) is brilliant. A "shaper" will take umbrage at the merest perceived slight to his manhood—or opinions—and will threaten the purveyor of such notions accordingly....Thus, Micko.

"Josser" (aka Dracula) Hughes was a mite more sinister and a more refined character. He was 6'3" and handsome—in a Gothic kind of way. He bore a striking resemblance to Boris Karloff. Others knew better than to call him Dracula to his face! "Josser" was restrained and exuded an air of authority. You got the feeling that he kept everything—and everyone—under observation.

Micko stepped into the cab of the cherry picker and closed the entry bar. He nodded to Josser and took the picker into the darkened aisle. He quickly raised the picker to the seventh level and stopped. A pallet full of boxes faced him. The pallet of small white boxes had been partially stripped and the heavy plastic surround was cut at the front.

He reached into the back of the pallet. Hidden were a number of small appliances—MP3 players, mini-televisions, Palm-tops, kettles. There were about 40 items. He threw them into the brown box on the floor of the cab, taped it up and with a black marker wrote "For attention of Michael Green, Cork". He continued down the aisle with his picklist and picked the rest of what he was supposed to be picking. He dropped the additional items from the racks into the steel box pallet until it was full. The steel box pallet was marked "Cork Drop Centre". Before he left the aisle, he took the marked box from the floor of cab and dropped it on the top of the contents of the steel pallet.

He took the machine to the main laydown area at the centre of the building and dropped the steel pallet box on the floor, with all the others.

Josser was waiting with a forklift. He nodded to Micko, picked up the steel pallet and drove out of the building to the outdoor loading bay. Eirtran had strict security on the Appliance loading bays to prevent "stock leakage" —another word for stealing. There was no value in the industrial side of the business, where Josser and Micko worked. On this side of the warehouse, no security was present.

Josser drove to an open-backed forty-foot trailer and landed the steel pallet on the back of it. The small appliance trade that he was running was a nice little earner! So long as they didn't get too greedy, they would all continue to do nicely. The important thing was to ensure that nobody in the Admin office, or any of the supervisors, got suspicious.

Josser went up to the driver—Alo Stenson, a distant relation of Micko's.

"That's the last pallet, Alo—you can start tying down now." Just before he turned away, he whispered: "It's on the last pallet—on the top—a box marked 'For attention of Michael Green, Cork'. He'll meet you at the usual place in Santry—make sure you get the £600 off him first before you tell him where the box is."

-o-o-o-o-o-

Ulser had left The Chasers at 11 for his rendezvous in Santry at 11.30 a.m. Alo better be on time this time. Ulser didn't like parting with cash unless he saw the goods first. Alo had been getting on his nerves lately. For the last two drops, Alo demanded the money first—in his hand—before he'd let him see the goods. Dracula was a bastard. Ulser knew Alo was afraid of both Dracula and him—but Alo was more afraid of Dracula...he always did whatever he was told by him.

Dracula better have loaded all the stuff he was looking for this time.... Last time he provided the wrong make of MP3 Player and Ulser's customer refused to pay. He took a hit of £60 on it—the oul' wan said she'd take it but refused to pay enough to make a profit. He'd already lost £100 on a red-hot tip the same day on the gee-gees. He didn't appreciate being stung twice. He had a busy day ahead of him and wanted Alo to make the drop on time.

He could see the forty-foot was sitting at the filling station where Alo was on his tea-break. Alo sat in the cab munching on a breakfast roll. Ulser pulled up in his beat-up Skoda a few yards from him. Alo had seen him and was already jumping down from the cab to stroll over.

"You got the gear?" Ulser demanded. There were no niceties with Ulser.

"You know the rules—I want the colour of your money first, Ulser", countered Alo.

"Fucking ugly bastard—he's up your arse again, Alo?"

"He's me brother-in-law, Ulser, and a cunt to boot. It's not in my interest to piss him off. Twice before, you got gear, paid only half with a promise of the rest later...ye didn't deliver and a few months later, Drac had to put the screws on you. Next time that happens, he promised me he'll get in the heavies—not just on you, but me as well....Green stuff first!"

Ulser shot him a look and pulled a wad from his pocket, handing it to Alo. "Well...where's the stuff?"

"Count first...then see", countered Alo.

"You're pissin' me off, Alo."

"Pissin' you off is nothing to pissin' off Drac—now eff off until I count...you're £100 short ..."

"For fucks sake, you know I'm good for the other £100", shouted Ulser. He had a sure-fire winner on the 3.40 at Wolverhampton and needed to hold onto the ton.

"Nothin' doin'—all or nothin'...what's the tip today, Ulser? I can smell the Guinness off ye. Your mate in The Chasers has a sure fire one today?" Ulser dug into the back pocket of his scruffy jeans and pulled out another two fifties.

"You're nothin' but a pain in the arse, Alo." Alo grinned.

"I love you too, brother...c'mon to the back of my Winnebago!"

He leaped up to the steel pallet and removed the cardboard box marked "For attention of Michael Green, Cork". He took the Stanley knife from his pocket and cut through the tape.

"Check it's all kosher, Ulser." Ulser had a quick rustle in the box and seemed happy enough that everything was in order.

"Happy?" asked Alo.

"Fucking delirious", retorted Ulser as he walked away to his car. He was hoping he'd catch up with some of his buyers this morning and have a ton for the bookies by the start of the 3.40 at Wolverhampton. That git Dracula always seemed to get on his tits.

-o-o-o-o-o-

"Jody" Martin and "Iano" Cullen worked the appliance racks. Jody was on large appliances—dishwashers, washing machines, tumble driers—and Iano worked the smalls—anything from hairdryers to TVs, and everything in between. Jody's brother was married to Iano's sister. Jody's brother only married the sister under duress—a good few years after her second child arrived. The brother was forced by Iano's Da to make things respectable—a shotgun had been mentioned!

As teenagers, Jody and Iano played football together for a team in Ballyfermot but hadn't known each other before that. Now they were inseparable and enjoyed each other's company, even outside work.

Jody was a bit of a trickster but was always first to get stuck into whatever job he was put to do. He had an easy way about him and was popular both with the lads on the floor and his superiors. The management recognised his good influence on his peers and had earmarked him as a future supervisor. Jody was in his twenties.

Iano was more reserved. He was never first to do anything and would spend time considering problems before applying himself. He was recognised as a good worker but not very forthcoming. Lads liked him when they got to know him, but he was happy staying in the background.

Jody was engaged to be married and was finding the money situation tough in the last few months. He was doing a few "nixers" for a mate who was a builder— labouring at night on a small development of new houses. He needed every cent to pay for his new house and the wedding. Word got around to Josser, who made it his business to know everything going on in the premises.

Josser took full advantage of Jody's predicament. Josser put pressure on him to assist a few others move small appliances in the warehouse so that he became implicated in his own little business. Josser provided him with "incentives" to get involved. The incentives included both money and threats—to Jody's family and property. Jody capitulated. He managed to justify his participation on the basis that he was only doing what everyone else was doing in the store. He hadn't found it difficult to get his mate Iano to work with him for the same incentives.

Jody drove the forklift among the aisles of the large appliances. He had the picklist attached to the dashboard in the cab. He went right to the end of one of the aisles, where it was quiet. He directed the forks to the top-most appliance in the rack, pulled it out and dropped it to the floor. He stepped out of the forklift, taking a quick look down the aisle. Satisfied that no-one was present, he pulled the Stanley knife from his pocket and cut the white tape down the centre of the box. He pulled back the two flaps. The top of the appliance was protected inside by a foam covering. It was a single square piece and he removed it completely. This left a gap in the box— between the top of the appliance and the top of the box. He re-closed the flaps without sealing them. He broke the foam packing up and threw it under the bottom of the racks, to be disposed of later in one of the rubbish bins around the depot.

He drove the fork-lift loaded with the appliance back down the aisle to the Load Assembly area. This was a drop zone where all materials, big and small, were placed together for loading onto the delivery trucks. Some trucks delivered directly into shop outlets and others delivered direct door to door.

The Load Assembly area consisted rows of assorted appliances placed in straight lines, each row directly opposite a loading bay door. Each line was made up of a combination of large boxes. The boxes contained freezers, cookers, washing machines and tumble driers, sometimes stacked two and three high. He drove between two of the middle piles and dropped the appliance to the floor. He stepped out of the cab and placed a small, luminous yellow piece of sticky tape on the side of the box.

Iano, meanwhile, walked along the racks with his trolley for the smalls (small appliances). In addition to what he was picking for the shop deliveries, he added in, as appropriate, extra items for Josser's little operation. He marked his "own" ones with luminous sticky tape kept in his overalls. That way, he could easily retrieve them from the cart when he needed extract them.

On finishing the pick, he headed to the Load Assembly area. Iano wheeled his carts between two rows. He spotted the yellow luminous tape on the large box left by Jody. He stopped and placed the trolley in the gap beside the marked box. He had room to step in between the marked box and the trolley. There was a cooker to one side of him and two cookers, stacked one above the other, on the opposite side. Even if a security man looked down the aisle, Iano was to all intents and purposes invisible.

He removed the marked small appliances from the trolley, opened the flaps on the cooker beside him and packed the appliances into the gap at the top of the box. He managed to fit in the 15 he had picked. He closed over the flaps and sealed it with black tape. He took out a marker and marked "Special: 15 Vernon Close" in large writing on one side of the box. Whoever came to load would know to leave this boxed appliance near the door of the van for ease of removal.

Security, for all their checks, never opened sealed boxes.

-o-o-o-o-o-

Ted had enjoyed the crack with the lads in the canteen. His initiative had gone down very well, and he had gotten a good response from the few lads he had met at the table. He was in good form considering the difficult start to the job over the previous few days. As the crowd was leaving the canteen, he felt a hand on his shoulder. It was Tom Hannigan.

"Ted, can I have a word?" Tom looked concerned.

"Yeah, no problem!"

They worked their way out of the crowd and found a corner at the end of the hall. Tom looked very uneasy. He launched straight into what he had to say.

"Ted, you're aware that we have a very high level of security on the premises? We brief the staff and let them know that they are being watched. The unions and staff are aware of security beams, alarms and the use of cameras because we've briefed them—keeps it above board. Daily, we do random checks on some of the loads going in and out of stores. Again, the staff know the routine. However, as you probably know, if we relied purely on stuff like that alone, we'd be fleeced." Ted was baffled, wondering when Tom was going to get to the point, but held his fire.

"In the last few years particularly, we've noticed that on the high value end of our electrical goods, leakage has been increasing. Lads are always on the look-out for little 'earners' and are quite ready to exploit any gaps in our security systems.

"Take our security men, for instance. They work for a pittance. Because the money's so bad, we don't exactly attract the highest calibre. Most of them are 'streetwise' and our experience is that they are easily bought off. For example, if someone is 'on the make' and starts threatening them or their families, they're quick to cave in. We've had a high turnover of security guards in the last few years and their value is debatable—except to provide high profile lip-service to security.

"In the last two months, we noticed an increasing number of faulty alarms on the appliance side of the building. We got them checked by the technical people and they can't find anything amiss with the system. They say they are genuine alarms. The result has been that security is getting fed up checking out false alarms. They have got blasé and are putting some of the alarms they should be checking down to faults on the alarm system.

"My gut tells me that this is a sign of increased activity by someone on the pilfering front. I believe an organised group is setting off the alarms, timing the response—if any—and helping themselves when they get their timings sorted. They've succeeded in creating a climate of false alarms and it is giving free reign for an insider group to dip their hands in our stock and line their pockets. Lads on security aren't bothering their arse with fifth or sixth alarms and things can happen...."

"Are you saying that things **are** happening, Tom? ..." asked Ted.

"I'm pretty sure, Ted...."

"How can you be that sure it isn't just an aberration on the system? ..." asked Ted.

"Let's say that we have other checks ...if the unions knew, we would get our balls cut off. I'll spell it out. We have a relationship with a PI (Private Investigator) and if things on the ground get a bit "iffy", we bring them in."

"BRING THEM IN?" asked Ted.

"Well, we create an atmosphere of "busyness" from time to time in the Warehouse and create a demand for temporary staff. The unions are delighted...we're recruiting a few extra members for them. As a result, it's now no problem to recruit seasonally. We give overtime to the lads in stores in addition to taking on the seasonal group. We take on these temporary lads around

Christmas for major stock checks, just like we're doing now.

"To all intents and purposes, it looks like we go through an interview process and select people at random from the masses. What we do, in fact, is employ one or two "moles" —provided and vetted by the PI. Sometimes the *temps* are even his own employees. These temps provide information to the PI—or sometimes directly to myself—around suspicious activity. In addition, we detail them to see if they can inveigle their way into any of the scams. They give us a low down on how it operates and how to break it up. Over the years, we have nailed a few bad pennies this way. It's obvious we need to keep these methods under wraps...whatever way we nail these gits, it has to be in a way that doesn't expose our less publicised methods...."

"You sayin' that DETAILS have come to your attention? ..." asked Ted. Tom continued on as if he hadn't spoken.

"In addition to the known cameras, we have hidden cameras and microphones around the store. We have some on the delivery trucks...all placed by our moles to provide us with ammunition. I stress that if we go to nail these gits stripping the stores, we have to do it legit and not expose our moles. There are too many possible IR issues so we must base our cases on strictly approved methods. We will have to construct any case against these gits so that it stands up in the Labour Court because—guaranteed—that's where this is going. Other Courts even.... In addition, it would be impossible to continue to use current methods of investigation if our methods were ever exposed", said Tom.

"I'll repeat myself, Tom—are you sayin' that details have come to your attention...that you think stuff is being moved out of the stores?"

"I don't think, Ted—I know. I have the route and I know the participants. However, they are shrewd bucks, and we need to tread carefully. Some of them are connected outside, and that's another complication. I think we better find a room to talk in private and I'll fill you in on some of the detail we have so far."

"I'm not sure I want to know what 'connected to outside' means. I have a pile of shite and management reports to get through. I have contracts to negotiate and figures to look at. In addition, I'm expected at a conference in Holland in three days time and I need to get flights booked etc. Some of our key customers are there. I need to butter them up, so we can retain their business. I need to get a feel of what they are looking for and how I need to bid. Can't this wait?" said Ted.

"The most important management issue in the stores is security. Did no one brief you on this? Some of the lads here have mates in the 'RA and others have connections with notorious criminals. Our lads are the small fry in the big picture, but the ramifications can be nasty from time to time."

Ted wasn't sure he liked what he was hearing. He just wanted a straight-forward management job—not this kind of shite.

Tom headed up the stairs in front of Ted without a word. He went along the upstairs corridor, opening doors to find a vacant room. The Safety Officer's room was in darkness and they stood in.

"Now, Ted, I'll fill you in on the position to date.

There's a small group in the stores who are siphoning off appliances—high value, small goods, to order. We knew it was happening, but we couldn't figure out how they were doing it. Just to make it even more interesting, a good friend of yours is to the fore...Ulser."

CHAPTER 7

Jimmy Spain was a small, fat man, a driver all his life. He was a grumpy individual. His only joy in life was driving. However, stopping for any reason—or deliveries— upset his delicate sensibilities.

The drivers of Dublin each day sated Jimmy's hatred for traffic jams and he never had a short supply of traffic events to allow him moan. Each stop for a drop meant he had to remove his bum from the driver's seat and exert himself to do physical work. Jimmy was allergic to physical activity. Any of his helpers, as a result, endured torrents of abuse in the course of each delivery. Jimmy cursed his way through every second of every working day.

Each new day was an opportunity for endless grumble—from early morning to late at night. The end of the world was always nigh. Every helper in the store dreaded a trip with Jimmy. He was born to moan—it was his *raison d'etre.* He moaned about tax, the government, taxi drivers, the weather, women drivers, his wife, his family, the publicans, barmen in Dublin not being able to pour pints of Guinness right, the layout of the cab in the truck, the position of the steering wheel, the size of doors, the Pope, Afghanistan, politicians...nothing was sacred. It was Jimmy's truck that contained the cooker marked "Special: 15 Vernon Close".

"Jayo" Tuite sat beside him in the cab, as the unfortunate helper for the day. Jayo and Jimmy didn't get on. Jayo turned the radio up enough to drown out Jimmy's tirades. Today the traffic around Terenure was awful. Jimmy was waxing lyrical on country drivers in the city. Cars with LH (Louth) and TS (Tipperary South) plates were ahead of him in the queue. They were all waiting to turn right at the filter light on Terenure Cross. He had followed the same two cars all the way from the Harold's Cross. The Nissan Micra with the TS plate was the target of his bile-filled hatred at this point. A few minutes earlier it had stopped in front of him where a truck was offloading at a local shop in Kenilworth.

"For fuck's sake, woman. What the hell are ye stopping there for? You know what I call that?", he said, trying to engage Jayo. "The Sherman Tank Syndrome. Do ya know what that is, Jayo?" Jayo had heard it a thousand times before. He grunted because he was more interested in the radio show—where there was a riveting discussion on wife swapping—than Jimmy's rant. Jimmy continued regardless.

"Sherman-fucking-Tank Syndrome. The smaller the fucking car, the more likely the cretin in it believes he's driving a Sherman Tank and can't get through the gap. The bleedin' car becomes inversely proportional to the space in bleedin' front of him. If it's a female, the fucking formula is to the power of 10. If it's a culchie, and worse still a culchie female, it's to the power of infinity." This was one of Jimmy's great rants—small cars, female drivers, culchies, and his mathematical prowess, all rolled into one great rant. He was at full throttle. He was so worked up on this one that he rammed his hand down on the horn to get her to move. She provided the V sign out the window in acknowledgement. That didn't improve Jimmy's mood.

"Move, you silly bitch", he said, gesticulating wildly with his free right hand. "For fuck's sake, me granny would put a herd of elephants through there."

Why Jimmy was in such a hurry was anyone's guess. Jimmy never got the truck above 25 miles per hour and always had traffic trailing in his wake for miles. It was just that he hated being stopped. Driving was an end in itself for Jimmy. The need to deliver product was a massive inconvenience to him. Now Jimmy was sitting behind the same unfortunate female at the lights in Terenure.

"For fuck's sake, the lights are bleedin' green. There's nothin' comin' down from Rathfarnham. Do ya want an invite from the President to go?...You don't need the fuckin' filter light—you can go now...." he ranted at the person who couldn't hear him. Jayo wasn't listening either. He was trying to find out what wives in Dublin 4 were getting up to every day and what website would allow him to get in on the action.

"Bleedin' culchies. There should be a border at the Pale to prevent them gettin' into the city. It's no wonder there's fuckin' traffic jams in this city every day. The bloody culchies and women cause them. Bringin' their brats 100 yards down the road to school, double and triple parking...and the lollipop ladies. What are they for? They stand at pedestrian lights. The minute the pedestrian lights turn effin' green, what do they do?

Jump out with their large bleedin' lollipop to let some mother walk back to her car. I think we should have a Spanish Inquisition again, where all the Lollipop ladies are rounded up, tortured, and hanged." He was in free fall on this one. Then Jayo's mobile rang. He was glad of any diversion.

"Where the fuck are you?" said the voice at the other end.

"Stuck in traffic at Terenure Cross. We'll be there in a few minutes", said Jayo.

-o-o-o-o-o-

Ulser was impatient. He had his mechanic's job to get to. He had spent the day tearing around, rounding up his buyers, getting rid of the goods and getting the cash in. Why they had chosen Jimmy the Snail to move this load, he'll never know.

He was sitting at the entrance to Vernon Close in Templeogue waiting for Jimmy to arrive with his second drop of the day. Then he could get away to his regular nixer as a mechanic. He was already behind time. He knew he had a full service and a cylinder head gasket to attend to. He'd be poxed if he was home by midnight tonight at this rate.

Jimmy's truck rounded the corner and Ulser was out like a flash.

"What's that wanker doing here?" asked Jimmy of Jayo.

"We've a bit of business to do. You just keep yourself to yourself, if you know what I mean? I've something in the back I have to give to Ulser." Jimmy's antennae went up straight away.

"What are you doin' with that scum-bag? I thought he wasn't fit for work, or so he tells us? Doesn't look too injured to me", Jimmy said to Jayo

"Jimmy, you just do your job and I'll do mine. I'll be a few minutes. You stay in the truck while I talk to this guy."

Jimmy observed the two talking in the mirror. There was a debate and Ulser handed a small envelope to Jayo. He then watched Jayo go to the side door of the truck. He lifted the roller door and got in the back.

Jayo, once in the van and out of sight of Jimmy, cut open the tape on top of the marked cooker and pulled back the flaps. Ulser threw up a cardboard box to him. Jayo offloaded the smalls to Ulser's box from the cooker box. He resealed the marked box with tape he kept in his overalls. Ulser closed over the flaps on the smaller box. It was over in a minute.

"Done", said Ulser. "I'm off. I'll be in contact." And with that he headed over to his beat-up Skoda, without as much as a glance back at Jimmy in the truck. Jayo closed up and climbed back into the cab.

"He's bad news, that Ulser. Don't know what you're doin' hangin' around with him. I don't know what you're at and I'm damned sure I don't want to. But if I ever get pulled for being part of any scam, I won't be staying quiet. I value my job."

Jayo said nothing but pulled a £50 note from his pocket. "If you know what's good for you, just take the money and keep your effin' mouth shut. Now move on and let's get these deliveries finished."

Chapter 8

It was 10.30 a.m. Thursday and Ted and Tom stood in the locker rooms of Eirtran. The main pick of the day was in full swing outside. The delivery trucks had all moved off. Tom was using a master key to open locker number 17. Ted was not happy looking into the lockers of the staff. However, he had been convinced by Tom that, as the lockers were business property, they—as managers—were entitled to check that each one was being used for legitimate purposes. Even so, neither wanted to have to explain to one of the floor staff what they were up to. If anyone caught them in the locker rooms (hopefully not looking in the lockers) their prepared story was that they were considering revamping the locker room and were doing a survey.

The door of locker 17 was covered with Page 3 lovelies from *the Sun*. Both men couldn't resist casting an eye over the collage of female flesh. The locker contained nothing unusual at first glance: a change of clothes, a pair of overalls (still in its cellophane wrap), an empty plastic lunch box, a bicycle pump, a few football magazines etc. There was a brown box on the floor of the locker. Tom pulled back the flaps.

"Ted, have a look at this!" The two men peered in. The box contained 3 items: an MP3 Player, a hairdryer, and a clock-radio, all in their original boxes and all products distributed by Eirtran.

"OK, close it up and lock the door. Who's next for shaving?" said Ted.

Tom went over to locker number 32. He opened it up. The stuff came tumbling out: boxes containing electric kettles and hair styling sets, all similar items to those distributed by the warehouse. Iano and Jody were going to have some explaining to do.

"OK, now the big one." He closed 32 and went to 47, Ulser's locker. The door was covered in glossy *Hustler* rather than paper *Sun*. The pictures were a tad more revealing. Ulser—for all his endearing qualities—certainly was not known for his subtlety. Ulser seemingly had a soft spot for Asian Babes.

They looked through the assorted rubbish in his locker. Nothing unusual—as you would expect from the leader of the pack. He would be foolish to leave traces. Tom could not resist searching the pockets of the donkey jacket in the locker. He pulled out a cellophane package of something. However, when he pulled it clear to view it, it was obvious he was holding cocaine.

"Christ, either he's got a bad habit or Ulser's got more business interests than even I was aware of." There was a sense of satisfaction in Tom's voice as he said it. Ted had had enough at this stage.

"Ok, close it up...what's the next step, Tom?" Ted looked uncomfortable. He seemed to have suddenly turned grey to Tom.

Ted was already thinking of the ramifications. This guy, Ulser, had to be dealing with some serious players. He thought to himself that however carefully he'd have to walk with IR procedures, he was now in the legal arena where he can't be seen to be tampering with evidence and that every move from now needs back-up proof. He could make no assumptions. He could feel his thoughts clouding and his heart racing. Everyone will look to him for leadership and he wasn't sure he was up to it. He needs his head to slow down and not knee jerk. Christ, he thought, why didn't I stay in my last job?

"I did expect something in Ulser's locker but not that. I think we need to get the cops in on this one...but when? My preference would have been to somehow get the lads to come in and open their own lockers. I would prefer to do it on a *random* basis, but we need to include all those we suspect in the random line-up. We haven't got time to go through all the niceties. We're going to have to make some quick decisions here. If we ask guys to show us the contents of the lockers, there'll be opposition to it. They'll get the union in on it and buy time until they remove the evidence."

Tom was talking fast now, and Ted's stomach was beginning to churn. This was heavy stuff.

"The staff'll raise a few red herrings. For instance, they'll go along the harassment route and it could get very unpleasant and messy. We know the stuff is here, but we must know legitimately. The problem we have now is that we could have been spotted skulking around and alarm bells are already beginning to ring out on the floor. We're going to have to work fast."

Ted's stomach was tightening at every word and was beginning to feel nauseous.

"What I suggest is that, firstly, we bring over one of the security guards to man the door of the locker rooms. That way no-one is getting in or out. We get Jem, the shop steward, to look at the opening of each of the lockers in the presence of the culprits. Of course, we don't have Ulser in situ, but we can, as a management group, open his anyway in the presence of witnesses, however unwilling. We cannot let the culprits know how we knew—our case for bringing dismissal procedures will be made up from the evidence we find in the lockers—not how we found it. Then we go through the disciplinary procedures and move towards suspension and sacking. Are you in agreement, Ted?"

Ted's stomach was churning as he tried to focus. He wasn't going to have time to make a considered response and he knew it. His instinct told him whatever decision he made now would have major repercussions for his future as manager of the business.

"What I suggest we do is bring over the individuals in question—with their union official—while opening the lockers. Because Ulser isn't here, we open his locker witnessed by the security guard and Jem but without the other two. The crap in Ulser's locker is in a slightly different league. Then we call in the cops today—only to look at the cocaine issue. We deal with the stealing issue through our own disciplinary procedures. I don't want concurrent court cases and IR hassle."

His mouth was dry and the rest of his mouth, to his throat, was as if he had just swallowed a bottle of vinegar. He had nearly repeated verbatim what Tom had already said without realising it. His mind was in a whirl.

"With Ulser, you're going down the legal route. You know that don't you?" Tom said, sending a shiver up Ted's spine as he said it.

"OK—let's go and get this crap over with."

-o-o-o-o-o-

Iano heard someone calling him as he walked back for the next pick with his trolley. He looked around and saw Tom Hannigan beckoning with his right hand to come over. Once Tom got his attention, he saw Tom turn away and whistle for his mate Jody, who was sitting in the cab of the forklift. Tom had a phone to his ear and was speaking to someone at the same time.

Iano and Jody walked towards Tom. They looked around to see Jem approaching from another direction. Tom said nothing and turned to face Jem. Tom looked stern and seemed happy to maintain an uncomfortable silence until they were all assembled.

"Lads, you might come along with me and I'll explain why when we get there." With that, he turned and marched ahead of them. Jem looked perplexed as he had no idea what was happening.

"What's all this about, Tom? I don't even know what I'm required for."

"It'll all be clear in a minute, Jem. Just stick with it...." This was clearly irritating Jem, who liked to have himself prepared for any possible situation. Not knowing the issue made him uncomfortable. Nonetheless, he fell in step behind Tom.

They assembled in the locker room. The three behind him were surprised to see John Fitzpatrick, the tall, thin security guard who was usually on duty in the appliances area, standing inside the door. Ted Black sat on one of the benches in the middle of the locker room. Jem pushed Tom aside and confronted Ted.

"What's this all about?" he demanded.

Ted felt peaky and hoped it wouldn't show in his voice.

"I'll show you", replied Ted, who stood up purposely and indicated with his finger for them to follow. Iano and Jody were feeling concerned at this point and knew something wasn't right. Ted stood opposite locker number 17, Iano's locker. Iano's heart began to pound. Ted placed the master key in the locker door.

"Ian, would you prefer to open this locker, or will I?"

"There's personal property in there—you've no right ..." interjected Jem.

"Wrong, Jem. I have every right to ensure company property is being used as intended—it's no different to checking that PCs are being used for company business, no more than a landlord ensuring that his property isn't being used as a brothel. I have every right. Now that we've cleared that up ..." he said evenly, realising he had the high ground and that Jem was on the back foot.

"Ian—will you open it, or will I?" Iano nodded to go ahead, fearing the worst.

Ted turned the key and opened the door. "Would you mind opening up the box on the floor of your locker, please?"

Iano stepped forward and pulled back the two flaps. The appliances were there for all to see. Iano was red in the face and Jody was starting to sweat profusely. Ted's stomach was in a knot with the tension.

"Would you agree that what we are looking at is company property, Ian?" asked Tom without emotion.

"Brother Ian does not have to answer that question, Ted", Jem chipped in, feeling totally outmanoeuvred.

"Remember—we're not in a court of law, Jem. You should know that. In accordance with Industrial Relations procedures, I am giving Ian a chance to explain himself. I am asking a question to give him a fair chance to provide an answer. You're not his solicitor and he's not your client, if you can remember your Industrial

Relations procedures? I'd be surprised if you couldn't reel them off, chapter and verse, Jem", retorted Ted icily, unable to suppress the hint of sarcasm.

Jem never liked being undermined, particularly in his role as a shop steward, in full view of the lads. He knew that Ted was right but was so stumped, he couldn't come up with a quick retort. Iano looked towards Jem with his mouth open, a desperate look on his ashen face. Jem was unable to form a sentence. There was an uneasy pregnant pause that Ted or Tom made no effort to break. When Iano received no direction from Jem, Iano turned to Jody who was looking away.

"I-I don't know how they got there. Someone is stitchin' me up."

"I'll ask you again, Ian. Are the items in that box the property of Eirtans? It's a simple yes or no."

"How the hell do I know? I've never seen them before...."

"Ian. You agree that this is your locker? You are responsible for its contents and for ensuring that it is used for legitimate business. I'm formally warning you that I am, pending an investigation, suspending you from duty on full pay. In due course, when the investigation has taken place, the company will give you a chance to put your case. You are entitled to representation at that meeting in the form of your shop steward. Until then, I am asking you to leave the premises. As I say, you will be on full pay."

Jody knew what was coming at this stage. He was numb and felt like a lamb to slaughter. He and Iano had got a little greedy in the last week. They felt Drac was taking too much of a cut while they were taking all the risk. To even things up and get better balance to the deal, they decided to "skim" a little more than previously. For Christ's sake, this was only the second time they'd done it and they were nailed! Someone had ratted on them. Had Drac got wind of it, or had someone told the manager about it? Drac liked to have everything under his control. He didn't like any opposition. You were either with him or again' him.

Iano felt crushed. His wife had warned him to keep his nose clean and stay away from any funny business. He was in line for a supervisor's job and knew it. It was important to stay out of harm's way. His wife felt they would get over the lean spell if they just ground it out. How could he go home and tell her he'd been suspended and was likely to be sacked?

In a blur, Jody now saw them opposite his—Jody's—locker. "Will you or I open it, Jody?" asked Ted. Jody just nodded to go ahead. No words would come out. Ted pulled the door open and all the appliances came tumbling out. Ted asked the same questions of Jody.

"I don't know how they got there", was the best he could come up with. Ted informed him also of the procedures and that he was suspended on full pay, pending investigation.

"I advise both of you to think seriously about your current situation and stay at home until we have had time to explore further. We will write to you formally explaining why you have been suspended, copy to your union, and we will also write to you—post-investigation—when we will discuss next steps with you. Please pick up any of your personal effects and leave the store immediately."

Both lads were hanging their heads. They collected one or two items from their lockers sheepishly whilst supervised and Ted asked John Fitzpatrick to escort both men from the premises.

When they left, Jem spoke. "How did you get this information? You seemed to know exactly where to go."

Tom was first to interject. "That is not the issue, Jem, and you know it. The issue here is that property belonging to this warehouse was discovered in the men's lockers and that you were there, in accordance with procedure, when it was discovered. How we knew is not the issue. We have no intention of going there. The improper placement of company property *is* the issue, and you know that."

Ted was glad that Tom was talking because he certainly didn't feel—nay, was not capable of—uttering a sound. He was sitting on the bench, burning a hole in the floor where he was looking, wishing this would all go away. He felt the burden on his shoulders and a little tension in his left upper arm.

"...and that's not all. Come with me, Jem."

Jem's heart began to sink when he realised that both Tom and Ted were making a beeline for Ulser's locker. Jem had a fair idea about the two boys and that something had been going on. He had warned them to stay away from Drac. They were decent lads, but probably weren't the brightest. He could understand how youngsters might get careless. However, Ulser was a different kettle of fish. He was careful, and it wouldn't be like him to leave anything incriminating around.

"Martin is not here at the moment, as you are well aware. He is on sick leave. However, I am going to open his locker and I want you to observe."

If Jem could have gathered his thoughts, he might have had the gumption to refuse the offer. However, before he had time to formulate a reply, the locker was open, and Ted pulled a pack from the donkey jacket.

"Do you know what this is, Jem?" Jem looked at the pack in his hand.

"I think I have a fair idea—I hope it's not what I think it is."

Christ, had Ulser taken leave of his senses? Jem knew straight away that he did not want to get involved in this. It was not just an IR matter. This was probably going to involve the polis.

"We're not sure either, but I have already rung the guards and they are on their way. If this is what we think it is, I think we both know the repercussions for our friend Martin."

Jem was trying hard to think straight. Ted had already rung an old friend of his, who was a sergeant in Pearse Street Garda station. He knew the patrol car would arrive any minute.

"Look, this is out of my league, and I have no intention of getting involved in this. This is between Ulser and yourselves. If that is what I think it is, it's illegal—and holding it on the premises cannot be condoned. I'm in agreement that I'm a witness to you discovering it but I don't want to get involved any further, at least for now."

A Garda sergeant strode in with John Fitzpatrick, the security man, just as he finished the sentence. Ted introduced himself and shook his hand. There was some mumbling as he showed him what he had. The guard asked a few questions of Ted and then said that all the people present must provide a statement around its discovery.

Ted realised he was knee deep in a major controversy and he was hardly a week in the place. He felt like a man drowning and did not like where all of this was going. He could sense imminent conflict and that he was entering a battle arena he wasn't entirely comfortable with.

CHAPTER 9

Ulser stood in front of the TV in Stanley Bookmakers. In the Goodwood 2.20 p.m. "Mennysthethyme" was holding second place as it passed the three-furlong marker. She was maintaining a good line on the inside rail. At 7/1, she was a great bet for a 6-horse race. His phone rang to the tune of Queen's "Another One Bites the Dust". They passed the furlong marker. She had her nose in front. The phone intrusion was unwelcome. He answered with "C'mon ye fuckin' beauty!"

The two old codgers watching the race had lost interest at this point and were tearing up their betting slips. A few words were spoken on the other end of the phone. Ulser said "Thanks" just as "Mennysthethyme" crossed the line a nose in front. He was up £350, but his humour had suddenly turned black. The old codger beside him sensed it.

"Bad news, Ulser?"

"With the greatest of respect, it's none of your effin' business, Joe." Joe turned to his mate and raised his eyebrows.

"Jaysus, if you're that happy when you win, I'd hate to see when you bleedin' lose.... I suppose a pint and a ride is out of the question?" He winked at his old mate, a twinkle in his eye. That didn't help Ulser's mood.

"Forget the pint...but I can sort the ride out for ye all right...*go fuck yourself!*" He spat out the words, phlegm flying in every direction.

With that, he turned and left without collecting his winnings. A girly "OOOH!" from the two oul' lads was left ringing in his ears as he slammed the door shut behind him.

-o-o-o-o-o-

Josser, aka Dracula, sat in the picker and had been observing Tom Hannigan's entourage heading for the locker room. He sat in the cab a few more minutes to figure out what was going down. Things quietened down but his curiosity had got the better of him. He made over towards the Administration office with a picklist in his hand. Some of the items on the list were not in the locations shown. He had legitimate reason to query the Admin staff. It was an ideal excuse to be at close quarters and get the lie of the land.

As he opened the door of the Admin office, John Fitzpatrick was escorting the sergeant through the main door of the building. He put two and two together quickly. Backing out of the office, he found a quiet corner to make a call.

"Get the word out to stop the business. Do it quick." He hung up and made his way back to the Admin office.

-o-o-o-o-o-

Ted told Tom he had something to do after everyone

left. He went to the car and drove out to Shellybanks, parking the car near the beginning of the great South Wall. He left the car and began walking the pier, sea breeze in his face. His throat was still dry, and his nerves were jangling. His whole body was on edge.

He thought about his dad, long passed on, who was so cool in difficult situations like this and whose advice had always been on point. His great saying, "Worry only about what you can control and leave the rest in the lap of the Lord", was running through Ted's mind.

Ted had lost his faith in the Church long ago, but without ever losing his faith in a Greater Power—Fate or whatever. He wasn't religious—but he was spiritual. Clerics he had no time for and even less so after he visited the Vatican in Rome. He saw the unimaginable wealth in the place and envisaged how the Man Himself might have reacted had he landed at that time. Ted suspected he would do something akin to what he did to the merchants and money lenders in the Temple....The wealth of the Vatican sickened Ted so much that he never went back to a church again.

Rebecca was religious in the traditional sense and tried to get him to attend services from time to time. Her rationale was that Church and its clerics needed support. She continued to pay dues to the local church via standing order. "Where would your sons and daughters get married if the Church wasn't there? Wouldn't you want a funeral ceremony when you passed on? Clerics have to be there to do it," she reasoned. Ted thought civil ceremonies would suffice but wasn't sufficiently engaged to argue.

He usually appealed to a Higher Power when things

got tough. It was a throwback to his Catholic upbringing. He passionately believed that a Greater Power was looking over him, steering him. He shared the burden of his fears and doubts with that Greater Being when there was no-one else to turn to. He also believed his father was in a different realm nearby, providing a guiding presence.

'Why am I being tested like this? I did all the right things to have more time with my family when I moved jobs. My work was perhaps a little more boring where I was—and less lucrative—but it wasn't a scourge like this. This guy hangs around with some low-lifes, and I'm not sure I'm up to the challenge. They're looking to me for solutions—I don't have them. I've heard what some of these gangs do to people. I don't know who Ulser knows, but they're not the most savoury, I suspect. When he finds out what has happened today, he—or his mates— may target my family and me. Rebecca won't thank me for that.'

Instead of calming his mood, his thoughts were running away with themselves. He felt slightly sick and had no appetite.

-o-o-o-o-o-

Micko Stenson was feeling uncomfortable. He was in the canteen eating his lunch, but his appetite had deserted him. He wasn't much in the humour; he had heard the law made a visit that morning. If the management had got hold of the two lads, who would be next? He kept himself to himself, staying out of conversation with everyone at the table.

He'd rung Ulser earlier to let him know the scene (i.e. that coke was found in his locker). Typical Ulser, he didn't seem to give a damn. He felt the need to tell him as a mate, but he didn't much like the guy. In relative terms, Ulser was in far deeper than Micko.

Micko had no time for drugs and hated all that went with it. His own son was an addict and he understood the mess it created. The fights at home; the violence visited on Micko's wife, Molly; the effect of his son's behaviour on his two sibling sisters—they now had regular nightmares; pushers breaking down the front door for payment...the list went on and on.

All his family were on tablets. His wife was shattered and suffered from anorexia and agoraphobia. She was regularly hospitalised. One of his daughters suffered epileptic fits and had missed a whole year of school. She never went out. His second daughter seemed to be handling it ok—as far as he could see. His son was in Mountjoy, serving 3 years for supply. He hadn't gone to see him since the court case—he was glad of some respite.

After all his family had been through, Micko wondered how he could justify tipping off a scumbag like Ulser, Christ, he dealt in the stuff! To satiate his conscience, he reasoned that if he didn't rat on Ulser, Ulser most likely wouldn't rat on him if the heat came on. The management were digging, and it was only a matter of time before they'd catch up with him if he wasn't careful.

-o-o-o-o-o-

Rebecca sat at the window observing Howth Head.

She inserted the needle into a vein on her left arm. The view was soothing—particularly as she had this chore to do. It distracted her from the damned needle. She was expert at injecting herself at this point. When she couldn't face doing it herself, Ted would do it for her. Rebecca's insulin shots were part of her life.

She had been diagnosed with diabetes 3 years before. In the run up to the diagnosis, she had a series of mystery illnesses. The shots had transformed her life. She had been so ill at one point she didn't want to consider having kids. However, once diabetes was diagnosed, Ted and she decided to have kids straight away. Jason arrived exactly 9 months after she was diagnosed.

The phone started ringing, but she left it. She had to get this chore out of the way first. Aaron was asleep in the cot upstairs. Jason was playing with his toy cars in front of her. She hated the jab of the needle and always felt nauseous at the thought. She could feel the pressure from the plunger in her veins. She could see her muscles tense at the back of her wrist. She hoped the ringing of the phone would not wake the baby.

When she finished, she gathered up the paraphernalia and insulin packs. She was extremely conscious of the children and could not afford to leave medication lying around. She had a special box for used needles, which she returned to the chemist regularly for proper disposal.

She opened the child-gate at the bottom of the stairs and climbed to the bathroom to put her stuff in the cabinet. The phone had stopped. As she came down the stairs again, the phone started ringing once more. She picked up the receiver.

"Hello ..."

"You looked great at the window. Your hair isn't up this morning. I like you better with your hair up ..." said an eerie, whispering male voice at the other end.

"Who the hell is this? ..." Her mind was racing. Someone had to be watching her. How else would they know?

"Does that stuff you inject give you a high? I can give you a bit more if you like...." whispered the voice.

In a panic, she slammed down the receiver. She was sweating profusely, and her legs were weak. She felt nauseous—both from the insulin shot and at the thought of the freak on the phone who had been observing her. Where was he looking from? Who was looking at her? Her space had been invaded.

Her body tensed. Instinct took over. Where were her babies? She bounded up the stairs, two steps at a time, to see that Aaron was still there. He was fast asleep. She went over to the cot and let down the side to hear him breathe. She could smell his baby smell and kissed his head. She ran back down the stairs and saw little Jason playing happily with his toy cars.

She breathed a sigh of relief, but her mind was still racing. Her tension levels were sky high. She needed calming. She opened the drinks cabinet. It contained a bottle of red wine – still open from the previous night. She poured a generous glass. She sat at the table and downed the glass in one go. Some of it dribbled down her front, staining the white blouse—blood on virgin snow. Her hand was shaking. It wasn't a good idea to drink so soon after her insulin shot. To hell with that, she thought. She needed Ted.

She rang his number. As usual, it was on answer machine. Ever since he went to this new job, he was constantly busy. He was never available when she needed him. Where was this person observing her from? She dropped the phone. She went upstairs again and looked out through the lace curtains of the back window.

The house stood on the side of a hill. The hill sloped away towards Dalkey village below and the sea. The room overlooked the roofs of adjacent houses beneath. She reckoned she could only be observed at an upstairs window from any one of those houses. She noticed the green area masked by trees where a lane ran through it. Could someone be standing there? Who was taunting her and why?

CHAPTER 10

Ted was back in the office after his unsatisfactory walk in Dublin Bay. Tom and Ted were locked in conference. The sergeant had returned from Pearse Street and was with them.

"We feel that we have IR issues with Martin Cullen that we need to address. Quite obviously, what we are confronted with here is a breach of his employment conditions and we must go through proper procedures. I also understand that this is now a legal matter and that you are obliged to caution the suspect regarding the drugs. For that reason, I would be keen that we both visit Martin together with our different issues. Would you feel that is possible?" asked Ted of the sergeant.

Ted was trying to give himself time to think and space to explore options.

"We'll be making a visit very soon. We have a bit of work to do yet before we can charge him. I think if you have something to do, go ahead and do it. He's unlikely to abscond for what's a relatively small offence."

"That's fine. We intend contacting him today and visiting him if possible. I didn't want to do anything that might upset the legal process. I appreciate you being so helpful. We'll go ahead on our own bat then." There were a few handshakes and "thank yous" before the sergeant left.

"Ok, Tom. I think we need to contact our friend Ulser and say that we wish to meet him. Although our preference would be to meet him on the premises here, I suspect that he may insist meeting him at his home...and that's fine by me. I think that we must let him know that he is entitled to representation at the meeting. I am suggesting that you do the contacting and I'll do the talking.

"If you can't raise him by phone today, go directly to the house. If you can't get him there, I'd have a written note giving him a time for our meeting, which you can slip under the door. It should state that we need to meet him immediately. If you do get to talk to him, don't get drawn into any discussion. Let's keep it all formal for the meeting. Would you make a move on that straight away? I want to talk to our HR people for guidance. I don't want to put a foot wrong here. You don't get too many chances to deal with a gurrier like this."

It still baffled Ted that he left drugs in the locker. Even if it had been only some stolen goods from the store—why in God's name drugs? In any event, he now had grounds to move towards his dismissal. He'd never dismissed anyone in his life before and wasn't particularly yearning for this new experience. His heart gave a flutter.

-o-o-o-o-o-

Ulser was working on a 95 Ford Escort in Dolphin Motor Repairs. He had been a joyrider as a youngster and got into a lot of trouble with the law. Part of the "rehabilitation" programme suggested by his probation officer was to be placed in work experience by FAS. Because of his "love" of cars, it was suggested that he might be interested in a mechanic's course. Ulser took to it like a duck to water. He started working full-time as a mechanic but found that he wasn't making enough money to support his lifestyle. People didn't pay on time and it was hard to make ends meet.

He believed that if he could do most of his mechanic's work in the evenings, he could hold down a fulltime day job as well. Eirtran's arrival in Ireland was timely. He was taken on because he had both fork-lift driving and mechanical skills. For his first year in Eirtran, he juggled the two jobs. However, when the Celtic Tiger hit, he found his work in the evenings expanding. More and more cars were being bought and his customer base expanded rapidly. He had difficulty balancing the day job with his own business.

The money was too lucrative at Eirtran to forego it. He found ways and means to make time during the day in Eirtran to catch up on the backlog of his mechanic's work. Sick leave was a regular means to achieve this, Mondays in particular. His increasing absenteeism from work resulted in a series of runs-in with various managers. He realised that he couldn't be touched if he didn't give them too much rope to hang him with. He briefed himself well on employee rights and charters.

Things got so busy on the mechanic side that he recruited an apprentice and another mechanic. He was forced to buy a ramshackle premises on Marrowbone Lane, not far from Guinness brewery, to provide enough space to cater for his expanding business. His costs increased, so he needed more and more business to pay the bills.

Today, Ulser was in oil-stained blue overalls and an old woollen monkey hat, black with sweat, oil, and grease. His hands were covered in oil, black lines clearly marking the meeting of fingertips and nails. He was under the car when he heard the mobile ring. He wriggled out from underneath, pushing the car creeper he was lying on.

"Yeah?"

"Martin, an issue which involves you has come to light and we need to have an urgent discussion. I suggest that you have representation in attendance at the meeting. We can meet you anytime today, preferably here at the depot. If that can't be, I'd suggest early morning, preferably at the depot but elsewhere if you wish. I know that you are out sick, but it is critical we meet you within the next 24 hours."

Tom was tense and his voiced cracked slightly.

"What's all this about...I bleedin' well hurt me back, I've sent the doctor's cert ..."

Ulser had been tipped off and knew exactly what was up. He'd deny everything, of course. The law would have to prove it. The management had to prove it. He knew the management were crapping themselves. He wouldn't give them an inch.

He knew plenty of local lads in Ballyer who had gone to court and were home long before the cops had landed a punch in the court room. The judges knew the prisons were full. The worst sentence any of his mates got, provided they hadn't murdered or raped someone, was a suspended sentence...and most who got that would have been on far more serious possession charges than his.

He knew their lawyer in any event, so he'd be fine. Feck it if a legal eagle cost a few bob. If others got no more than a slap on the wrists, he might get community service. That's nothing to get worked up about. Sure, the Courts system here is shite....The only thing solicitors and barristers are worried about is getting paid. 'Justice, me arse!' He thought, 'It's all about precedence...and precedence is soft on criminals. The whole system can't touch the likes of us.'

"Its an entirely different issue. I suggest you be here at 4 pm this evening...."

Ulser just about heard Tom, as he was jolted out of his reverie.

"Well, what's it about then? I amn't goin' into any shaggin' meetin' with you—or your mate—without knowin' what it's about. If it's an IR issue, I'm entitled to know what the issue is."

"And you're goin' to be told that at the meeting. You have the option to speak then or not. We're payin' your salary 9 to 5—during working time; that means you're at our beck and call and you attend a meeting if we call it, whether it suits you or not."

The tension was palpable. Ulser knew well enough not to push too hard or they would pay an *unplanned* visit to his home. Better play the game and deal with it.

"OK. My house tomorrow at 4 pm...and I don't need that dozy git you call my shop steward. That muppet's head is so far up management's arse he's only able to speak out through your hole! I don't need him. You know where my place is?"

"Martin, I think that I could drive blindfold to where you live at this stage ..."

"See you—with the new love of your life—in my gaff at 4 tomorrow." He clicked off his phone and uttered an expletive. This was inconvenient at best, a complete pain in the arse at worst.

-o-o-o-o-o-

Ted turned the key in the door, glad of respite from the day's events. He was looking forward to a nice dinner, bottle of wine, and unwinding in front of the fire. He called out. No response. He could hear Aaron crying in his cot upstairs. Jason walked out from the kitchen; his face covered in chocolate.

"Daddy—Mammy not well. Come."

He took Jason's hand and followed him into the kitchen. Rebecca was slumped on the floor beside the cooker. Two empty bottles of wine were beside her and she was snoring.

"Good God!"

He ran over and pulled her head to his.

"Becks! Becks! Are you ok?"

She started to come around.

"Ted", she mumbled. "Ted...love you...you my best friend...ooh, I'm bit pissed, amn't I?"

Ted didn't know whether to laugh or cry. She looked so funny, but what had brought this on?

"Becks...what were you thinking? You ok? Have the kids eaten?"

"Man rang ..." She started to go back to sleep. "Scared me...kids...kids ..." She shot up into his arms.

"Ted...the kids. Are they here? Are they ok?" She was frantic. Ted held her.

"No, honey. They're ok. What the hell happened? How long are you like this?"

It took multiple cups of coffee, a lot of crying and sobbing, an amount of prompting, and consoling before he heard the full story. He was frightened to see the impact it had on her. She was in a dreadful state. He knew she wasn't the strongest. He eventually got her to bed and tucked her in. By the time he had the kids changed, fed, and put to bed, he was exhausted. Dinner was beer and a cheese sandwich.

As he lay in bed that night, trying to sleep, his mind raced. His heart pumped hard, the adrenaline flowing through his system. Rebecca mumbled in her sleep, tossing and turning. The prospect of a good night's sleep was remote. Nonetheless, by 4 a.m., he had slipped into an uneasy doze ...

...The phone beside the bed was ringing. He banged the button on the clock. 4.30 in the morning. For Pete's sake, the one night he needed kip. He picked up the phone.

"Hello?"

Maybe some relative had died, he reasoned. Rebecca's dad was always a bit frail. His mind started to race with possibilities. But no answer. He thought he could hear breathing.

"Hello?"

Still no answer. He thought that someone might have set his number off accidently by failing to lock their mobile phone in their pocket. With a B in his name, he was often fast-dial 1 or 2 on someone's phone. They had pressed the fast dial by accident possibly. He put the phone down. Then he took it off the receiver and fell back into his uneasy doze.

CHAPTER 11

Tom rang the bell of a small house in the estate, which was close to Ballyfermot Village. It was a typical Council house of late 40's vintage. It had a small garden to the front. An iron railing—the base encased in concrete—separated the front garden from the footpath. The garden was no more than six feet deep. It was overgrown and unkempt. The 2-storey house was pebbledashed with a white plaster band across the middle—some 10 feet up—to break the monotony. The pebbledash was painted in a dull brown colour. The front-doors of Ulser's semi-D, and that of his neighbour's, were only feet apart. A small iron railing separated the two properties.

Tom waited a minute for a response. He looked to the heavens. He pressed the bell again. Still no reply. He heard noise inside in the hall. There was a rattle of chains. The door opened slightly—a security chain prevented it opening any further. A pretty woman's head appeared at hip level.

"Yes?" It was a pretty face but a little vacant. The woman was in her twenties. She sat in a wheelchair.

"Martin?...He was expecting us? ...We were to meet him here at 4 o'clock."

"No. Martin alway ring if someone gumin'. Di'nt say no-one gumin' today. Not heaw. Said he'd be late de night." The eyes never wavered from Tom's.

"You're certain he's not on his way?...Would you mind if I rang him just to check and you could speak to him?"

She nodded.

Tom rang Ulser's number. The message came up straight away. "Martin Cullen. If I owe you money, hang up. If you owe me money, then leave a message and I'll ring you back"...BEEP...

"Martin, its 4 o'clock and we're here at the house—there's no sign of you. Could you let us know where you are and when you are coming? You know my mobile. Tom." He hung up.

Tom wasn't surprised or annoyed. It was what he expected. He looked to Ted and threw his eyes to heaven. He turned back to the lady at the door.

"He has the phone on answering machine. We'll wait in the car for a while, if that's ok? ..." he said.

"I'm Tom Hannigan and that's Ted Black," he continued. "We work with Martin in Eirtran. If we don't come back, would you tell him we called?" The girl nodded and closed the door immediately.

Ted opened the squeaky metal gate and they both strode over to the car.

"That cute hoor...he's messin' us around again. This is fucking deliberate. He had no intention of meeting us. Guaranteed he'll have some excuse." Tom tried to get himself worked up over Ulser's no show.

"He's done this before? ..." asked Ted.

"Umpteen times. He'll claim he had to go to the

chemist, or his granny was giving birth to a canary or his car ran into a train. He'll have some implausible excuse. We can wait, but I'm pretty sure he's not going to show."

"Let's give it 20 minutes. You can try again on the mobile ..." offered Ted. This was really pissin' him off.

What annoyed Ted even more was that if he, as a manager, didn't dot every "i" and cross every "t", irrespective of what this toe-rag did, the IR legislation would favour the "worker". What a misnomer that! The unions might even construe that by Ted following up today at Ulser's house, during working hours where Ulser continues to get sick pay to doss around, was worker harassment or bullying. He'd seen it happen to other managers before. In Ted's view, he should have the power to sack this miscreant on the spot. Look at the hours of management time that was being wasted while Ulser swung the lead. The sense of injustice was eating Ted. It was clear to him that there was no justice, that the systems were set up to erect roadblocks against active managers at every opportunity.

-o-o-o-o-o-

Ulser sat in his car 200 yards from his own house watching proceedings. He took delight in pissin' off management. He needed time to think. He was tipped off that the fuzz and management had discovered the stash. He had a number of explanations but needed to work out which one would work best with both groups—the fuzz and the management. He knew that whatever story he told it must to stand up to legal scrutiny. He knew the managers would wait – it was their job. They would wait at least half an hour. Let them stew, he thought.

-o-o-o-o-o-

It was approaching 4.30, and Tom and his new boss had run out of things to say. There was a tap on the side window. Ulser nodded in the direction of his house.

"Nice of him to show up!" said Ted sarcastically.

They followed Ulser to the door. He didn't turn to apologise, just opened the door and let them follow him in.

"Martin. I' tha' you?" the girl cried from one of the rooms. "There were men heaw lookin' fer you. Are you in twuble?"

"Its ok, Mel. The men are from work and they're here to meet me...."

"Aw, dat's ok den. I'm just watchin' de telly."

"Leave us alone for a few minutes, Mel. I have to talk to them about somethin' a' work."

The three men walked into the small living room. It was surprisingly homely. A traditional picture of The Sacred Heart of Jesus was prominent on one of the walls. It had a red cross mounted underneath, which was lit. A three-piece suite was neatly laid out, filling the floorspace of the room. The room contained a black metal Victorian fireplace, complete with the original tiled surround. The mantelpiece was decorated with little knick-knacks and small vases. Another wall featured three flying ducks. Martin turned and faced them for the first time.

"What the fuck's all this about? I'm bloody well on sick leave and tired of this. You're harassing me."

"Yeah, Martin—I noticed the severe limp as you

127

walked in. You look like you're about to breathe your last!" Tom had it out before he could stop himself. Ted glowered at him. He knew the cost of just one loose word.

"Look, smart arse. I'm on pain killers and they're starting to kick in. The doctor told me to do some walking to prevent me getting stiff."

Ulser was annoyed at forgetting to limp. Not good. He was concentrating so hard on working out smart answers that he was letting things slip.

Even though Ted had glared at Tom, he was delighted that Tom had rattled Ulser's cage. Ulser looked at his watch.

"It's twenty to five. I'm on the company clock until five. After that, you're not welcome in my house and can eff off. Get on with what you have to say", said Ulser.

Tom and Ted were still standing. Ulser stood as well, leaning against the mantelpiece. He made no effort to offer them a seat. Ted took one pace forward and cleared his throat.

"Martin, there was a random search of company lockers carried out today. You and others were found to be using the lockers for purposes not intended...."

"Who the fuck gave you the right to open anyone's locker? They're personal and private. I have personal stuff in there, and you've no right to be pokin' your nose where it ain't wanted."

He fixed a threatening stare at Ted. Ted didn't flinch.

"That is not correct, Martin. The lockers are company property and are given as a privilege to staff. We, as a company, are entitled to protect our good name and reserve the right to ensure that lockers are being used legitimately."

"I'll have my lawyer on you. You're infringing on my personal rights and my dignity as an employee", Ulser ranted.

'Dignity. Is this guy for real?', thought Ted. It galled Ted that he couldn't just punch his lights out. He could feel himself tensing and his throat drying.

"I would suggest that while you're ringing him you seek further advice from him on criminal matters. We discovered a substantial amount of cocaine in your locker. We called in the guards, who confirmed our suspicions. They will be in contact with you in due course. However, you are in breach of company regulations and we regard this as a very serious disciplinary issue. Have you anything to say?"

There was complete silence. It didn't seem to Ted that Ulser was in any way surprised and was weighing up his options.

"Fuckin' right I have sumpin' to say. The gear isn't mine."

"Well, no one else has access to your locker...." said Tom.

"Oh yes, they bleedin' well have!"

Ted froze and hoped that Ulser hadn't noticed. Ulser had the rapt attention of both Tom and Ted.

"When the company took on the temps a few weeks ago, there weren't enough lockers to go round. Remember that dozy git of a shop steward of mine?...He looked for extra lockers from management and you refused. Well, I was forced to share my locker with this Enzo Rossi bloke—his Ma and Da run a chipper in Ringsend. I guarantee that you didn't check out his form when you employed him, did ye?"

Ted was dumbstruck. Was this little rat goin' to wriggle out of it again?

"What's more, I haven't been around for a few days because of my back. That little git obviously took full advantage."

Ted's heart sank. He could see that Ulser had got a tip-off and was prepared to sacrifice someone else to save his skin.

"If you're accusing me of dealing in this stuff, I'll have my lawyer on you like a hot snot. These are serious allegations and if you have anything else to say, say it to my lawyer. If I was you"...pointing accusingly at Ted..."I'd be very careful about making false accusations. You're only a wet week in the place, and it wouldn't look very good with your director if you get this one wrong. I'll have a picket on your depot before you can blink if this harassment continues. Now rev up and fuck off out my house. You're not welcome. I need to get on with my recuperation."

With that, he opened the door and beckoned them to leave. The two men passed Ulser and could smell the alcohol from his breath. However, they knew already that they were leaving the winning enclosure.

-o-o-o-o-o-

Ted was on the mobile as Tom drove.

"I'm aware of the fact that we are struggling with the cost base and that profits are well down...I know you said that it was my key target when you employed me but, we have this very difficult IR situation...(long pause)

Ted was onto his European Director.

"...I know you wanted me in Holland to meet key customers but I didn't expect this to blow up...(another long pause)...I can't at this stage—I've cancelled the flights—this guy is quite difficult and is volatile: I have to be here to keep an eye on it...."

Tom noticed that Ted's face was flushed and that he had his arms folded across his chest. This was indicative of the tension in his general demeanour. Ted was rushing his answers—impulsive answers—keen to garner a level of empathy, or sympathy, or both, from his director. It was clear from the conversation that his director had no interest in his predicament. He was demanding the impossible from Ted. There was a level of desperation in Ted's eyes which Tom hadn't noticed before.

"I know that these contracts are crucial and that I need to meet some of these people...but I'm sure you can do that...they won't want to hear that this asshole has caused a strike at the depot...(long pause)...Look, I know that you're not happy but I feel its crucial that I'm on top of this...I...FUCK! He hung up. Can you believe that? He hung up! This little bastard better be fucking worth it."

Tom had a bad feeling about the coming days. A manager on the warpath—and who isn't thinking straight—is not a good thing. He had more bad news to give him, which he knew wouldn't improve his humour.

"You know that you have a retirement speech to make for Georgie Monday night? You'll be expected to be there and buy a few drinks, mingle and all that." He waited for the explosion.

Ted faced him, incredulous.

"What?...The fucking place is fallin' down around my

ears...and you expect me to do a speech about the life of some oul' fella I barely know? ..." He paused for breath.

"I take it you've a speech written out for me, then? Can't you do it?...For fucks sake, I've enough on my plate." Ted was feeling overwhelmed just now.

"Ted, I'm sorry...I can't ..."

"Course you can!...I haven't time for this...my wife needs me home at the moment...I've hardly been home since I've taken up this job. It's taking over my life right now."

Ted felt Tom was just landing everything on him at once. Hadn't he got any initiative himself? Had he been waiting for Ted to arrive in the job just to dump all he didn't want to deal with on the new manager?

"Sorry, Ted. Its Georgie Hartnett, the longest serving member of our staff. He's hitting 65 and he has worked with the company since it was founded. It was the old Ringsend Freight Company then and he's the only member of Eirtran that has been with the company through all its take-overs. He's getting a very special send-off. The most senior manager in the place has to do it."

"Any chance we could keep him and retire Ulser in his place?" Tom shrugged and said no more. He could feel a level of hate for Eirtran and all it stood for run through him. Right now, he'd be happy to be anywhere else.

-o-o-o-o-o-

On his way home, Ted was close to St. Vincent's Hospital. His mind was foggy, and he was fuming over what he was being asked to do. It felt impossible to keep all the balls in the air. He was totally drained after today. The whole world wanted a piece of him.

'I'm just not functioning', he thought. 'There's no-one I can even bounce things off. All my mates are in banking, teaching, or finance. Handy jobs, I bet. Can't see them having to deal with trash like this. I'm sure their jobs have their pressures, but I can't imagine its anything like I'm having to deal with.' He knew he was being irrational and unfair, yet he couldn't stop himself from having a pop for no good reason.

Drizzle had started and was adding to his gloomy demeanour. Night had long since closed in and a string of red taillights extended into the distance. He needed time to himself, to allow the world to slow down and for him to take stock. The lights of Merrion Road Church shone through the stained-glass windows from the road. He indicated and pulled into the car park in front.

He blessed himself at the font and the entrance door squeaked loudly as he pushed in, echoing down through the vast chamber.

He sat into the first pew available. When did he last even sit in a church? God knows. The silence in a vast space he found somehow soothing. The only audible noise was the hum of traffic outside. What had drawn him to this place? It felt peaceful, shelter from the storm. How could he square this with his views on the Church as an institution? Why did he seek comfort from an establishment he detested?

If God spoke directly to us in bibles and gospels why, in all honesty, do we need theologians to interpret the Good Books and the Word of God? Perhaps it serves a purpose for the Vatican to control, indoctrinate, and subjugate the otherwise agile, sensible minds of resourceful individuals and imprison their minds with rules, articles of faith, and doctrines in order to scare them to conform and consequently, surgically removing the (dangerous) free mind which is inquisitive and would explore the natural and innate curiosities of the Soul. The membership rules suit the vast majority of the sheep-like herd, or flock (to use the Rome's wording), who are willing to surrender blindly their critical faculties at the Church door to shadowy figures in the Vatican so that they can retain membership to the club and suitably demonstrate their loyalty to the gang strictures by devoting themselves, in ever increasing levels of sanctimoniousness and devotion, to rituals that should ensure a place in Heaven and the Hereafter, rather than deliberating on the bleakness of life and the fatuousness of Man in the Here and Now. Followers—feel free to turn your brain off and follow the herd.

What ran so deep inside him that he ran for succour to the very place he disdained? But the truth was, he did feel a level of solace. Perhaps he would have felt just as protected in the womb of a synagogue, a Hindu temple, a Mosque, or a church of some other religion?

Perhaps it was the vast enclosed space where he and his problems seemed diminished somehow. He seemed to occupy an infinitesimally small zone in comparison with the larger expanse. His problems seemed small in comparison to those of the world. His troubles seemed an irrelevancy in here. Maybe that's what perspective is?

The vastness of the sanctuary seemed to cocoon him from the life that was closing in all around him. He thought of the tree house he had as a kid, where he ran to if his parents scolded him. It was a haven of peace. It was his private space.

He sat still and vacant and let his mind empty. The low hum in the distance, together with the intermittent slow whistle of wind through a door behind him, made him sleepy.

He was awoken by a cleaning lady who was about to leave the church.

"We're about to close", she said.

He looked at his watch. It was 8.30. He'd been asleep for over an hour. He felt a little embarrassed.

"I'm sorry. It was a long day", he mumbled, pulling himself from the seat and heading for the door.

CHAPTER 12

Ted pulled up outside the detached property that was his house. His neck was extremely tense. He noticed himself opening and closing his fists to relax. He felt tension along his temples. He felt drained. It was late. He stood out of the car and went to the boot to pull out his briefcase. Only then he noticed. At the corner of his eye, in the streetlight, he saw the red paint daubed on the front wall of the house. "BASTURD" had been written in two-foot high letters by someone with a shortcoming in spelling. Maybe turd was to make it even less complimentary? He noticed the swastika sign, in the same red paint, on the yellow front door.

He had a sharp intake of breath. He could feel a burning sensation across his chest, just below the "v" of his neck.

"Fuck! What the hell is goin' on?"

Only then did he think of Becks and the kids. He ran as fast as he could to the front door and threw it open.

"Becks! Becks! Are you here?"

No response. Her car was in the driveway. Where the hell was she? No sign of the kids. He checked all the rooms. Everything looked normal. He went back to the kitchen and sat down.

"Think! Think! Did she say she was going somewhere today?"

His imagination was racing. Maybe this nutter who rang some days ago came to the house. But there was no evidence of a struggle. The writing on the wall was Bastard—well, with a U—not Bitch. Someone was having a go at him, not her! Maybe, whoever it is, is trying to get at him through her. He better not hurt her or the kids. NO...no...no! There must be a perfectly logical explanation.

He heard the door-key turn in the latch. Rebecca backed the buggy in the door. He met her arrival with a mixture of relief and exasperation.

"Jesus, Becks, where have you been? Have you seen the door and the walls? I was petrified about you and the kids. Why the hell didn't you tell me you were going out?"

Rebecca turned and met his eyes evenly and coldly.

"I would if I could make contact with you. Jennifer from across the road came over this evening to tell me what was done out front. How can I bloody well tell you when you never answer the bloody phone?" Her lip started to tremble. Jason looked up at his mother and started to cry.

"I'm sorry, Becks. This job...it was another bad day...I'm having problems with one particular guy and I have to keep on top of it...."

"Is he more important than our family, Ted? I needed you today and all I got was your bloody answering machine. I'm sick to my stomach all evening. The reason I'm coming in now is that we had no milk or bread—I went down to the local shop to get them. I needed to get out of this house anyway. The last few days are frightening me, Ted—strange phone calls and now this. What's going on? What have we done?"

Ted thought it better not to tell her about the strange call last night. He took Jason in his arms and told him it was ok. He relaxed in his father's arms.

"Have you rung the guards?"

"Of course. They were out earlier, took a look around and took a few pictures...."

"And?" Ted felt impatient with her. He knew immediately this was unfair. She must have felt awful. He instantly wanted to take back the impatience in his voice, which at best must have sounded ungrateful.

"Don't 'And?' me!! Have you any idea of how I've been feeling all day? Having to sit here knowing what was on the walls outside. I'm petrified. What is going on that we deserve this?" Her eyes were moist but defiant.

"The guards didn't give much hope they'd find anyone for it. They asked who I thought might have done it and if we had any enemies. I don't. Do you?...They told me to ask you to ring them when you arrived home. What's going on? ..." and with that she started to cry.

-o-o-o-o-o-

Ted had asked one of his elderly next-door neighbours about a painter, to cover up the unholy mess on the walls and door outside. It had taken a little while to get agreement with him to come tomorrow, Saturday, and do it. He was a retired man and was quite happy doing odd jobs around the local neighbourhood.

Ted rang the guards after putting the kids to bed. The

guards arrived at 11 pm to interview him about possible suspects. From the look on their faces, it was clear they didn't believe him when he said he couldn't think of anyone who would want to get at him. He could see it in their eyes.

Rebecca's only concern seemed to be with the neighbours and what they might think now that the squad car was outside again. At one stage, she even asked Ted if he could ask them to park their cop car down the road a bit! This drove Ted mad. "For God's sake!!...and the state of the walls and doors!" In his mind at least, the squad car might at least draw attention away from the crap written all over the house!

After the guards left, the parking of the squad car developed into a full-blown argument. Ted lost it, got a drink from the cabinet and Rebecca sulked and stormed up to bed.

When Ted eventually went to bed at 1 am, he lay there, his mind racing, not sleeping. He was too hot, and he threw the clothes off. It wasn't particularly warm, but he was roasting; adrenaline pumping probably. And now this effin' speech for Monday night had to be done...he'd spend most of that night at a function he didn't want to be at, with people he didn't give a toss about! He looked at the clock. 3.30 a.m. and he still couldn't sleep. The phone rang at the edge of the bed.

"Mr. Black?"

"Yes"

"A-Line security here. We've had a break-in at the depot in Ringsend and we need you to come in. We're not sure if anything was taken but there has been a fire outside which damaged one of the doors. The guards need to talk to you." Ted tried to gather himself.

"And your name is?...and your phone number?"

"Alex Brennan of A-Line at 081.2372370. Sorry for having to ring you at this hour but you are the contact on our list. We also have asked Mr. Tom Hannigan to be there as soon as possible."

"Thank you. I'll be there in about half an hour."

Ted needed this like diarrhoea needs a laxative. He could sense Rebecca was awake, but she didn't turn towards him or ask him what was going on. She was still sulking. In his own mind, he thought, 'Fuck her.'

He dressed in the dark and pulled the keys from the dresser. He wanted to tell her where he was going but pride wouldn't let him. He could feel more tension at the back of his neck.

-o-o-o-o-o-

Tom saw Ted coming through the entrance hall. Ted looked haggard. A 5 o'clock shadow didn't improve him. Ted looked less like a manager with his red, sunken eyes, black from lack of sleep and without his Italian suit. He wore a grey pullover and blue ill-fitting jeans. He didn't look a happy camper.

They spent a few minutes looking at the security control panel. It was clear that there were some breaking of beams around the perimeter of the building. However, CCTV didn't show any intruders on screen.

Tom and Ted went around the building with the security guard and checked all doors for signs of forced entry. However, everything seemed intact.

The area of the fire was a small door in the yard.

There were fragments of a smashed bottle in the vicinity, blackened by smoke. It would seem a Molotov Cocktail was lobbed over the wall. Luckily, nothing had caught fire and the only damage was scorch marks to the door.

"Perhaps there was no break-in? The beams sometimes get set off by papers in the wind or on account of passing cats and dogs—the wind has been howling tonight. I was concerned we had a break-in when I saw the fire. I'm really sorry I disturbed you tonight." The security guard spoke as if he meant it.

Ted was back in his car in 5 minutes. "Riders on the Storm" by the Doors played on the radio and seemed appropriate in the circumstances. He felt exhausted heading out the Merrion Road early Saturday morning. There were few cars around, and he was pushing along nicely at about 50 mph.

His mobile phone rang in the cradle. He answered in automatic business mode.

"Ted Black."

"Tough day?" a gruff voice asked.

"Who's this?" demanded Ted.

The phone went dead. He stopped the car to look at the caller ID, which was blocked. He felt uneasy and jumpy. He could do without this hassle.

CHAPTER 13

On Monday morning, young Enzo Rossi walked into Ted's office, flanked by Jem. Ted immediately felt sorry for the spotty, lanky, and shy young lad. It was obvious that before he opened his mouth, Enzo was an innocent abroad.

"Enzo—can I call you Enzo? ..." He nodded.

"You have probably been made aware of an incident that happened last week. We must investigate, as the matter is serious. I am using today to give you an opportunity to hear your side of the story. In addition, I will set down exactly the circumstances that have led up to this interview.

"To come to the point, we have found an amount of cocaine in your locker. We know that you are sharing the locker with Martin Cullen. We have already interviewed Mr. Cullen. As you share the locker with him, we need you to know whether you knew anything about this substance in the locker and how it got there?"

Jem nodded for Enzo to reply.

"Look, I'm only employed here as a temp for a few weeks. There is absolutely no way that is mine. I don't know how it got there and it's certainly something that I don't condone in any shape or fashion."

"My Brother here feels that he is being targeted unfairly. He is only new to the warehouse", Jem interjected.

Ted went through the motions of seeking further clarifications and taking notes for the record. However, his mind was wandering—he would learn nothing new. In conclusion, he said that he had no option but to suspend Enzo on full pay until the investigation was complete. He felt tightness in his left arm, reminding him—as if he needed reminding—that he was tense. His face was flushed and dry. His mouth was parched and his thinking fuzzy.

He could hear the voices droning on around him. They were like Medium Wave radio channels, competing for the same wavelength. He'd hear a bit of one channel in English before competing Spanish and African channels kicked in. There were intervening periods of poor reception, just noise. He was taking nothing in, nor could he focus on anything concrete.

Ted went through that morning in a daze. The lack of sleep and the tension he felt meant that his recollection and concentration was poor. He thought about who was ringing him. Who was targeting his house? Who was hassling Rebecca? Was there a connection between them all? Would it ever end? There was a sense of panic. The same words and questions repeated, repeated, repeated.

At the weekly management progress meeting he found it hard to take any interest. The Accounts Manager raised the issue of security because of the incident over the weekend. Ted struggled to think how security might be improved. The Technical Supervisor raised the issue of accidents and near misses reported. The trends were moving in the wrong direction. What could be done with the staff to change things? He did a slide show on some possible proposals. There was also a need to provide better PPE to the staff because of an independent Safety Audit—had they money in the budget?

The Transport Supervisor went to town on high sick leave rates in his area. Deliveries had been missed—or delayed—as a result of no shows by helpers and drivers. He wanted action against those involved—all of whom had notoriously bad sick leave records. He had done everything he could at his level and now it needed action by the manager. Could we pull them in next week to outline our concerns and put it firmly in the disciplinary area? He needed management support. There was also the issue where ABS on one of the trucks had locked up on 2 occasions—the Transport Supervisor needed capital approval to replace the braking system on this truck.

Ted's accountant was concerned about the rising unit costs. He had commissioned a survey of their competitors and the competitors were better in every area of pricing. Eirtran needed a productivity drive to get charges under control. He provided a PowerPoint presentation to the group on how this might be achieved; the usual accountant's suggestions—cut overtime, increase delivery hits, reduce some of the services (stop stripping the packing at the customer's house etc.).

Towards the end of the meeting, Ted realised he hadn't taken in a word said. He used his guile and asked that they all email their slides to him. It would give him an opportunity to consider their suggestions in depth when he got some quiet time to review the issues. He felt the whole world closing in around him. They wanted decisions but, without being able to focus and feeling a little nauseous, he just wished that the meeting would finish.

Ted's concentration continued to wander away from the meeting to his own personal issues. He couldn't actually see the figures in front of him. He constantly had to ask for clarifications. He called the meeting to a close without making a single decision. He stated that he needed to take the items away for further review.

Ted worked through his lunch trying to find out what had been said to him and understand what was required of him. Constant phone interruptions ensured that he was still on the very first point of the meeting after one hour. This only added to his feeling of frustration.

Tom didn't produce the speech for the retirement until 3 o'clock that evening. Ted had a quick read of the badly written document. As a result, Ted sat with Tom for another hour trying to piece together a speech that was halfway coherent. It was obvious Tom had cobbled a speech together without any thought. Ted worried about how the speech would go down with the staff. He really needed sleep.

-o-o-o-o-o-

Ulser was propped up at the bar in "The Widow Scanlons", downing a pint of Harp. He was the only man left in Ireland who still drank the stuff (nicknamed Harpic by most Dubs as it had a reputation for being so acidic it could strip wallpaper). While everyone else was in conversation, Ulser was happy to stand on his own. He was intent on maximising his share of the free drink. He had given enough to Eirtran and the least he was entitled to for his efforts was a free pint, now and again, on the company tab.

He wandered over to Georgie, who was engaged in animated conversation with some older members of the staff. As Ulser approached, the conversation stopped. Josser looked up at him and broke the silence.

"How's the back, Ulser? I hear you won't be back to work for a few weeks. You must have a great doctor for certs....Suspect he must get his car serviced for free down your way, does he?" Josser held Ulser's gaze evenly. The group knew that Josser was treading thin ice. It wasn't exactly a friendly greeting by any standard.

"I'll give you his number so you can use him, Josser. Mind you, he doesn't take dodgy goods in payment for services—strictly cash. Doubt you'd be his type of customer on that basis so, Josser?"

The air was crackling between the two. Old Jem sucked in some air and the rest lowered eyes to their pints, waiting for the explosion.

"Well, at least it might be an honest buck from a few dodgy goods and not on the back of some kid's misery. I prefer white goods to white powder. What about you, Ulser?" It was obvious to Ulser the word was out on the stash found in his locker.

"I can't help it if some young fella's got a problem. It's not my gear."

Ulser had no intention of giving them any satisfaction. What I do for my family is none of their business, he thought. Just because they don't have the balls....

"Hey, you'd let your granny hang if it meant you

could have a few extra pints for the night." Josser wasn't going to be outdone by this scrote in front of his mates.

Georgie was feeling edgy. His night might be destroyed if he didn't say something.

"Look, lads, I don't know what's eatin' you both...but you're my guests here tonight. If you want to have your little squabble, don't do it on my patch. My wife and family are sitting over there, and I don't want a bar room brawl as my going away gift. So, cool it. I want everyone to have a good time of it. If you can't manage that, then find another bar to have your fight in." Ulser looked at Josser and then at Georgie.

"You're right, Georgie. I shouldn't be wasting words on that pile of shite. He's a complete tosser and I'm really sorry I've wasted so much time talking to such a complete arsehole." Ulser smirked as he said it. Georgie was a good sort in his eyes, but sure, he was leaving after today. Ulser wouldn't have any use for him again.

Josser bolted from the seat, but two sets of hands restrained him. He jutted out his chin and went nose to nose with Ulser. Ulser didn't as much as take a step back. They stared defiantly at each other. Ted Black walked into the bar just as the two men were locking horns.

"Calm the fuck down. The boss has arrived. I don't need this shit on my last day. You two got a problem, get a room! Otherwise, behave yourselves." Georgie was livid.

"Yeah, yeah...ok, Georgie. I'm not going to let a scumbag like that wreck the night." Josser backed off as he said it.

In his own mind, Georgie couldn't decide who was worse. Both of them caused nothing but trouble and he was glad to be getting away from it all. Josser sat down and Ulser moved back to the bar, to resume a pose of standing on his own.

-o-o-o-o-o-

Ted looked around at the assembled throng. Tom stood at his side.

"Tom, are these all our people? I don't recognise a fraction of them. What is expected of me here? In the last job, the first thing I'd do is sit with the person due to retire and his family. Is that the done thing here?"

"Boss, I haven't done too many of these things myself—so—go with the flow. Whatever you think ..." Tom wasn't exactly a well of information.

Georgie caught Ted's eye and beckoned for him to come across and join the group. Ted smiled and made his way through the noise and the crowd. Georgie reached across his mates for a handshake. His eyes were warm and his handshake strong and friendly. He introduced Ted to the lads sitting beside him. He called the bar girl and ordered Ted a drink. Tom was nowhere to be seen when Ted looked back.

Ted exchanged a few pleasantries with the assembled guests, asking each of them what part of the business they worked in. Very quickly, the conversation got around to football.

"I'm telling you. Best leaves Gazza in the shade. He's the best player I've seen...."

"You think the world revolves around United. Stephen Gerrard is doin' it week in, week out—if only that stupid manager of his, Houlier, put him in the position he plays best in. What is he doin' playin' him on the right wing? The man's the best centre field player since Roy Keane...."

"That wouldn't be hard. Keane has no skill but a big mouth. The only thing he brings is that all the rest are afraid of him. I'll give you he has a great engine—but skill and vision? ..."

"Maybe Keano's the Ulser on the arse of Ireland! ..." (Laughter)

"Ulser never kicked a ball in his life unless it was attached to the scrotum of someone owing him money! He couldn't kick a habit either by the looks of it...." (more laughter)

"And Berkamp...how in God's name do all the pundits reckon he's a great player?...as good as George Best, Pele, Maradona, Beckenbauer? The last 7 matches I saw him in, he barely kicked a ball in anger ..."

And so, on it went. Heroes created and reputations destroyed. The hurler on the ditch whose sole claim to fame was a beer belly the size of a small mountain, a mind as deep as a puddle and a view subtly formed by the literary opinions of *the Sun* and *the Star*. These are the opinions that form the mind of a nation. Night after night, in every watering hole in the country, similar esteemed "pontificators" drunkenly create the legends of our time.

Ted was able to sit back and enjoy the craic. He laughed with a group that not long ago he wanted to disown. How strange that. The atmosphere seemed to help lift his spirits. And boy—did he need it.

At a certain point in the proceedings, Georgie took Ted across the room and introduced him to his family.

His wife, Madge—somehow Ted knew she would have to be a Madge—homely, quiet, and motherly. She had a ruddy complexion and seemed at home with her children around her. Georgie had been busy—he had six!

The eldest boy—nearly 30—had come home from America, where he had worked as a Systems Analyst in California. He was a slim, tall version of Georgie but much quieter. Georgie had two very good-looking daughters in their twenties—one of whom was engaged. They sat either side of their mother in animated conversation. Their boyfriends talked across the table to each other, but it seemed slightly strained between them.

At some point, Ted ended up talking to Georgie on his own. Georgie was a good conversationalist and had a wide range of interests. He was a well-read man. He explained that as a youngster, he left school early. However, later in life, he saw the value of education and vowed to redeem himself. He became an avid reader. He acquired an interest in psychology and had enrolled for a full-time Arts degree as a mature student—due to start soon after his retirement. He had learned to cook. His wife then, who had been earwigging, joined in to extol his virtues as an accomplished chef, particularly Asian cuisine—"anything with rice", as Georgie put it.

His other son was a chef and the son thought highly of his dad. He had got his dad a job as a chef with a local Thai restaurant, which he would start on his retirement—"now my real career begins", he said to Ted.

"Surely you don't need to fund your studies by working, Georgie?...Sure, you'll be made up with your lump sum?" said Ted. Georgie laughed.

"Madge owns that, not me, after putting up with me

all these years. She had always wanted to go on a cruise, so now she can."

"I take it you'll be joining her?"

"Not a hope! That's not for me. Herself and the daughters are heading for the Caribbean. Can you see me sitting out, with this beer belly, in the sun? The "blue rinsers" would be dying for some of me body. They wouldn't be able to keep their hands off me." He winked at Madge and she gave him a playful slap.

As well as being a family man, Ted could tell that Georgie was a man who aspired to improve himself at every opportunity. His retirement wouldn't be wasted. This was all additional material for Ted's retirement speech. Three quarters of an hour flew in the company of Georgie and his family. Ted felt comfortable enough in his company to ask him about Eirtran.

"I noticed that Josser and Martin seemed to be having a bit of a disagreement as I arrived? ..." Ted enquired. Georgie smiled.

"Long time since I heard that git bein' called Martin. You mean Ulser?"

"Yes. Didn't know if the boss could use that name", replied Ted.

"I don't think anyone in this place would know who you were talking about if you said Martin." Georgie laughed as he said it.

"How did Ulser get his name?" ventured Ted.

"You obviously never heard the story? It's Ulser with an 's'. He used to be known as Ulster—after the province, you know. Ever see the way Ulser is always the first to help you out—?" he continued. "...I'm bein' sarcastic, of course. Ulser thinks of no one but himself.

"Well, one of the lads said that he was just like Ian Paisley...never says yes—always No...." Georgie continued.

"ULSHTER SAYS NOOoo! ..." he boomed in a voice reminiscent of the Great Orator...his whole family were caught by the force of his voice and turned around when he said it....

"The name Ulster stuck...at least for a while. Then one day, Ulster arrives into work complaining about a boil on his arse. He moaned about it for days, pissin' everyone off. I got fed up listening to him as well. I just couldn't help myself one day when he came into the canteen...and I had an audience. You know the way it is when you have a few lads around you. I quipped to his face that the boil suited him.

"'An' how the fuck do you make that out, you old cunt?', Ulster said to me—pardon the French. You don't ever call old Georgie here a cunt...beggin' your pardon for the vernacular, sir. Anyway, the canteen is full and everyone's listening. Georgie, if I do say so myself, was on form that day. In fact, I was lightning!" He smirked as he said it.

"'Well', I said, 'I was just talking to Mikey about the boil on your arse and do you know what?'...I paused for effect.

"'Everyone in this canteen is agreed on one point, Ulster...and you know how fucking difficult it is for these bastards to agree on anything!...but it was a unanimous decision, Martin.' I stopped so he'd ask me the question.

"'So, an' what did you all agree on, y'oul fart?' He teed me up brilliantly. 'Martin'—he hates it when I call him Martin—'**we all agree that you're an ulcer on the**

arse of Humanity!'

"It brought the house down. Ever since then, we dropped the **'t'**...ergo, Ulser!" Ted snorted when he laughed. That always happened when he had a pint or two.

"Georgie, you know I shouldn't be laughing."

"Don't worry, sir—I won't be telling", and he winked.

Tom had joined the group. Ted had been enjoying himself at this point, a welcome respite from the last couple of days. His tiredness was forgotten. Even for his pending speech, he felt no tension. The finger food was being passed around—cocktail sausages, sandwiches, salads—and he ate with relish.

Tom indicated it was time. Ted mounted the small stage, usually reserved for the guitar player on Friday night, and took the mike. In the din of the pub, he couldn't hear his mobile phone ring.

CHAPTER 14

Rebecca was frantic. Jason was thrashing around on the ground. It seemed that he was having a sort of seizure. She had turned him on his side and covered him with one of her jackets. She was trying to placate Aaron at the same time, who was bawling in her arms. She had the phone in her hand and could only hear her husband's number ringing out. She flung the phone across the floor in temper.

"Stay, pet...Mammy has to get someone to help." She didn't know where to go but ran out the front door, Aaron in her arms. An elderly man was getting out of his car on the other side of the road. She recognised him as one of the neighbours.

"Please get a doctor quickly. My child...there's something wrong with my child....I need an ambulance. Please come and help!" The man looked at her with concern.

"It's ok. I'm actually a retired doctor. What's happened?"

"Oh. Thank God. Come quickly. My child is having a fit."

The elderly man was finding it hard to hear because of the high-pitched screams of Aaron in her arms. He came across to her.

"Let me have a look at him...." as he ventured, making a move to look at the child in her arms.

"No. No. My other child! He's having a fit on the floor in the hall. Please come quickly." They ran into the house. Jason was still thrashing on the floor. The kindly doctor knelt beside him.

"What age is he?"

"He's just gone 2. Is it an epileptic fit?" The elderly man was pulling up Jason's eyelids as he spoke. The child looked out vacantly.

"It's highly unlikely. Did he have the MMR recently?"

"Yes, I had him with the doctor two weeks ago for it. Is it linked?"

"It may be. Have you a cold shower somewhere?"

Rebecca pointed to the doorway opposite. "There's one in the downstairs toilet."

"Get the clothes off your little boy immediately and I'll get the cold shower running. Strip him down and do it fast!" The man wasn't asking—he was telling.

Rebecca pulled the clothes off Jason whilst he kicked, punched, and thrashed. The man returned, helping to hold him still while she stripped him down. Aaron was laid on the ground, screaming in the middle of it all. They ran in where the shower was running. She stepped into the shower fully clothed—Jason in her arms.

The cold water caused her to gasp. It was on, full blast. Jason started to quieten quickly as the cold water hit. Within thirty seconds the kicking had stopped. After a minute, he was limp in his soaked mother's arms. The man stood watching Jason all through this. Jason opened his eyes and looked at his mother.

"Mam. Code!" Rebecca, hair stuck to her head, looked down and started to cry.

"Oh, baby. I know you're cold but thank God you're alright. And...I'm sorry, I don't even know your name...." She turned to here kindly neighbour, who stood in silence.

"Bernard ..."

"Bernard...oh, thank you for coming to help. I was frantic. How can I thank you? I couldn't get my husband and I didn't know who else to turn to. I fell on my feet getting a doctor. Does he need to go to hospital?"

Rebecca was smiling with relief as she spoke.

"Yes. I think as a precaution, although I'm pretty sure he'll be alright. We won't take a chance. I'd be quite happy to bring you—that is if you want to? Perhaps you need to change into dry clothes? We don't want you catching pneumonia on top of all of this." She looked down at her clinging dress, which was wringing wet.

"What do you think it was? You seemed to know straight away", Rebecca asked.

"If I'm right, it's a thing called Febrile Convulsions. It's unusually common in children of his age. Basically, it's where a child's temperature spikes very quickly in an extremely short space of time. The brain is inclined to shut down as a protection mechanism—so that's why he didn't respond. You did just about everything right. You laid him on his side to prevent him swallowing his tongue. You also had him on the floor—you'd be amazed the number of people put them on a bed and they fall off, hitting their heads. The only thing which wasn't required—and you weren't to know—was not to cover him—but strip him down to cool. It's perfectly natural to try and keep the child warm but—in this case—it's the exact opposite of what is required.

"Any ill effects from an attack are unlikely. It can be very scary when it's happening. Even though I've seen it many times, I still find it upsetting. Is your husband at work—maybe we can get him to meet you at the hospital? My wife is at home, and she'd be happy to mind your other little boy while you're gone. Maybe you want to put a few things together—bottle, change of clothes, nappies? We still baby-sit our son's kids, so we've a cot in one of our rooms!" He smiled.

"I'm so lucky I have Superman living next door to me! You are very kind. I don't know how to thank you."

"That's what neighbours are for...I'm sorry; I don't know your name...."

"Rebecca. I'm sorry. With everything that was happening, I didn't get time to introduce myself."

Within an hour, she was sitting in the waiting room of the Children's Hospital in Crumlin in deep conversation with a man she barely knew. It seemed that this stranger was more of a friend to her than her own husband, whose only interest at this time seemed to be his work—morning, noon, and night. Despite repeated attempts in the car on the way to the hospital, they had firmly failed to make any contact with her husband.

-o-o-o-o-o-

"...and so, just to finish, I'd like to compliment the bar on the food they prepared. It was excellent." The beer was getting the better of Ted at this stage and he felt he was on a roll.

"However, I'm told the bar should look at engaging Georgie's cooking skills. With Georgie's wife here, Madge, and the encouragement she is providing so that he can embark on a new career in the art of cuisine, a word of warning in the form of a joke about food...." He was determined to roll out one of the few jokes he could ever remember, even under the influence.

"Paddy the Englishman, Paddy the Irishman, and Paddy the Mexican worked together and met at lunch every day to eat. They were working on the Empire State building and sat out on a beam 500 feet above the ground as they ate." A few groans from the audience as the boss attempted to tell a joke. Ted was undeterred.

"This day, Paddy the Englishman opened his packet of sandwiches...'Aw, no. Cucumber again. I'm sick to death of cucumber sandwiches. If I have to eat these one more time, I'm going to kill myself tomorrow!' Paddy the Irishman opened his lunch. 'Aw, no. Calvita cheese sandwiches again. This is depressing. If this happens tomorrow, I'm with you, Paddy. We'll jump together.' Paddy the Mexican opened his." Ted attempted his best Mexican accent, learnt from Warner cartoons in his childhood.

"'Aw Jeez! Burreeeto again. A canna take it ...'" he sounded more like a bad Scottified Indian...."I'll make a pact weet you. We all jump together eef I get burreeto again!'

"So next day, it's 1 o'clock and lunchtime....Paddy the Englishman opens the sandwiches. 'Aw no—cucumber. I've had it, lads' and he leapt to his death. Paddy the Irishman is distraught at the loss of his friend. He's now petrified to open his lunch. 'Calvita. I don't believe it. I'm with you, Paddy' and falls to earth as well. Paddy the Mexican has now lost his two best mates and his appetite. He opens his lunch. 'Aw, no. Burrito. I'll meet you in heaven lads'—so he jumps to his death also."

He tells a story well, and the crowd are hanging on his every word. There was always a bit of a showman in Ted.

"...so, the three wives are at the church...it's a joint funeral service for the three best friends. The wives are sitting in the front pews, some of them beside themselves with grief. Two of the wives are inconsolable. Paddy the Englishman's wife looked to the other wives. 'If only I knew he didn't like cucumber sandwiches. All he had to do was say so ...'

"Paddy the Mexican's wife shared her sorrow with the other two. 'If only I knew he didn't like burritos. When we got married originally, he said he married me for my burritos....(large guffaw—Ted pauses for effect)...for my burritos....' he repeated slowly, as the guffaws die down, milking the innuendo for all its worth.

"'I hated the things myself. If only he had told me....' They looked around at Paddy the Irishman's wife. She didn't seem to be grieving much. She had her emotions under total control. Paddy the Englishman's wife looked at her. 'You don't show emotion very much. Don't you feel somewhat responsible?'

"'Responsible? No—why should I? Paddy was a total gobshite...he made his own sandwiches!'"

There was a second that seemed an eternity to Ted...then an explosion of laughter. He got a standing ovation for his speech and his finishing joke. He felt relief because his first real public obligation had been received well.

"Now, I'll hand you over to the man of the moment...Mr. "Satchmo"—Georgie Hartnett!"

-o-o-o-o-o-

Mel heard loud banging at the front door. She felt afraid. She could hear men shouting and roaring. She felt too afraid to answer. She turned off the television and the lights. She had the mobile phone in her hand and dialled 999. The phone was answered quickly.

"Which service do you require? Gardai, ambulance, or fire brigade?"

"Gaadee!...Men banging doaa...on my owen and afwaid. Send someone—help me? 15 Elmpark Drive—Ballyfe'mot Village. Quickly."

"There'll be someone there in a few minutes." Mel hung up.

"Ulser—you thievin' bastard! Come out here. You've got our gear and we want it." This was given added emphasis by another kick to the door. The whole house shook. Mel had heard it all before, and she knew not to get excited.

"We'll sort you out...and that little sister of yours as well." It always amazed Mel how no one in the houses nearby heard the racket or came out to tell them to get lost. Martin always seemed to be out when she needed him around.

-o-o-o-o-o-

Ted stood at the urinal relieving himself. He was glad

to be on his own for a second, giving him time to reflect on his oratorial magnificence. The main door to the toilet slowly opened and a man stepped up to the urinal beside him. Ted felt uncomfortable, as the 10 other urinals were free. Ulser spoke.

"That'll be another one less at work tomorrow. For a man who hardly knew him, you did a decent speech. Did you spend as much time on his file as you did on mine? The doc says I need to take it easy and not strain myself. Georgie is one of the best. Did you hear him sing yet? Give him an hour or so and you'll hear him in action."

Ted was dumbstruck at his audacity. The last time they'd met, Ulser had thrown him out of his house and threatened him with a solicitor. Now here he was, bold as brass, talking to him as if nothing had happened. However, Ted had drink on him, and his defences were down somewhat.

"I'm sure that your doctor doesn't recommend mixing alcohol with pain-killers. At least mine doesn't." He felt duty-bound to say something, although his mind was telling him to keep quiet. His sense of outrage at the audacity of this toe-rag made him righteous.

"I'm not answerable to you outside working hours. I'll do whatever I fucking-well please." There was a sense of menace in the reply. Ted was nonplussed.

"I may not be in charge of you right now, but I want to see you in my office first thing tomorrow morning. I'm sure that if you're capable of making it to the pub on Monday night, you're more than capable of attending a meeting in my office Tuesday morning. Considering I'm paying your wages while you're 'sick', you can get your arse to a seat in my office 10 o'clock tomorrow morning.

I'm not asking you—I'm tellin' you! You're obviously well enough that I don't have to visit that house of yours again. Got that clear in your head, Martin?"

Ted knew that his bravado was certainly alcohol induced. He knew the minute he stopped talking that he'd pushed the boat out further than he intended. What the hell was he going to say in the morning that would change anything? He'd put himself in an impossible situation and he knew it.

"Don't bite off more than you can chew. You'd better be sure of your ground...." He zipped up aggressively and leaned into Ted's face.

"I've seen off better managers in this place than you. Just watch your step." With that he turned, and by the time Ted made for the basin, the toilets were empty again.

The shock of what he had said hit him while he washed his hands. He started to shake—a delayed adrenaline rush—and was breathing fast. He leaned on the basin to support himself as his legs felt weak. The phone started ringing in his pocket. He looked at his watch. It was 10 p.m. He pulled out the phone and saw seven missed calls on it—all from Rebecca's mobile. He rang the number immediately.

"Yes? ..."

"Where have you been? I've been trying to get you for the last few hours and no answer...."

"I told you that one of the lads was retiring and that I had to give a speech at his going away function. I'm still here. What's going on?"

"It's Jason. I'm here with him in Crumlin Hospital. He's had a fit and Bernard—from across the road—

brought me here. His wife is minding Aaron...."

Ted was struggling to focus again. The shock of how he had reacted to Ulser, the effect of too much drink and hearing that his son had some kind of fit while he wasn't around, made him weak.

"I'll get up there as quickly as possible. Is he alright?"

"Ted—have you been drinking? Don't take ..." Ted had already hung up. It was about 10 minutes to the depot, where he could collect his car. He'd be ok to drive, and then Rebecca could drive them from the hospital home. But what if they had to keep Jason in? What would he do then?

He pulled himself together, wet his face two or three times in the sink and took a few deep breaths. He straightened his tie and walked back to the assembled throng. He went to Georgie and explained that one of his kids was in hospital and he'd have to leave.

When he stood into Pearse Street, the cold air hit him hard and helped revive him. Although he had eaten some finger food, he had a hunger on him now brought on by the few pints.

He devoured a "single" from the local take-away on his way back to the depot. He downed a bottle of coke to kill the thirst. With the ten-minute walk and some food in his stomach, he could feel himself sobering up—enough to realise he shouldn't drive. By that time, he had turned into the badly lit street that led down to the depot. At this point, he felt it would be better to turn back and get a taxi near Shelbourne Park.

Something moved behind him. He caught a glimpse of something moving in the shadows. Two men seemed to be following him.

They broke into a run, bearing down on him. He caught a flash of light from a knife in one of their hands. They were on him before he could react. Both wore balaclavas. Before he could raise his fist, he felt a kick to his groin and collapsed to the ground. The kicks rained in—to his ribs, his head, his legs. He went into the foetal position, trying to protect his head with his raised hands. He last remembered throwing up on the pavement. He could see the chips swimming in the noxious fluid in front of him. The savage beating continued and his glistening vomit on the ground was the last thing he remembered before passing out....

-o-o-o-o-o-

The men outside the door saw the blue flashing lights before the Garda car ever got close to the house. Mel heard a brick come through the window, and a few obscenities uttered, before they ran off. The guards, as ever, didn't really want to catch them. More squabbles between thieves in their view. The familiar blue pulsing illuminated the front room when they stopped outside. She was dialling for Ulser as the Guards emerged from the car, slowly starting to pursue the disappearing figures in the distance.

The phone kept ringing, until his usual voice message came up.

"Martin, this Mel. Bad men came again t'night. Rock in window. Guards—but they gone. Pleade come home. Afwaid." Mel then waited for the bell at the front door to ring. It was one of many similar nights. She felt that these guys, whatever they wanted with Martin, were getting bolder each time.

Before this, they would ring and leave horrible messages. She would pretend to Martin that she didn't listen to them. But she did. Then notes were pushed through the letter box in the early hours. Silent, unseen messengers! But now they didn't seem to care. This was the second time they had come to the door, kicking and banging. How could the neighbours not hear?

Eventually the doorbell rang. The bored Garda stood and listened to what Mel had to say. She struggled with her words. They asked where her brother was, and she said "out". Martin always said not to say where he was. As usual, she was asked if she wanted to make a statement. As usual, she said no. Martin always said not to tell them anything but only call them to scare off anyone if they came. When the door closed, she started to cry and felt very alone. If only her Mam and Dad were alive. Why so much misery in one lifetime?

-o-o-o-o-o-

Ulser had brought a prostitute he met in "The Widow's" to the depot with him. He had a few cans under his arm, which he was quite willing to share with the Eirtran security guard. Ulser explained he wanted a quiet spot to have a bit of fun and the depot was the first place he thought of. She was game for a laugh, though, and if the security man wanted a free leg-over as well, she'd have no qualms. The security man jumped at the chance. He was an oul' retired fella who hadn't looked half-way handsome, even in his prime. Ulser said he'd stay on watch while he took advantage. He explained that all the staff were on a free bar and wouldn't be back for at least an hour or two.

In the half hour the security man was occupied, Ulser had the run of the depot. He'd instructed the woman to give him a minimum of a half an hour. He'd knock on the door when it was time.

Afterwards, Ulser drove her back to "the Widow's" in silence. He dropped her off at Ringsend Bridge and paid her off. He passed an ambulance on the way, which seemed to be picking a drunk from the road.

He parked near the railway bridge on Barrow Street and soon was back among the singing throng, as if he was never away. He knew the security man couldn't mention Ulser's visit for fear of incriminating himself. The security man had told Ulser that he couldn't risk losing this job. He had been sacked from the last one for drinking on the job. As the singing got louder, Ulser couldn't hear the phone ringing in his pocket. He was feeling so good he even joined in with Georgie when he gave a rousing rendition of "What a Wonderful World".

CHAPTER 15

Rebecca was frantic. Four hours had gone since Ted had said he was on his way. The hospital doctor had decided to keep Jason in as a precaution. She had thanked Bernard for his help. She told him to go home, as Ted would be arriving soon.

She tried to sleep in the armchair beside Jason, but her mind kept racing. She told Ted not to get in the car. Did he hear her? It was obvious he was drinking. Had he crashed on his way? Was he in hospital somewhere else? Worse...had he killed someone? Was he breathalysed? Was he in a cell somewhere? Did he go back to that damned retirement function, get pee-eyed and just forget about her? Was he at home, passed out on the bed while she was worrying about her son? She got mad when she thought about it. She had tried his phone on numerous occasions, and all she had gotten each time was an out-of-order tone.

She started to think of recent events...the graffiti, the strange calls during the day to her, at night to him. Had someone been trying to get at them? What had Ted done to make people hate them so much? Was there a part of him that she didn't know that had caused it? Had Ted gone home to bring some baby stuff to the hospital and been attacked in the house?

She started to breathe fast. She was panicking. Her head was spinning. She stood up to catch her breath. She had forgotten her medication with all that had happened. All the rushing, and she felt weak. She had missed her shot by a few hours, and now realised she needed it. The room around her was rushing away and black night was screaming in to replace it. She managed to hit the panic button near Jason's bed before slumping to the floor. Jason remained sleeping.

-o-o-o-o-o-

When Ted awoke, he thought he was in Heaven. All was white. He could hear distorted voices in the distance. Blurred figures moved in and out of his eyeline, all in white. A white light made the back of his eyes ache. He couldn't feel his body—no feeling in his arms, legs, fingers. He must be in Heaven. He couldn't focus on the shadowy figures. Where was he? Where was he supposed to be? He knew he was to be somewhere, and what's more, he knew it was urgent and important. His head thumped. Jason...Jason...Jason was in hospital! God, he had to go and see if his son is all right. Where was he? He attempted to form a sentence.

"Hotpit-AL. God do go do de hotpital. My dun." He had a mouth of wool. A dark blur appeared that blocked out the white light. He heard a disconnected voice stating that he was coming around.

"Yes. You're in hospital. You've had an operation, but you've got to rest." The voice was female, kind, and reassuring—that was all fine except he had to see his son.

"No. No. God do go do dee my dun i de hodpidal." He got agitated because they failed to understand. His head moved from side to side. His neck felt very sore.

"No. You are very ill. Please do not move. Get him sedated—quickly." He felt the dart of a needle in his arm as the palliative was applied. Within seconds, he was overcome with a warm feeling before falling back to sleep.

-o-o-o-o-o-

Ulser stood at the front door of his house in Ballyfermot. A car door opened on the road opposite. In the silence of the early hours, the sound of the door closing echoed between the houses. A voice called out.

"Ulser. I need a word." The walls of the narrow street resonated to the deep timbre of the voice. Ulser recognised the distinctive Cork accent of Sergeant Gene Millar. The detective was based in the plain clothes division of Garda HQ in Kilmainham Castle. He rolled the shoulders of his large 6' 4" frame as he strode towards Ulser. He had a confident gait which showed no sense of urgency. Ulser looked slight beside him.

"Your friends came calling here tonight. Our lads had to make a visit to keep your sister from freaking. She's a little shook, so I suggest that you keep an eye on her. It's clear they're coming out of their shell, which is good, but we need you to keep rattling their cage. It could get a bit rougher. I also hear that you got into a little bother at work. Since when did they start going through lockers at your workplace? You need to be a step ahead. I don't like having to explain myself to the uniforms, but we've made sure there won't be any charges. By the way, I think that your front window needs repairing." He nodded in the direction of the front room window.

"Now, I'd suggest that before you get a good night's sleep, have a word with your sister to calm her down. I know that I've asked you this before—is there anyone else can mind her 'cos I don't think that this is going to get better in the short term?"

"I can look after her. I've always done it. You just keep out of my family affairs." With that, Millar melted into the night. Ulser tried to open the door. The bolts were fast on the other side.

"Melanie. Melanie." He shouted as loud as he dared without waking the street. He heard the wheels of her wheelchair roll across the floor and the bolts going back. It was obvious when he looked at her that she was scared out of her wits.

CHAPTER 16

Ted stood washing the pots in the kitchen. His face was black and blue in equal proportion. The stitches were prominent on his forehead. His top lip was purple, but the swelling at least was starting to go down. His ribs ached and he limped a bit on his right leg. He was in pain. Ted's father-in-law, Mick, sat with the remains of the breakfast at the kitchen table, Irish Independent held aloft. His beloved Mayo had played a match on Sunday and he was devouring every last column inch the paper had devoted to the men from the West. The Connaught Tribune lay unopened on the table. It undoubtedly had further unbiased coverage of Mayo's latest bid for All-Ireland glory. Ted understood why Rebecca's parents needed to be here—both Rebecca and he needed every bit of support right now—but it wasn't easy to have them all living under one roof.

The door of the kitchen opened and Maura, his mother-in-law, came in with Rebecca who was supporting her Mam on her arm. Jason and Rebecca left the hospital the previous Saturday, but Ted knew that something wasn't right with Rebecca since she came home. She was listless and was finding it hard to mind the kids. No wonder, he supposed. The stress of the previous week with Jason, her subsequent panic when Ted never got to the hospital, the shock of hearing that he had received a beating and the vision of a barely recognisable husband after surgery seemed to affect her delicate sensibilities. She told Ted that she needed some help, and would he mind if her parents stayed a few days to give a hand? How could he refuse? He didn't object although he wasn't their greatest fan.

Ted liked his own space and they cramped his style. He was in recovery and found their presence intrusive. However, he knew the kids liked them, but he felt a stranger in his own home. He felt compelled to talk whenever they were around. It annoyed him that they seemed oblivious to the intrusion and they seemed perfectly at ease in *his* home! Mick was comfortable reading *Ted's* paper, smoking the pipe on the patio, sitting at *Ted's* TV to watch kids' programmes with Jason and telling Jason and Aaron stories on their way to bed. What took the biscuit was Jason looking for Nana and Grandpa before looking for him. Everywhere Ted went in the house, they were there. He wouldn't complain, though, because Rebecca was just not well enough for him to give out about them.

They always knew best—when Rebecca needed rest, when Rebecca needed a cup of tea, what Jason was crying about etc. Did they not know that he had managed his family quite nicely up to now without their interference? The last few days had been a severe strain for Ted. The physical pain was one thing—the incessant familial loving care for his wife quite another! Was Ted not sick as well? He was annoyed at himself for being annoyed—in fairness, Mick and Maura were doing their best for

Rebecca.

He felt guilty for being so negative towards them. In the current situation, he felt responsible for all that had happened recently. It scared him. Since he had taken up his new post with Eirtran, his world had started to unravel. He remembered his dad telling him to be careful what he wished for. Surely it was just a bad patch? Everyone gets a bad run. He was having his now. The fact that he might have inadvertently created this mess tugged at the back of his mind.

He scrubbed a stubborn stain on the pot with more vigour than needed. Water splashed from the sink onto his trousers, wetting them at the crotch.

"Bollocks!" he exploded out loud. All the anger in his head found its way through to his speaking orifice and ergo the outside world. The paper lowered and paternal eyes were raised. He could feel the daggers from his mother-in-law, Maura. Rebecca didn't respond at all.

'They're always fuckin' here', he thought to himself but "Sorry" thankfully found its way to his mouth instead.

How could they understand? Since Rebecca and he came home from hospital, they were still receiving stealth calls in the middle of the night. He was called names by a malevolent, disconnected, whispering voice in the early hours. He didn't like to admit it, but it frightened him. He wasn't getting enough sleep as a result. Was the physical attack linked to the calls or was he just in the wrong place at the wrong time? What would they do next? What about his kids and Rebecca? Were they capable of hurting them? What was this all about anyway? Was Ulser at the back of it all?

Ted reasoned that he'd had plenty of difficult IR issues to deal with in previous jobs, without repercussion. He'd had to deal with strikes, issue suspensions, take legal cases against customers. He'd never had a problem. These recent events were just a coincidence. Some sicko had got hold of his phone number and was intent on satiating their sick desires at his family's expense. He'd bought a phone call ID unit.

When he checked back on the stealth calls, the numbers were blocked. He'd reported the calls to the guards at the time they interviewed him about the attack. The guards were looking for any lead on the attackers. Could he think of anyone that might have a grudge against him? He was slow to divulge stuff about work and said very little to the guards as a result. The guards suggested that he change his phone number. Deep down, his instinct told him that this had to be linked to his new role in Eirtran. Maura's pronouncement brought him to his senses.

"Ted, I really think Rebecca needs total rest. I've had a chat with her, and she'd like to come home with us for a few weeks—with the kids. The peace and quiet of Clifden will help her." Sure, Mammy always knows best. Does she ever stop meddling? It wasn't really a question from her, more a statement. The next few sentences bore his worst fears out.

"There's a bus leaving this evening from Busarus. We're going to pack this morning and get a taxi into town. We've arranged neighbours to collect us from the bus when we arrive in Clifden. The sea air and the beach at home will do her good. Our local doctor is particularly good and if she's not feeling the best, he'd be happy to see her."

In his head, Ted wondered what the problem was with the sea air in Dalkey, with walking the pier in Dun Laoghaire or relaxing on the beach in Killiney? The doctor here is every bit as good, I'm sure. They're meddling again! But when he looked at Rebecca, he knew he wasn't capable of caring for her. He hardly had the strength to keep going himself.

He'd committed to return to work tomorrow, even though he knew he was probably going back a bit too early. He knew that Rebecca was in no state to fend for herself at home. While he wanted Rebecca to remain at home, the thoughts of an extended period of providing familial hospitality to his in-laws did not appeal. He was impulsive but knew that he had to hold his tongue. This was an offer he had to take.

"How do you feel, Becks? It's whatever you want. I can manage on my own. I'll be the chipper's best customer if you want to stay in Clifden!" She gave a wan smile.

"I really don't feel the best. I haven't been home for a while. Jason is mad keen to see the cows in the field next door. Dad's been telling him about Rocco, the sheepdog. Jason is keen to pet him. Maybe it's as good a time as any to take a break. But I'll only go if you promise to keep going back to the doctor. Ring me each day to let me know how you're getting on ..."

"You know I'll be ringing to see how you and the kids are. I want to see you're getting better. If you stay away too long, I'll start piling on the pounds from the chipper. I assume you want to remain married to the lean, mean, six-pack machine and not return to the Michelin Man, don't you?" Even Mother Misery Ireland—Maura— managed a laugh at that.

"Sounds like you might be easier to contact from Clifden than from here." There was hurt in Rebecca's voice. It was a low dig that he didn't need.

"You know that I've been very busy with the new job recently. I just have to get up to speed. It won't last forever. It'll soon settle down. I promise I'll be on to you every day."

Ted was afraid to catch Medusa's disapproving gaze for fear of turning to stone! Rebecca's mother believed that the role of Daddy, the wage earner, was to be home at 5.30 p.m. on the dot, sit with his family for dinner, say grace before meals, check the children's homework—she conveniently forgot that school-going age was 4 and not 2, as in Jason's case—read bed-time stories, say the rosary and walk the dog before bed. She placed this expectation on Ted for her daughter. In addition, she'd expect Ted at Mass Sundays and Holy Days and to attend Confession every Saturday if she had her way. Her puritanical views were not for turning. He reckoned that, in her view, he was on the Highway to Hell.

She had a view on everything. She disapproved of taking kids to restaurants— "they'll have done everything by the time they're 10—they'll have nothing to look forward to as adults." Why did Ted and Rebecca go out for meals in restaurants ALL THE TIME at night? — "Hotels give such great value at lunch-time in the carvery." Why are tables so close together in Italian restaurants? —"you can't swing a cat in them." Ted reckoned he would find room to swing for her, though, if she kept nagging much longer. The old saying—see the mother to see how your wife will turn out—came to mind and scared him witless. Surely Rebecca won't end up a crotchety old crone like her mother?

Ted reckoned he'd lose his marbles if Maura Medusa and Mute Mick were here a day longer. He married her psycho family when he married Rebecca. Mute Mick, Medusa's godforsaken lapdog, had developed a coping mechanism over the years. He had the knack of emptying his mind of anything to do with the present. Nothing Medusa said permeated his grey matter. Mick just read the paper, smoked, took a pint in the local and answered "Yes, dear" at appropriate intervals. She took this to mean he agreed with everything she said. She misinterpreted Mute Mick's disinterested verbals as support for her ever more radical and batty views.

Despite his reservations, he knew Rebecca would be in caring hands. Wherever there was misery, Maura Medusa would sniff it out! Ted mused which came first—Maura or the misery? Did Medusa impose her misery on otherwise happy people so that she could pursue a cause, have a meaning to her life? Was Medusa akin to a blood-hound—capable of smelling misery from afar and arrive, Superwoman-like, in time to save wretched souls in the nick of time? He smirked at the thought. Maura Medusa thought he was smirking at her. He was.

-o-o-o-o-o-

Tom felt under pressure. Jem was leaning so close that Tom could smell the stale Guinness from his breath. Jem's eyes were bulging, and his face was flushed. The drivers had refused to leave the depot that morning. Jem was flanked by two of them. Tom sat on the other side of the table on his own and, boy, did he feel isolated!

"We will not accept management rummaging through our personal belongings. This is a matter of Human Rights! In our view it's bullying by management. I don't care what the IR rulebook says. My members are on the road all day and don't expect managers to be rooting around in their personal belongings while they're away. How would you feel if every Tom, Dick, or Harry was coming in here, looking through your presses— particularly those you have locked—and then say— 'Hey, this is company property. We have a right to rummage through it anytime'? Guaranteed you wouldn't be happy about it? Well, we're not happy either. I want a commitment from you this minute that this won't recur— otherwise there'll be pickets on the gate. As it is, I'm having trouble calming the troops."

Tom started to burble and splutter. He felt exposed without Ted at his side. He didn't feel he could ring him at home considering what happened to him in the recent past. He had to use delaying tactics until his return. He didn't need this crap.

"Look, Jem. You know the boss isn't here right now. In his absence, I'll guarantee that this won't happen again for the foreseeable future. The matter ..."

"Foreseeable future?...foreseeable fuckin' future? ..." Jem glared at Tom with contempt.

Jem's response sounded like a line from Monty Python. It caused Tom to smirk. He realised smirking was not appropriate at serious IR meetings. He attempted to hide the smirk with his hand and feign a cough. The result was disastrous. He farted, startled himself, and poked himself in the eye with the smothering hand. As water streamed from his eye, he decided the meeting needed to rapidly conclude before further injuring himself.

"Look, Jem, there will be no further locker check-ups. Isn't that what you want to hear?" All three looked curiously at the injured party on the other side. Jem uttered concern.

"You ok, Tom? Your eye looks very red. I'd say it would be a good idea to see a doctor. I'll meet the lads and put it to them to go back to work. The minute the manager comes back, though, I'm expecting we'll meet as soon as possible to make sure we don't have a recurrence."

Tom watched them push back the chairs and leave the room with his one good eye.

-o-o-o-o-o-

Val Somerville, the Safety Rep, tugged at his newly developing wispy beard. He looked like Cat Stevens on "speed". Val was a traditional Irish music fan. From observing fellow traditionalists at gigs, he had noticed it was nearly compulsory to have a gnomish beard in order to demonstrate traditional "Oirish" values. By complementing the beard (it really was just a few hairs sprouting from his chin) with a beer belly, jeans, Fainne Nua badge (displayed despite the fact that he couldn't speak a word of Irish) and a plaid shirt, he knew he was welded into the Irish trad music, Gaelgeoir Diaspora. Even though he looked a total prat to everyone else, he thought his new beard gave him gravitas at work. He needed gravitas for the lofty position of Safety Representative in Eirtran.

Val was surrounded by several staff. Mickey Stafford, a fat, stubby man, was speaking.

"Look, Val, the law says that they must provide a mechanical device to eliminate the possibility of us hurting our backs through manual handling. Management is pushing this notion that we can offload from the side doors without using the tail-lift—to get appliances out quicker, get numbers delivered up and costs down. For whose benefit? Not ours, that's bleedin' clear. If I try liftin' a washing machine from the side door, I could drop it on me foot and crush me bleedin' toe. Do me back in, as well as lose me balance and hit me head if I fell." He was in full flow. He didn't give a toss about how they did work really, but he loved upping the ante for management.

"Jaysus, Mickey, you couldn't fall on the floor if you tried. You'd roll over and bounce away first!" Jayo's comment got a laugh from the assembled throng.

Jayo had stirred the unrest earlier that morning after a phone call from Ulser. Ulser felt that management were on his back a bit. Ulser needed diversions to keep management busy while he was off work. It would disrupt their little business on the side if management came down hard on Ulser. They'd discussed the tactics they might use. When they came up with the idea of resisting the use of side door offloading, they loved it immediately. Management would be terrified of the Health and Safety implications. They knew Val would be both stupid enough—and stubborn enough—to run with it all the way. Val was so thick, they reasoned, that once he was playing with this particular ball, management wouldn't be able to pull it from him.

Jayo planted the seed during the tea break. Mickey Stafford took the bait and was running with it. The whole debate was music to Jayo's ears.

"An' fuck you too, Jayo!" However, he was laughing as he said it.

"Anyway, the serious point here is that until management come to their senses, I want you ..." pointing into Val's chest..."to tell them that we only offload using the tail-lift at the back of the van—<u>for everything</u>—washing machines, freezers, tumble driers, heaters, kettles, deep fat fryers—I don't give a rat's! The law doesn't state what weight you need a mechanical device for. We use the tail-lift for everything!" He puffed out his chest with the pronouncement, proud of *his* great idea. He looked about the group for affirmation.

"Yeah. Stuff management. Go on, Val, give 'em hell."

Jem was listening to the assembled throng wondering how this had raised its head. He didn't like the sound of it. The company was struggling and had lost some contracts recently. This wasn't going to help anyone, least of all those on the shop floor. However, he thought it best to hold his counsel until he established where it had come from. He moved strategically away from Val to escape his overwhelming body odours. Did he ever wash, he wondered? There was obviously an EU soap mountain in Ballyfermot!

"I'll demand a management meeting on the matter. In difference to the meeting, I'll put together a cohingent argument to afflict the intermediate introduction of mechanical affiliation to replace manual intersection." As usual, no one understood a word of what Val said and cheered (with a heavy hint of sarcasm). However, the sarcasm was lost on Val, in a wave of pomp and circumstance. He took the cheer as an endorsement of his assertive action style.

"Val, before you meet management, I suggest we have a talk on how best to move this on. Give me a call when you get your thoughts together later today", Jem said. 'That won't take long', he thought. Val's labyrinthine mind skills were akin to the juggling ability of an egg.

Jem moved away to try getting his thoughts together. This issue had come from nowhere. No one had been giving any grief on this subject—ever. They were all doing well on over-time. It didn't make sense.

He mounted the stairs to go to the toilet. Half-way up, as he turned to mount the third flight, he caught sight of Jayo in conversation with Micko Stenson and Dracula. They were standing adjacent one of the unloading doors. It was an animated conversation between them. It finished when Jayo did a "high 5" with Micko, who received a slap on the back from Dracula. Jem somehow felt that this group were generating the unrest. He'd only just sorted out the mess with the lockers. He'd soon be upstairs again trying to sort out another one.

-o-o-o-o-o-

Tom was minding his own business as he drove along the Clontarf seafront. He was heading to a meeting with Janus, a supplier based in Raheny, with whom they were having supply problems.

He stopped at the lights where the road onto Bull Island met St. Anne's Park. To pass the time, he was looking around absent-mindedly. He noticed an Eirtran truck three vehicles back in the queue of oncoming traffic. Jimmy Spain was in the driver's seat. He didn't recognise the helper beside them. Then realised why. He was a she! A well-endowed woman, wearing a revealing, fluffy white blouse, was reaching over to kiss him. God— Jimmy wasn't exactly in his prime, thought Tom. She wore a red leather jacket and her knees, clad in black fishnets, were propped up against the dash.

The lights changed. Tom was still glued to the figures in the van. Jimmy indicated left onto Bull Island. Before the van turned off the road, Tom got a clear view of Jimmy's face and that of his passenger. She was a dyed blonde, probably in her mid 40's. As Bull Island is a bird sanctuary, there won't be any house on Bull Island expecting a delivery, thought Tom. Nonetheless, it was clear to him that Jimmy was intent on providing some sort of service!...

Tom's mind was racing as he continued towards Raheny. Should he stop Jimmy and take him to task? He would have all the IR bullshit to go through: seek a suspension, endless meetings with the Unions, assemble all the paperwork for the case, get statements, the location of the drops for that day, root through his personal file to see whether it was an isolated incident, go to a disputes council. After all that, senior managers would likely take the case over and baulk at doing anything concrete. And yet...how could he let it go? He decided that he would haul Jimmy in next morning and look for an explanation.

CHAPTER 17

Ted decided to slip in late to Eirtran the evening before he was due back and bring himself up to speed on developments in his absence. He sat, chin cradled in his palms, at the desk in his office. The only light was that of the brass lamp on his desk. He had kept the lighting low deliberately in order not to attract the attention of anyone in the building. He didn't want to waste time on social chit chat—he had work to do.

He had been pretty pissed-off after Becks left for Clifden. The house felt empty, and without life. No kids, no noise, no smell of cooking, no knowing that Becks was working somewhere else in the house, no companion to share the day's events with—just 4 walls and emptiness: loneliness even. He couldn't bear the thought of sitting there for the night, nursing a whiskey. He always hated being in the house alone. He decided therefore to make the journey to the office and occupy his mind.

He pored over a document sent by his manager from the European HQ in Brussels. The more he read it, the more he wished he'd stayed at home. He was aghast at the contents of the document. It was innocuously titled "A Board directive on Positioning European Logistics to better meet Customer Requirements".

European Logistics was the parent company of Eirtran. It had several bases throughout the UK and the European mainland. Whereas business was fairly good in Ireland, the business on a wider front had been struggling for some time. What he didn't know was the extent to which it had been struggling. Operating costs were the biggest bugbear. The European Board had engaged consultants—Aleventura—to review the business and how it might be improved. He was aware that changes were required, but the extent staggered him. For the first time, he was seeing the proposals for the Dublin site which started on page 51.

'We, Aleventura, recommend that the Dublin site be upgraded to a modern, computerised pick and put away Warehouse. This requires the installation of a fully computerised warehouse management system, using tried and tested computer technology, to allow faster and more accurate tracking of stock without the need for human intervention—except for the purpose of the biannual stock check. The introduction of such systems is known to reduce the warehouse staffing component of "pick and put away" by up to 90%.

The Stockholm site invested in this technology some 5 years ago. The staffing levels on the floor reduced from 35 general operatives to 2. Stock reconciliation during regular audits moved from an average of 80% before implementation to 99% within 2 years. The reduction in leakage alone paid for the system. The overall savings in operating costs per annum amounted to £4 m.

It is suggested that the implementation of this system will take 18 months to introduce in Dublin, based on the Stockholm experience. The investment in the new *equipment, like that already in place in our Stockholm site, has a payback of 3 years.*

Tenders have been placed for both the automatic equipment and the IT software system for the Dublin site. 4 contractors have to date replied. It is expected that the project in Dublin will be ready to start within a few months....'

Ted's head was reeling.

"For fuck's sake! How in God's name has it got to this stage and no one even told me? No one at the interview thought it might be helpful to tell me that this was in train? Is this the real reason they got me in here—to be the fall guy to negotiate with unions on this one? Who the hell knows about this? There'll be war!" His words were lost in the evening gloom.

His stomach churned at the thought of broaching this with the floor staff, the drivers, and the shop stewards. Christ, he was in the honeymoon period and already he was being nailed to the cross by his own management.

He read the attached letter from Michael Davis, General Manager, European Logistics.

Dear Ted,

The attached plan sets out the company's new European-wide vision. I see you playing a vital part in leading this exciting new direction for the company. The Dublin plant was selected by the board as the flagship project for the rest of our European operations.

We successfully introduced this new system of operation as a pilot in our Stockholm plant 5 years ago. Hans Larsson led up the project on our behalf at that time. We realise the Dublin operation is a much larger enterprise. To introduce a similar system there will require skilled planning and outstanding management leadership.

I see this as a great challenge, therefore, for someone of your considerable ability. In selecting you for the management post recently in Dublin, you clearly demonstrated your ability to lead change. In your previous posts outside the company, you demonstrated great resolve when implementing changes in the face of difficult circumstances. Eirtran management were greatly impressed by your leadership ability.

I realise that you will need support for the change process. The project needs to be introduced in phases, with minimum interruption to the existing business. You will therefore be glad to know that Hans Larsson has been appointed as Lead Project Manager for the project. He will arrive in Dublin on Wednesday next week to discuss how the project will be delivered and to view the Dublin operation at first hand. He will be accompanied by Aleventura Lead Consultant for the project, Michel Bouffon, who has introduced a number of these systems successfully in Germany and Spain. I would ask you to assist them both in every way you can.

Please ring me as soon as you come back from leave. I hope you are feeling better after your recent unfortunate accident.

There is a need to brief your own management team on these developments as soon as possible. I have emailed a PowerPoint slide show—which includes a video of the operation in Stockholm—which will be delivered to your team on Wednesday afternoon next week. Hans, as Lead Project Manager, will deliver the presentation. Please organise a special meeting of your team for this *important event.*

We need to discuss how best we can develop a communications strategy for the staff around these exciting new developments. There is a need to discuss the appropriate mechanisms to right-size the business over the next 18 months. There will be obvious IR implications and we need to ensure our strategy is able to cope with the range of issues arising.

I look forward to talking to you in due course.

Yours sincerely,

Michael Davis.

General Manager,

European Logistics

For 'challenge', read 'poisoned chalice'. For 'considerable ability', read 'fall guy'. For 'great leadership', read 'axeman cometh'. For 'Lead Project Manager', read 'management stooge'. For 'Lead Consultant'. read '26-year-old high-flyer with an MBA from Harvard—just out of short pants, ready to conquer the world and guaranteed to be a total asshole'. For 'communications strategy' read 'war'. For 'good health' read 'stamina'. For 'exciting' read 'shitty'. For 'discussion on IR strategy', read 'implementing what's already been agreed in Brussels'.

Obviously, the previous incumbent in his job was aware what was coming down the tracks and fled the scene. Ted should have known that if the salary seemed too good to be true, it was too good to be true. Even without this additional workload, he was feeling under ferocious pressure. How would he manage this on top of it all?

He felt tension at the back of his neck and near the

top of his left arm. He was sick in his stomach. He stood up to get relief from the tension. Stars appeared in his eyes and he felt dizzy. He had to sit down again. Eventually the stars stopped flying around and he felt a little better. It was time to go home and get some sleep.

CHAPTER 18

Jimmy Spain pulled up a chair and sat opposite Tom. Tom had a small manila folder in front of him on the desk. He had thought long and hard about whether he should involve Ted in this meeting. In the end, he felt that, as it was his first day back, he could do without the hassle. Jimmy opened the conversation.

"I met Bruno this morning and he said you wanted to see me straight away?"

"I did, Jimmy. I'm going to come straight to the point. You were delivering appliances in Clontarf yesterday morning?"

"What's all this about? Is there something wrong with my work?" Jimmy placed his hands between his legs to hold the seat and sat forward in a slightly aggressive stance.

"Look, Jimmy, I just want you to answer the question." Tom eyeballed the glowering Jimmy Spain.

"Sure, you know by looking at the printed schedules where I was. I can see them on the table in front of you. You know I was in bleedin' Clontarf yesterday." Jimmy wasn't backing down and felt threatened.

"Yeah, Jimmy...and so was I. I saw you—with a woman as a passenger—in your van near Bull Island."

Jimmy didn't answer.

"Let's say she was being more than friendly with you." Jimmy still didn't answer. Tom felt a coldness descend into the room.

"You know the company policy on this as well as I do. Cavorting with women in a company van certainly isn't in your job description."

"CAVORTING, WAS IT?...Is that what you are suggesting?"

"Well, let's say that I saw a blonde woman—dressed to kill—sitting beside you. She seemed to be showing more than a passing interest in you...as well as showing off more than a little of her...er...ample frontage ..."

"Yeah? ..." No further elaboration by Jimmy. The oddness of Jimmy's responses was disconcerting for Tom.

"Well, let's put it this way, Jimmy. I'm not aware of any housing developments on Bull Island in dire need of our appliances. The whole island is a conservation area. I don't think you'll find Bull Island on any schedule, no matter how hard you look. Unless, that is, there's a rare breed of toad who'd just ordered a large American fridge freezer recently?

"Bull Island is where you were headed when I last saw you. Whatever service you were providing this woman with, it wasn't delivering a washing machine!"

Jimmy remain stony-faced and threatening. He still refused to speak. Tom continued talking to fill the space.

"Jimmy, she was dressed like a hooker. I saw the low-cut top she was wearing—and the fishnets. She seemed more than willing for business." Jimmy's face had reddened at this point and was swiftly changing to purple.

"You calling me a fucking incestuous bastard, you long streak of misery? ..." Tom was totally thrown and didn't know how to react.

"I never accused you of incest. Where'd you get that from? I just said that you were doing business that wasn't necessarily Eirtran business."

"That's my fucking daughter you're talking about! You calling her a tart and me a dirty old man—is that it?"

With that, Jimmy lunged across the table, caught Tom by the throat and the two of them fell to the floor behind the desk. Jimmy caught Tom with two punches to the face before Ted opened the door.

"Jesus Christ! What in God's name is going on here?"

Two faces, of contrasting hues of red, appeared above the upturned table. Tom's was red with blood and Jimmy's red with rage. Jimmy still had Tom by the collar.

"This bleedin' cunt is calling my daughter a hoor and accusing me of incest. I'm not taking that from anybody...what happened your face?" Ted's face was still battered and bruised from his hospital stint. The battered threesome looked in silence at each other.

"Get up, the two of you, and sit down. Explain to me, in one sentence, Tom, what you said to this man...." He lifted his eyebrows towards Jimmy. He stared through Tom.

"Jimmy Spain, sir, is my name. I drive one of the vans...."

"...what you said to Jimmy. Then Jimmy, you might give me your side of the story."

"I'll give my side of the story aw'right, but I'll definitely be bringing in the union and my solicitor in on this. I'm 30 years working for this firm and this is just beyond the pale." Ted looked to Tom with a frown.

"It's very simple, Ted. I was on the Clontarf sea-front yesterday, going to a meeting, when I saw Jimmy in the van with a woman passenger. She kissed him, and then he turned onto Bull Island. We have no deliveries on Bull Island, and I asked Jimmy to explain himself." Ted held up his hand and Tom stopped. He sat down after speaking.

"Right, Jimmy. I think Tom has a right to an explanation, don't you think?"

"I was going to explain, if he only gave me time, but the fucker started accusing me of all sorts of things."

"Language, please, Jimmy. I can understand you may have been upset but I believe that Tom's question is legitimate?"

Jimmy gathered himself so that he had the attention of the real boss.

"It's fairly simple. I had a delivery run yesterday around Clontarf, Kilbarrack, Raheny, and Howth. I got a call about 9 o'clock from my daughter on the mobile. Her car had been stolen the previous night. She needs it for work in town. She works on the beautician counter in one of the chemists in Grafton Street.

"Anyways, the guards in Kilbarrack rang to say that a car fitting the description of hers had been found on Bull Island, and could she come down and confirm it? The feckers who stole it had taken the number plates and given it a bit of a once over. She'd no way of getting there and rang me—all very upset. It just so happened I was nearby and offered to bring her down to Bull Island, as it was hard to get to. Well, what would you do if your daughter was in the state mine was in?"

Tom looked sheepish at this stage. Ted felt queasier than he did the night before. The human element of this case would destroy any basis for sanction Tom might have thought he had. In the run up to the other bombshell he was about to drop next week to staff, issues like this were fuel to the fire.

"Anyways, I made a delivery only 5 minutes from my daughter's house and detoured to collect her. I dropped off my helper sayin' I'd come back for him. There isn't room in the cab for 3. I rang Danny Slevin at the radio centre to explain what had happened. I said I'd be unavailable for about a half an hour.

"When Tom 'Plank' here saw me yesterday, my daughter was just giving her father an affectionate peck on the cheek for having helped her out. You can check the story out with the guards in Kilbarrack—and with Slevin on the radio.

"Then this gobshite starts making all sorts of rash accusations just now. Me, like an idiot, spent the rest of the day yesterday catching up on deliveries and not claimin' overtime. I tell you, the next time you ask for cooperation, you can take a run and jump. This isn't the last you'll hear of this!"

"Look, Jimmy, I'm really sorry...." Tom bumbled a little.

"Ye can ram yer bleedin' apology up your arse. You'll be looking at assassination of character, harassment, defamation—you name it, my solicitor will find it. On top of that, I'll be getting the union involved. You're going to have some explaining to do." With that, he turned to walk out.

"And by the way, I feel so stressed, I'm off to the

doctor. So, stuff you and your deliveries today." With that he turned on his heels and stormed out. Ted glared at Tom. His neck was stiff and his left arm tense. He lost it.

"What in the name of fuck were you thinking? I leave you for a few days and all hell breaks loose. You know you're supposed to do your homework before making rash accusations...." The door opened and Val Somerville poked his head in.

"Ah, beggin' your pardon, sir, I see you are back in attendance. I was hoping that I could meet with you today on a matter of utterest indulgence. The men, sir, have a major issue with the tail-lifts and the instruction to offload from the side. I think that it is endemic on you to entrust your fullest consideration to the ablution of this matter. Could we say 11 o'clock this morning?" Ted raised his eyebrows and glowered over at Tom.

"Yes, I'll see you then for half an hour. Tom, make it your business to be there. In the meantime, I suggest you go and clean yourself up." He spat the words out.

Val looked at the embattled supervisor.

"Tom, I suggest you fill an accident report form—that looks very nasty." Tom fixed him with a look to kill but it went straight over Val's head. With this valuable advice, Val turned and left. Two battered faces remained looking at one another.

"Tom, I need to call a meeting of our management staff today. A major issue has cropped up and I need to brief you all on it. Have you any idea what Val wants?"

"No." The reply was clipped.

"Could I get you to round up all the managers, get the staff room set up with a projector and make sure they're all there for 2 p.m. sharp?" Tom nodded.

-o-o-o-o-o-

Ulser sat at the bar watching the door. The "Grunt" appeared with his two henchmen. The Grunt looked neither left nor right but strode straight to the counter. He sat on a high stool beside Ulser.

"Black Bush for me," he said nodding towards the barman. He stared straight ahead.

"You got the cash?" he said without averting his gaze. Ulser grunted.

"The bag's on the ground: it's all there. By the way, I don't need reminders in the middle of the night. My sister isn't part of this. I told you I'd have it."

"The lads were short of practice. I need to keep them keen. I was close to charging you interest. I heard on the grapevine that you had some grief at that workplace of yours. I need to protect my assets and don't you ever forget it." The Grunt's gaze remained fixed on the mirror behind the bar.

"Ever hear the phrase: 'Don't place all your fucking eggs in the one bleedin' basket.' Well, I don't place all my gear in one single locker. I'm well covered—I don't make mistakes. By the way, Billy Connolly got it spot on when he said that if you crap in my shoes, I'll piss in your Bovril... keep that rat pack away from my house and me." Ulser's even tone was little higher than a whisper, as he looked straight ahead at the mirror behind the bar as well.

"Martin, you never really knew your place, did you? Don't you ever threaten me, or some day you'll be found in a gutter eating your own prick-meat sandwich. Get my drift?"

Without waiting for a response, the Grunt threw back the whiskey, slapped Ulser on the back and beckoned to his mongrels to leave. Ulser felt a rush of cold air up his back as they exited the main door. His eyes remained fixed on the flapping door through the mirror.

-o-o-o-o-o-

Ted looked in exasperation at Val Somerville.

"You cannot be seriously suggesting that a fully adult man, built like a tank, annually trained in the art of Manual Handling Techniques—courses designed to help such Mister Irelands to lift items in a way so as not to injure themselves—and who is experienced at doing the self same manual handling job for over 20 years, is insisting on using a tail-lift to remove an electric kettle from the van?"

"That is the presumption on which my thesaurus is based."

"I assume you mean thesis?" Tom chipped in.

"Val, why does Eirtran spend so much money on manual handling, if you are saying the men won't use it in any shape or form? On your premise, I assume that when these self same Samsons use the canteen to fill a kettle full of water for the morning tea—which kettle, according to the laws of physics, will be heavier full than empty, the kettle which you are saying we can only lift off using the tail-lift out in the yard—that you'll be demanding a tower crane in the canteen at the sink to help him fill his mug of tea? This is just ridiculous." Ted sank back in the chair, incredulous, with his hands behind his head.

"The Safety Act puts no limit on the weight to be lifted. It just states that mechanical devices are to be put in place wherever possible to remove manual handling...." Val patted the Safety Act on the table as his comfort blanket. Ted was losing patience.

"The Safety Act doesn't ask us to leave our brains and common sense at the door...doesn't say we act like imbeciles...or maybe there is a page I missed in the Act? This is totally ludicrous. The HSA only recently audited this site for safety compliance, and we received a clean bill of health. You were present during that self-same safety audit and our methods of van off-loading were approved. So...it's very simple, Val. The status quo remains. We are within the law. Why didn't you raise this issue then?"

Val remained nonplussed. To Ted's eyes, Val remained as vacant as usual. Val pushed out his chest and pronounced.

"My members won't be happy with this ..."

"May I remind you that you're not a trade union official, Val. You don't have members! You're a Safety Rep." This flustered Val somewhat.

"The lads on the floor axed me to resent their views to you...."

"Present, not resent, Val." Ted was getting snappy and impatient at this point.

"...resent their views to you. I've done that and I'll be bringing back what you said. It won't be the end of the matter. I'll be raising it with the shop steward, and we'll be back to you in due course."

"Hopefully, we might get some sensible dialogue at that point and, with a bit of luck, sanity might prevail", Ted retorted.

Val pushed back the seat and backed out of the room; head bowed low as if leaving the Queen's chambers. Ted didn't watch him leave as he rooted around in a drawer. Tom turned to Ted.

"I've organised that meeting for the afternoon. Everyone will be there. It's important then?" Ted was still rooting in the drawer.

"Yeah. And the shit I've had to contend with this morning won't make breaking it to the staff any more palatable." He stayed mooching in the drawer. Tom took the hint that it was time to make himself scarce.

After Tom left, Ted stood up quickly and saw stars in his eyes. He felt light-headed and sat back down on his leather swivel chair. He noticed tension at the top of his left arm again and his neck ached.

He could hear a blackbird singing in the trees outside. The bird sang with freedom and without fear. It surveyed its world from the comfort and loftiness of its perch. It was all seeing. It was in control.

-o-o-o-o-o-

Ulser stood against the bench where he had stripped down the gear box of a Volkswagon Golf. He had the phone stuck to his ear. His solicitor was on the other end.

"Mr. Rosenberg, I want to ensure that you hit them for everything. Serious back injury, long term impact, that the manual handling courses provided by Eirtran are inadequate as they only cover lifting light carboard boxes from an even floor, lack of serious investigation of my accident, harassment at my home when I was ill, loss of overtime, future earnings....I don't give a toss, so long as we hit them everywhere we can. We are taking proceedings to the High Court etc. etc...(silence)...Ok, you got all that? Get it on a fax as soon as possible today so that it's on his desk by the afternoon." With his usual grace, Ulser hung up without as much as a 'by your leave'.

He smiled and looked back to the item on the bench. He wrapped his two arms around it and carried it all the way across the garage floor and placed it alongside a lathe.

-o-o-o-o-o-

Jimmy Spain walked from the surgery. He had a sick cert for two weeks in his hand. It stated he was suffering from stress and the doctor had also provided him with a prescription for tablets. Jimmy had no intention of getting them. He strode down the road and straight into the solicitor used by all of Eirtran staff. The solicitor was cheap—no foal, no fee. Jimmy was lucky enough that court proceedings had been cancelled for the day and Abraham Rosenberg B.L. Esquire was available for a "consultation" immediately.

In 15 minutes, they had a draft letter pulled together which had the appropriate "legalese" in it to satisfy Jimmy's torrent of rage. The letter alleged that Eirtran had seriously impugned his dignity at work, the supervisor had libelled his daughter and himself with scurrilous allegations, the supervisor had defamed the character of both his daughter and himself and that he was taking an action to the Circuit Court seeking £30k in damages.

As Jimmy sat there, Mr. Rosenberg realised something was amiss with Eirtran management. This was his second client this morning. He thought it might be useful to plug for a little business there. He asked Jimmy if he minded placing an advertisement on the Notice Board in Eirtran offering his services. With the humour Jimmy was in, he was more than happy to oblige. He took two pamphlets and said he would give them to one of the lads he was meeting for a pint that night. Mr. Rosenberg had a broad smile on his face when Jimmy left. He was like the cat who had the cream.

-o-o-o-o-o-

Val stood talking to Jem, briefing him on the reaction of management to his tail-lift issue. Jem patiently probed to find out where the push for the use of the tail lifts was coming from. It was clear there had been no build up of steam on the floor on this issue. It had come out of the blue. He tried to let Val think he was taking him seriously, nodding solemnly at appropriate intervals to each of the lofty concerns expressed by Val. However, his mind was elsewhere.

Jem would run with the hare and hunt with the hounds for the moment and get agreement off-line on a strategy with the manager. There were a variety of stalling tactics available—establish a joint management/worker group to review off-loading procedures, engage a safety consultant to review best practice in the industry and compare to Eirtran methodology etc. There were plenty of ways to kill this until he got to the bottom of it. He made a mental note to meet with the manager in the afternoon.

CHAPTER 19

Hans Larsson, Lead Project Manager, had just finished his presentation. You could hear a pin drop in the course of his tour de force. Ted's team of eight direct reports sat dumbstruck, their eyes fixed on Mr. Larsson. The room was stuffy and warm. Ted could feel the shirt sticking to his back. Michel Bouffon sat next to Larsson and said nothing.

Ted had met Bouffon earlier and found it hard to understand his thickly accented Parisian English. Eventually, he gave up trying to converse. The two foreign visitors had not gone unnoticed by staff in the building. In fact, Jem had bumped into Ted at the front door on their arrival. Ted didn't introduce them. Jem found that odd.

"I think I can say that you provided us with food for thought in your presentation. The issues are cogently expressed, and the timescale of the project is extremely challenging. Any questions for Mr. Larsson?" Ted could sense the quiet before the storm. Tom was first up. He stood tall, clearly to make his presence felt.

"Ted, have you any idea what you are asking here? If this goes ahead, we are talking about decimating the workforce in the stores. Are we just going to sack them?

Put them on the dole? You won't need a supervisor for what's left. I don't see myself in the picture anywhere. Am I in the same boat as all the other staff? All we heard from Mr. Consultant here"...Tom was starting to warm uncomfortably to his subject and Ted could hear the noise of the hurricane in the distance about to arrive . . "is how this marvellous system is going turn Eirtran fortunes around. Is that the company directors' fortunes—or—the fortunes of unfortunate plebs like ourselves? I don't think it's going to benefit me, or anyone else in this room, from what I heard." These words were accompanied by a grand inclusive sweep of his arm to indicate all his colleagues adjacent for emphasis.

"Anyway, since when did IT systems work as they were supposed to? Yeah, Stockholm was great. But what he forgot to tell us was that Stockholm has two depots and if they fecked up in one, the second one was able to handle day to day deliveries. Stockholm was all teed up nicely to make sure it couldn't fail. AND the depot they used as the guinea pig was much smaller than the main depot...AND in the end, it got so bad, that they stopped deliveries altogether from the smaller one and used it solely to sort out problems with the system. The facts were all laid out in the company magazine some years ago – I dug it out and here it is!" He lifted the magazine triumphantly for all to see.

"I also went digging about the Warehouse Management System that is being proposed. It's developed by a crowd called "LLogistix". Do you know what the overriding advice was to prospective buyers?" Ted wasn't sure he wanted to hear.

"DON'T BUY IT! Don't buy this bleedin' software! The website has comments from European Logistics staff involved in the project in Stockholm about their experience. Everyone says that the Warehouse Management System is basically a disaster. Even yet it has serious problems in the invoicing module, problems that were never resolved. The Put Away module regularly gets confused when new stock items come on stream and old ones are retired. Because of delays at the central site in Poland updating the item codes, the put away cars are stopping in the middle of the aisles because they are confused and have to be manually removed and reprogrammed. The outcome was delivery chaos. And that's not all.

"The back-up servers are based in the UK, but the bloody software provided by LLogistix has back-up agents in Israel, not even in the EU. This means that if the local server goes belly up, we have little or no back up. We can't get stock in or out!

"And now we're going to do the same in Dublin? What is this company at?"

Tom was red in the face at the finish. The colour in Ted's face had all but disappeared. Why did he give Tom a preview that morning and provide him with grenades to lob? Mind you, he'd obviously done his homework. Ted had to agree that he'd seen such systems before, which were going to change the world, tying businesses up in knots. What you imagine you thought you were getting and what you get are never the same.

The meeting then descended into a total chaos, headed by Tom. Questions and allegations flew from every angle. Ted found it impossible to control the timbre of the meeting where his guests came under full scale attack. The meeting ended in total disarray, with people standing up and leaving at different points of the meeting in disgust.

Jem found out earlier, from Ted's secretary (who had a thing going for Jem a few years before), that an important meeting was being held in the conference room. Jem had been standing in the room adjoining for the duration. This room held all the cleaners' mops, brushes, etc. and was normally locked. Jem had managed to unearth a spare key a few years ago and held onto it. He knew that it would give him opportunities to eavesdrop on management meetings in the boardroom from time to time and keep him ahead of the posse. His foresight had paid dividends many times in the intervening years, particularly today. This was dynamite.

He couldn't hear all the conversations but had heard enough. It shocked him. This was trouble. He locked the door behind him and slipped down the back stairs without being seen.

-o-o-o-o-o-

After the meeting, Ted rang Michael Davis in the European HQ in Brussels to brief him about the outcome of the meeting. To say the phone call was tense would be understating it. Ted ate Michael Davis for dropping him in it and for exposing him to the frontline supervisors and managers without adequate preparation. He told him the general mood had been horrendous and trying to remake the ground was going to be exceedingly difficult. Michael didn't seem particularly perturbed.

To add to Ted's problems, Michael insisted that Ted fly to Brussels on Monday for a managers' brief on this new project. He was to organise flights for Sunday night and be at HQ at 9 a.m. the following day. Ted tried to tell him about his wife and the difficult position Michael was putting him in. He needed to be near home. Michael was unsympathetic—saying that her parents could do the needful. Ted spent the rest of the evening organising flights and hotels on the web because Marie Connolly, his secretary, was too busy with other work he had given her. He got nothing else done.

To add to his woes, Ted had been handed two solicitors' faxes—one relating to Jimmy Spain and one in relation to Ulser. He was given them by the world's least intelligent—and most unattractive —secretary soon after the chaotic meeting in the board room. Marie Connolly felt he would probably like to see them urgently. He needed this added pressure like diarrhoea needs a laxative. 'Bleedin' bastards', he thought, 'always looking for an angle.'

Ted went to the managers' WC which was attached to his office. He felt dreadful. He was sweating. His arm ached and his chest felt tight. He stood over the toilet bowl and dry retched. He feared for the future and his inability to manage it. He felt under siege. He was a bird locked in a cage.

CHAPTER 20

It was Sunday night. The figure in the garden flung the Molotov Cocktail at the window of the house. The window shattered into smithereens. Flames took hold immediately in the front room. The figure stood listening to the whoosh of the flames. The alarm on the wall went off. The figure in the dark lingered, curiously watching the flames rising, licking feverishly at the walls of the house. There was a familiar roar from the fire which pleased him. He could feel the heat on his face. That was invigorating. The figure slipped through the bushes at the side of the house and disappeared into the night.

Within minutes, neighbours were standing agog, congregating around the fire brigade personnel as they tried to douse the flames. The area was sealed off for forensic examination. About a third of the house was destroyed by fire.

-o-o-o-o-o-

Ted sat listening to the presentation in the luxurious offices of European Logistics in Brussels. Michael Davis was providing a very compelling financial argument for introducing the LLogistix Warehouse Management

System Europe-wide.

The HQ is sited in the business district of Brussels, where tower blocks vie with each other for the heavens. Each business tower looked like a tree in a forest, the odd treetop reaching closer to the wild blue yonder than others. European Logistics HQ was one of the taller trees. The view from the conference room over Brussels was breath-taking.

A screen had been lowered from the ceiling for the PowerPoint presentation. The seats were luxurious, each one like the Pullman seats at the back of a cinema. The seats were tiered—as in a lecture hall. A mini soft drinks cabinet was installed under each seat.

Ted's phone vibrated on silent several times during the presentation. His phone was unusually busy. He tried to concentrate on the presentation, but his mind was wandering...was there something new happening at home? Was Becks ok? Had something else happened at Eirtran? He was nervous at leaving Tom in charge after the last escapade with Jimmy Spain.

He had a look at the numbers on his phone but didn't recognise any of them. Then a text came through from a number he didn't recognise. "Ring Sgt John McGuinness at this number immediately".

Ted panicked and quietly made his way out of the room. He rang and was answered by "Gardai, Kilmainham". What in God's name had happened?

"I was told to ring this number and ask for you. Has something happened my wife? I'm at a meeting in Brussels right now." Ted wasn't really sure that he wanted to hear the answer.

"No. Your wife is ok—there was no-one in the house

..."

"What do you mean? Has something happened in Clifden?" The Sergeant was totally confused.

"No—your house in Dalkey. It went on fire last night...." replied the Sergeant. Ted paused for a minute to take in what he said.

"What do you mean? My house in Dalkey was set on fire?" His chest started to tighten.

"Yes...and we have reason to believe it was started deliberately. That's why the investigation is being led from Kilmainham Central Detective Unit and not the local Dalkey unit. I need to have a chat with you as soon as possible ..."

"I'm in Brussels at a meeting just now...I can't get home until later today ..." Ted's mind started to race.

"I would suggest that you get home quickly and view the damage. I'm not sure it's habitable—a lot of smoke damage. Sorry to bring you such bad news but I'll talk to you on your return." He hung up.

Ted was stunned. He was sweating. His flight was due out at 4 that evening. It couldn't come soon enough.

-o-o-o-o-o-

Tom had decided. It was war on Ulser. He spent the morning at the offices of Mark Devins, Private Investigator. The office he sat in was dingy, above a sex shop in Capel Street.

Mark Devins PI was a scruffy individual. In his 50's, he was a retired detective. Tom noticed his dirty nails and his pockmarked face—one of abject depression—with two scars, possibly as a result of knife wounds, where dwelt deep pools of eyes staring out from the abyss within. Devins wouldn't have looked out of place in the dingy sex shop below wearing a dirty cream trench coat. In fact, if he wore a trench coat, it might have improved him.

Tom didn't like him. Devins was a complete scrote. Maybe years of detective work, observing the scum of this earth, had made him that way.

Tom provided Devins with as much detail as he could on Martin Cullen; where he lived, his known movements, his associates, his phone number, his car registration, any illnesses he had, his doctor, etc. He provided him with a few photographs taken from his file. One photograph was quite recent.

Devins only worked on day rates. He gave no guarantees in relation to results except to say that he would provide a report on Ulser's movements every two days—more often if deemed necessary. He would accompany each report with photographs and videos when required. Devins's name was not be used under any circumstances by Eirtran and would not appear on any reports provided. In the unlikely event that he was rumbled, he would ensure that no record of dealings with Eirtran could be found—either on a file in his offices or at his home.

He had his methods. The reports would be sent by courier but not by An Post. Either Tom or Ted had to sign personally for any package delivered—otherwise the package would be returned to him. A later drop of a similar package would be attempted next day.

Tom had used Devins before to build cases on difficult employees. While he didn't like the man, Devins had been very successful and was discreet. Tom couldn't risk further conflict with the union, particularly after the last few days. Eirtran could never openly use the information Devins' gathered but it gave them leverage for tackling the likes of Ulser.

-o-o-o-o-o-

Jem demanded to know why Dracula was stirring unrest over the tail-lifts. He'd worked out the answer already. He just wanted Dracula to know that he knew. Dracula denied all knowledge.

Jem, on reflection, came to the conclusion that it suited him to piggy-back on the unrest after hearing last week's revelations in the cleaner's room. A few stoppages would steel the staff for the fight against the modernisation which was being imposed by Brussels. If there was to be decimation of the stores staff, he concluded he wouldn't survive either. He had to pin his colours to the mast.

He was better off lining up with his peers and fighting for a good deal, rather than being a stooge for management. There was no value in tying his future to Eirtran anymore. The easy life he once had was now over. The next year would involve toughing it out for the best possible voluntary redundancy deal with management.

"Josser, I'm right behind you. I'm going to let you in on a secret. Sources tell me that Eirtran is just about to modernise this place. It'll mean all our jobs—in the stores anyway—will be gone. It's all going to happen in the next year and a half. It's already a done deal.

"Don't get side-tracked on this tail-lift issue. Work with me. We've a bigger fight on our hands. However, I think we'll use this issue to get leverage and get management to the table.

"I'm suggesting a work stoppage this week to highlight safety concerns and get management to come clean on how many proposed redundancies are on the cards with this new plan. We'll complain about lack of communication with the unions, lack of care around safety incidents and now lack of consideration over the future of 45 loyal floor staff who are about to be thrown on the scrap heap. We'll get it out in the public domain that we now know that Eirtran's future plans are to make profit on the back of depriving us of our livelihoods. We will claim staff are at breaking point and want management to come to the table to discuss this proposal from Brussels.

"I've a friend working in RTE. We'll get a few cameras here to highlight the loss of jobs in the Ringsend area. I'll make sure that some local councillors get wind of the stoppage and how it's affecting their constituents. Guaranteed they'll turn up with some protestors—local shopkeepers, publicans, and the like—who would lose business if we left. Ted Black won't know what hit him!"

He was happy that the word would spread like wildfire from Dracula. It was every man for himself from here on in.

-o-o-o-o-o-

The back door crashed to the ground. Mel screamed. The two men towered over her.

"Cash—where does he keep it?" Mel was told by Martin to hold out for a while if this ever happened. However, if it ever started getting dangerous, Martin had told her to point them in the direction of the small safe.

"I...I...I dunno." She tried to stay focused on what Martin had told her.

The bigger of the two masked thugs grabbed the two arms of her wheelchair and the other put a Stanley knife to her nose.

"Ring that bastard brother of yours and ask him where the money is!!" He pushed a mobile phone into her hand. She punched in the numbers. It answered.

"What's up, Mel?"

"Men in house. Wan' money. Where it?" Mel stammered a little. "They wan' fast."

"Are you ok?...tell them about the place behind the TV. Tell them to talk to me." The thug was listening and shook his head. He turned off the phone.

"If you want to keep that pretty face, tell me where the fucking money is, bitch!" She was frightened at this stage. She pointed to the TV cabinet.

"...pull out cab'ne...safe...o-6-8-9 code." The cabinet was flung aside by the other thug and the television died as it crashed to the floor with a thud. He pounded in the code and the door flew open. He grabbed what seemed a lot of notes from the safe.

"At least two grand. C'mon, this'll cover it."

"I like the look of you...." The first thug looked smugly at Mel. He then looked to his mate in crime.

"You stay on watch. I've a little lady here that needs a lesson in love!" ...

-o-o-o-o-o-

...Ulser knew that things were really bad the minute he stepped inside the door. He felt a breeze from somewhere. He stepped into the kitchen and saw the place had been ransacked. The back door was open, and a gale was coming through. The door was flat on the floor where it had been kicked in.

"Mel?...Mel??...MEL!"

He heard her whimpering in her downstairs bedroom. There wasn't a mark on her, but she was looking vacantly at the ceiling. Her wheelchair was on its side and her dress was around her waist. He knew at that point that he was in deeper trouble than he ever thought possible.

'If they've touched my sister, after all I've done to put things right, I'll kill them', he thought. 'Mel and I have fought to get to this point where I can nearly get away from this kip... we're that close. Fuck the world.'

"What happened, Mel? Who did this? ..." Ulser asked.

Mel didn't seem to know he was in the room. The trauma had numbed her. She couldn't respond. Ulser, where things never go to him, was numb inside. His little sister. He pulled her head towards his chest and anger filled his every pore. His eyes glistened at the thought of one of those scumbags laying a finger on his sister.

Ulser, nor anyone else, would ever hear Mel speak again.

-o-o-o-o-o-

Ted felt that he had to tell Rebecca about the fire. She

might be ringing the house, getting no reply, and worrying. The fire might be reported in papers. He knew she was frail, and the shock wouldn't help her. However, her finding out any other way might be worse.

He rang from the airport in Brussels before embarking on the plane home. She wept on the phone at the thought of their beautiful home being destroyed. Her parents rang back to say that she cried for hours afterwards and was inconsolable. If there was anything they could do?...He told them that it was better they take care of her. For the first time, he felt they were really concerned for him as well and how he might cope. He found that strangely comforting.

When he arrived back at Dublin airport, Ted thought about booking himself into a hotel. However, some years before, his uncle had willed him his home place. The house was in a rough area, just off the Coombe, close to the Tenters. There was a block of Corporation flats around the corner. Opposite was an old stone warehouse, which had fallen into disuse many years before. Ted had converted his uncle's house into two flats and rented them on an ongoing basis. The upstairs flat had been vacant for a few months. Ted had taken to using it from time to time after drinking sessions in town when he wasn't fit to drive home. He decided he would stay there tonight, after having a quick look around his home in Dalkey.

The roof was intact, but the downstairs was gutted. The walls were black with the flames. Some of the bushes near the house had been scorched. The smell of the burnt-out shell caught in his throat. He would have to organise to remove what hadn't been smoke-damaged to a lock-up during the week. He needed to organise an architect to assess the damage and price a rebuild soon after the assessor looked at the damage. The thought of all this—and the pressure he already was under at work—made him perspire.

At 2 a.m., he eventually got his head to the pillow in his new temporary quarters in the Tenters. He parked the car up Thomas's Road, where he felt it would be safer. He fell into a fitful sleep.

It took the whole of the following day to go back to the house, meet the guards and answer some questions, meet the assessor, fill in insurance claim forms, talk to an architect on what could be done with the house, organise a removal firm to take whatever was salvageable from the house to a lock-up and arrange boarding up the remainder. At best, if he were to rebuild, the architect told him it would be 2 years before he could be back in his home.

The insurance firm would agree to temporary accommodation of his family for up to 6 months. However, as the property was under-insured, the rental on offer would not provide them with anything close to what they were accustomed to. Things just got worse as the day wore on and Ted took to drinking eight pints on his own in the Tenters Pub that night. It shut out reality for a while.

'Jesus, what kind of hellhole have I landed myself in? Whatever gains I thought I'd make in salary and standard of living by moving job have all but evaporated, at a huge cost to not only myself, but my family and home as well.

'I hadn't realised how indolence—and insolence—was so well rewarded by worker legislation. Is this where we are now? Managers are fair game. It's impossible to tackle anyone anymore: these wasters are untouchable. The touchy, feely, liberalistas, brown sock and sandals brigade, have created a monster of an Industrial Relations Process without ever looking at how the manager might hope to tackle difficult staff...all rights and no responsibilities for the worker. All responsibilities and no rights for the managers.

'...and the Employment Appeals Tribunal. Now there's another crock of shit!

'It's like Statler and Waldorf from *The Muppets* in there the last time I was forced to appear on behalf of an employer. The Tribunal members, I mean. They were all but covered in cobwebs—and the average age seemed to be 95. Some may have been older than that—older than Methuselah himself. The defendant didn't turn up on the first two occasions we were there and on the third, the Tribunal was ringing him and begging him to attend as he was a no show again. The defendant had no case in the first place. It seemed the Tribunal only wanted to justify its existence by having more and more cases ruled on. A pure numbers game. We didn't even get our costs for attending on the three occasions. What kind of a broken system is this? There's no justice in it for anyone, either for the manager or all those other employees who put in a fair day's work for a fair day's pay. What do other employees think when they see wasters like this getting away with murder?

'I didn't know that managers could be targeted like I've been, to the extent of ruining all I have, without leaving a trace. The guards have no idea who burnt my house—but I have! But could I prove it in a court of law?

Wouldn't stack up on the basis of what I know.'

He could feel the hate building up inside him—hate for Eirtran, Ulser, the "Systems". The more he drank, the more the hate consumed his every thought.

'This isn't me. I've got to get a grip. I've never hated anyone. All right, I've lost it in the heat of the moment on a football pitch—yeah, even taken a player out when the red mist came down. But hate? I've never experienced this before. Where has that come from? I just feel I want to be rid of this person. I don't want to step away. I want justice. I want retribution. If only I had someone to talk to about it, but I can't burden Rebecca with anything more. She's delicate enough....

'Dad, what about you, if you're nearby in the ether?' He thought of his departed dad, and the long talks they'd have about the state of politics and the nation. Ted defined politics not by right or left wing but by right and wrong.

'Give me a sign—mind you, not the big lightning bolt from the sky?! If you were around, you'd help me keep my sanity and keep perspective. But look at me?...and God?...does He really exist, as we believe? If He is about, would you mind putting in a good word for me because it doesn't seem like I'm His pet in the class! It seems Ulser has that honour. Untouchable. A fair and just God? I don't think so...just a load of old baloney....'

CHAPTER 21

Tom pulled the package apart. He viewed the clear black and white photos showing Ulser working as a mechanic at "Dolphin Motor Repairs". For a man with a sore back, he clearly had no problem lifting heavy objects around the yard.

Devins had done his homework on the Register of Small Businesses. Ulser owned a premises and a business registered as Dolphin Motor Repairs.

'Obviously we're paying him too much overtime', thought Tom.

Ulser visited the bookies every day. 'Nothing unusual there', thought Tom. However, Devins shed some further light. He had someone posted in the bookies to overhear Ulser. The report stated that Ulser liked to bet big and pay in cash.

Devins' people had tailed Ulser when he visited Island Motor Repairs in Dalkey, just off Barnhill Road. It seemed like a similar set-up to Ulser's own—a small backstreet mechanic's business—and Ulser seemed on friendly terms with the owner. They would do further investigation to see if Ulser had any financial interest there.

The owner of that business was a man called Enda Hartnett, brother of Georgie Hartnett who had just retired from Eirtran. It was interesting for Tom to see the web of family connections in Eirtran. This was one he hadn't known about. A picture of Island Motor Repairs showed that Georgie was working part-time there after his retirement. Ulser paid for and collected some spare parts on the day he was tailed.

Ulser had his house in Ballyfermot—15 Elmpark Drive. He had a paraplegic sister, Mel, living with him. They had lost their parents when he was 19 after a fire at their parents' home. Ulser had managed for the two of them since.

He checked Ulser's record with the police. He was known to them but had never been charged with anything. He had been targeted by small time criminals from time to time. The word on the street was that he was questioned about dodgy goods sold in the pubs to pay off gambling debts. However, he had never been arrested for anything. It finished saying that a further report would issue in 2 days.

Tom had been in contact with the HR department earlier. They had wanted Ulser to meet the company's Occupational Health doctor to get a second opinion on his back injury. It was company practice to seek such an opinion for any back injury exceeding 3 Lost Time Days. Ulser had supplied additional sick certs to say he was still unfit for work due to a back injury. He was out a few weeks at this point. HR had set up two appointments in the last week and he'd attended neither. They asked that the manager and supervisor visit his home and insist on his attendance.

Ted had spent some time organising a new date for the doctor and had left a message on Ulser's phone with the appointed date. The pace was hotting up and Tom wasn't sure that he liked the way things were evolving. Eirtran was under attack on too many fronts. In addition, his own appetite for the war on Ulser was waning in view of the company's recent announcement on modernisation.

-o-o-o-o-o-

Jem stood in front of the assembled rabble in the canteen. You could hear an ant fart. He was flanked by Jimmy Spain on the one hand and by Josser on the other. Jem pulled in Jimmy as assistant shop steward in preparation for the upcoming negotiations with management.

"Brothers, a number of incidents have occurred recently that are causing us all a bit of concern. Eirtran is pushing for more and more productivity. They claim that we are falling behind other competitors and our cost base is too high...but where are they cutting the corners? Cutting management? Cutting admin? OOOH...NO! Cutting us, that's who. We are being asked to change our custom and practices to get deliveries up.

"Management are demanding we offload from the side of the vans in order to speed up deliveries. Those side doors are man doors—they're not designed for offloading gear. Why have we tail-lifts on the vans? For bloody offloading, that's what, Brothers. Those tail-lifts are there in order to protect us from hurting our backs and from accidents, that's why.

"And do they have any sympathy when we try to accommodate them? Look at Brother Martin, for instance. He offloaded in the racks, hurt his back, and has been off work since. Did he get any thanks from our management team? No! Not a sausage! Not as much as an accident investigation. We have been offloading from those racks for as long as I remember. It's awkward, we all know that. It's poor ergonomic design, Brothers. They kept the HSA away from the area during the last safety audit...and why? Because they knew the HSA wouldn't wear it, that's why.

"We make a reasonable request to offload using the tail-lifts—and what does management do, Brothers? They try to ridicule our Safety Representative, Brothers. They try to make out *he's* in the wrong. He's just applying the correct safety procedures. But we're not going to take that from anyone, are we, Brothers?"

He was in full flow...in Baptist Preacher mode. It was a tour de force. Val Somerville was delighted to see that his role was being acknowledged. There were various choruses of "No bleedin' way!", "Stuff management!" and "We're not takin' shit!!".

"As a result, Brothers, I am proposing we have a 3-hour stoppage tomorrow at the gates...*and*...there's more, Brothers. I have it on good authority that there are proposals afoot to reduce the staffing of this depot substantially. I mean substantially, Brothers! To the extent that only a handful of men will be here in two years time. Our mother ship management, European Logistics, have decided to run this place down to the bare minimum of staff. And have they come to discuss it with us, Brothers? No! Being done by stealth, like everything else in this place. Are we going to give our jobs up that easily, Brothers?"

He was working the crowd into a lather. He had his

peers in the palm of his hand. Comments flew from the assembled throng. "No shit from management!", "Stuff management!", "Let's teach them a lesson."

"Yes, Brothers, we need to take action. I want everyone on picket duty tomorrow. Placards will be there at quarter to eight. Let's give them a run for their money."

Jem felt happy at the outcome. He had played the game exactly as planned.

CHAPTER 22

She sat at the window, looking without seeing. Her face was pretty but vacant. At that moment in earthly time, she existed physically. Mentally, she was in another dimension. Her face remained passive, expressionless, and tilted to one side. Her body listed at an angle in the wheelchair. It was frail, slightly emaciated. It was as if someone had left a ragdoll in the same position earlier in the day. It looked as if she hadn't moved from the moment she was placed there. A plastic mug, with a dome cap and straw, containing something that resembled a yoghurt drink, stood half empty on the table beside her.

Her hair caught the ray of sunshine shining through the window. In the beam, one could see the flecks of dust flying, floating through the stuffy air of the room. The rays highlighted some stray wisps of hair which stood out from the body of the rest of her hair. A bluebottle, which had been trapped in the room for some time, droned angrily at window-ledge level, signalling it was preparing to die.

The ward was modern. It had a timber floor. Three modern black and white pictures adorned the pastel cream walls; one depicted steel erectors high on the New

York skyline, eating lunch, another of the Golden Gate Bridge in San Francisco, and the last one a soft focus shot of Marilyn Monroe.

The ward nurse walked into the room and said:

"Mel, pet, you have to eat something. Maybe if I took you out into the air it would help?...I'll wheel you out if you like? You might feel like eating afterwards?" They were rhetorical questions—only because Mel wouldn't speak.

The nurse looked to Ulser. He didn't respond. He wasn't hearing. He had driven Mel to Tallaght the previous evening. They ran a number of tests which confirmed she had been raped. They carried out further tests for AIDS, but the results wouldn't be known for some time. A Ban Garda had attempted to get a statement from Mel, but she just couldn't—or wouldn't—talk. Ulser had never seen her like this.

Ulser didn't like the police around but had no choice but to make a statement. He was asked who he thought might have had a grudge against Mel—or even himself. He said no one. He knew he had a lot of enemies out there. Maybe the Grunt didn't like being pissed off by him and had given some of his henchmen permission to take retribution on his behalf.

The guard persisted. Ulser pleaded ignorance of anyone out to get him. Having thought about it, he knew it could be any badass living in all of South County Dublin. For the first time in his life, he felt pangs of conscience. However big a mess he had gotten himself into, he had never wanted Mel affected by it. They were a team, pushing to improve on their current shitty lives. He wanted away from here. That's what he had worked for over the years. Now that it was getting in sight, this had happened.

-o-o-o-o-o-

Ted couldn't believe what he was seeing. The entrance gate to Eirtran was completely blocked by pickets. What in the name of God had Tom done this time? When he stopped the car in front of the crowd, there was a tap on the window.

"RTE. Would you mind making a statement? We believe that you intend laying off 40 staff in Eirtran and there has been no consultation with the staff?"..."Would you like to comment on the union contention that the company is trying to impose unsafe work practices in Eirtran?" ..."Is it true that you failed to initiate an accident investigation after a worker had a serious back injury recently?".... Ted's head began to spin. He foostered around, looking for the driver's window switch. He lowered and raised the back window twice before eventually raising the correct one.

He edged the car through the crowd of faces. They banged on the roof and hammered on the windows as he went through. His chest was extremely tight, and he was sweating. He was aware of the pain again in his left arm. The car park was nearly empty save the few management team cars. He could see a queue of forty-footers from their suppliers through the fence waiting to be unloaded. Obviously with the chaos outside, that was a highly unlikely scenario today.

He stormed into Tom's office, knowing he had to be there. With no staff, he shouldn't be anywhere else!

"Jaysus, Tom, what in God's name have you done this time?"

"What've I done? What've you done, more like? They somehow got wind of the proposals for this place before you got to brief the union officially, and now they're on the warpath! Who is the far-sighted git in Brussels who decided to brief management first? Could he not see it would leak like a sieve? I've no idea how the staff got to know—but they have, and they're livid. They've even got local councillors out there with the TV crews."

Ted looked out the window to survey the scene. He could see the harsh lights of the camera crews in the street down below.

"Ted, this is your mess and I object to the way you accused me. If you want a management team to stand behind you, you had better be a bit more diplomatic in how you treat them." Tom stared at him—looking abject in the process.

"Ok, maybe I was a bit previous and I apologise...but the last day I came back, I had hell to pay. I better get on to Michael Davis in Brussels before coverage hits the papers and the TV. I assume we have some PR dude that deals with the press for us?...I'm not going to be fed to the wolves to explain the vagaries of Brussels' mismanagement. Let them send someone from Brussels if they want." Ted did not feel well.

"Ted, you might want to look at these letters and the report from the PI on Ulser as well. The one on Ulser I think you'll find interesting."

"Christ, Tom, I think I have enough on my plate with what's going on outside, don't you think?" Ted became edgy and sharp again. Tom decided a reply wouldn't make relationships any better and buried any thought of a swift retort. Nonetheless, Ted grabbed the report from Tom and left.

The rest of the day left Ted exhausted. After consulting with Michael Davis, who hit the roof when he told him of the situation, Brussels instructed the Industrial Relations expert from the UK to be in Dublin in the morning. Ted was to calm things as much as he could and try get them back to work.

Ted worked flat out that day. He managed to convince the union to meet with him and hear their grievances—but only on the basis that the staff went back to work. He got agreement on the basis no pay was docked from any employee for the stoppage.

That evening, he presented the union with the slideshow given to management. It was met mostly with stunned silence and disbelief. He had to come clean on the number of staff reductions—as it was out in the open anyway. Of course, he thought to himself, no sign of our esteemed Project Manager from HQ when the shit was hitting the fan.

It was 6.30 p.m. when he eventually had time to glance at the file on Ulser. In the twilight, he read the references to Dalkey. The mention of Georgie caught him off guard. He felt he was a good reader of people. Georgie, associating with this kind of undesirable, surprised him...surely not? He saw the references to arson—arson wasn't unknown in Ulser's previous life. The more he read, the more things began to fit into place.

As he stood to leave at 7.45 p.m. the phone rang. His mother-in-law was on the other end.

"...It's Rebecca. She saw you on the 6 o'clock news

tonight...interviewers were pressing you on the television...I don't know what happened...she's just left in the ambulance...she collapsed and didn't come around...I think you better get down to Westport Hospital as soon as you can...."

'What is it with this so-called God we call on in times of desperation. He's the one creating this chaos. He's not only cracking me up but He's allowing it to destroy my family. Dad, if you are floating in the ether somewhere nearby, you mustn't be that well in with the Big Guy because I'm not seeing His helping hand.

'I think I know how Your Man on the Cross felt when He shouted *Why hast thou forsaken me?* You're not really there at all, are You? The whole Church institution is built on a con and shifting sands. Not that any of the other religions are much better. They all seem to bring misery. They're just big gangs and we all want to be members of gangs. They attract fanatics who take things to extremes. Celtic and Rangers—there's not a fan in their midst who is churchgoing or has read the New Testament while they take lumps out of one another for their *beliefs*. No understanding—just blind loyalty to a brand. Fanatics just want to be right and foist their poisonous views on everyone else. They move Heaven and Earth to prove everyone else wrong, killing and maiming in the process.

'Most wars I can think of exist because of one crowd saying to others that their version of God is the definitive one. They can't all be definitive, can they? Muslim against Hindu in India, Catholic against Protestant in Northern Ireland, Jew against Muslim in the West Bank and Gaza Strip, ISIS forming a Caliphate and murdering their own in Iraq and Syria for the privilege, Vatican Crusaders killing Muslims, The Inquisition torturing and killing those who dared have a thought or doubt about Catholic beliefs. If God was meant to be easily understood by children, why in God's name do we need theologians to tell us what to think? I thought the basis of all these religions was love of God and one another? I'm afraid I don't see any evidence of that. Quite the contrary, in fact.

'In addition, for all my praying and contacting the other side, I'm beginning to lose hope as well. Right now, I've lost my house, my family whom I rarely see, my wife who is severely ill, and I'm living a dog's life everyday'.

Ted's thoughts didn't give him any solace. The opposite in fact.

Ted didn't even know he had been on television. The enormity of it all got to him. The rain was beating down outside. The Gods were crying. Ted broke down into a flood of tears. The crying was in no way cathartic. He just felt the will to live seeping away. The tears weren't washing away the hurt or the loss.

-o-o-o-o-o-

Ted secured two weeks leave to be with his wife in the hospital in Westport. He was shocked when he arrived at the ward. She seemed to have lost a lot of weight. It showed particularly in her face. She had little weight to lose in the first place and now looked gaunt. She smiled weakly. Whilst Ted had told her about the house being burned down, he had been economical with the truth. He couldn't bring himself to tell her about more graffiti and that it was suspected arson or that he reckoned it was related to what was going on in his work.

When she asked what had happened to cause the fire, he white lied. He said that the fire officer believed it was an electrical fault. He felt she had enough to contend with without knowing all the detail. He wasn't sure if she was really believing him. He knew he was a poor liar—she'd told him often enough. It would only cause unnecessary stress.

Ted asked what happened her, how she was feeling, what the doctors and consultants had said, how soon before she'd likely be let out, how the kids were coping with being away from home and how the relationship between her, the kids, and her father and mother was working out. The kids were happy enough, but they were missing him as their Daddy. They asked where he was every night. They had been upset the nights he hadn't rung before bedtime.

Even though she was getting tired, she asked him about the pressure he must be under at work after seeing him on television. In addition, he now had all the issues with the house to deal with as well. How was he faring? Was he eating properly? Had he gone to the doctor to get advice on stress? Was he working too hard and doing long hours into the night? He white lied on every count. Eventually, Rebecca's eyes began to close. He kissed her gently on the forehead before making his way to the in-laws. He was looking forward to seeing the kids—but not his wife's parents.

He went back and forward to the hospital over the weekend. He brought the kids to a "fun factory" to give Beck's parents a break. He tried to relax in the in-laws' company at their home but was failing spectacularly. There were constant questions relating to the job, about which he didn't want to divulge anything. When he was with the kids and away from the house, he was on edge waiting for the next fall, the next bawling, the next nappy, the next kid to fall on top of them, etc. His head was spinning with everything going on at present; Ulser, strikes, insurance, claims, solicitors, etc. He had given his mobile number to Tom's PI so that he would keep him up to date on developments with Ulser—even though he was supposed to be on holidays.

On the first Monday morning in Clifden, the phone rang from the PI. He had pictures of Ulser (the PI kept referring to him as The Target—very MI5!) lifting heavy engine parts in his garage yard, pulling heavy chains to drag parts of engines around and various other mechanic activities, clearly indicating he was quite fit for work. Ted was pleased and anxious at the same time. He knew that he couldn't use the information easily—he'd have to catch him in the act. He wanted to move fast on that. He decided on the spur of the moment that he had to get back and arrange a sting with Tom and catch Ulser in the act of working.

He explained to the Bat-in-law, Maura, that something urgent had come up about the house and he needed to get to Dublin. Would she mind keeping an eye on the kids for the next few days? He got the steely stare he expected. He said he would call in by Westport hospital to see Becks along the way. He expected to be back in Westport on Tuesday night.

Becks was a more doped up version than the previous day. He got talking to a doctor who said that she had been highly agitated during the night, was having nightmares and thrashing about. They had made the decision to give her something to settle her down.

Ted tried to talk to her, but she was struggling to stay awake. He left a note to say he'd been. He asked a nurse to tell her he had been called back to Dublin, had visited and would return Tuesday night.

He got to Dublin about 12 p.m. where he had arranged to meet Tom at The Inn, at the top of Harold's Cross Park. You could park easy enough and they did a good sandwich. It wasn't a long trek to Dolphin's Barn from there.

"How's yer wife and kids doing? Surely you should be with your wife?...yer mad to be back here when yer supposed to be on a break?" Tom wasn't sure he ever heard Ted mentioning his wife's name.

"Fine. She just needs rest...." The answer was needlessly curt and defensive.

"Look, this cunt is acting the prick and I'm going to nail him. Devins has someone watching him all day. He'll let me know when to go in. We wait a street away until he gives the nod. We'll walk in and surprise him. He'll have no idea he's being watched—our PI has a great viewpoint and hasn't been rumbled in over a week. He has two or three people interchanging who are keeping him informed. I want to catch him when he's in full flow, working. He'll have no idea....I can't wait to see his face." Tom detected a peculiar and unpleasant sense of malevolence from Ted as he said it.

Ted tore at the sandwich wolfishly and slurped a large mouthful of tea. Tom was a bit unnerved.

"You sure this is the right thing to do, Ted?"

"You getddin' code feed Tom? ..." Ted snapped back through a mouthful of sandwich, a long dribble of tea running down his chin.

"Nooo...I'm not sayin' that, Ted...but this guy is a cold fish and cool as ice. He knows how to play the game...."

Ted reasoned that Jem, as a union official, was invested in the choreography and the rules of the game. Jem was only interested how he played his position, not the outcome of the game. Ulser and himself were invested in the game; how they played was irrelevant so long as they won. Ted was a winner. Ulser would be a loser.

"He haddent med domeone like me...." Ted gobbled menacingly through more sandwich. The dribble of tea was quite pronounced now, a small river dripping over the front of his shirt. He noticed and swore.

"Shid...tha'd jud been washed...." He swallowed hard and nearly choked. That started a fit of spluttering and coughing. The people at the next table looked over to see if the man with the now red face wasn't going to pass away in front of their eyes. Ted saw them looking, raised his hand and waved during his fit, to indicate he was going to be ok. There were tears coming from his eyes and Tom looked concerned.

"You ok? ..." Ted gave him a hard stare as he tried to regularise his breathing. Eventually he managed to say

"Fuckin' marvellous! ..."

-o-o-o-o-o-

They drove in the car in silence. Both had a sense of foreboding. Both were also determined to nail Ulser. Both felt they were entering a final act. The tension was palpable. Tom wanted to break the ice.

"I feel like a commando going into action...."

"What?...." Ted said irritably.

"Don't know why that entered my head just now?...just the tension of going into action I suppose."

Silence.

"Reminds me of the joke where the nuns got locked out of the convent after been out drinking? ..."

"What the fuck are you on? ..."

"...on a bender...Mother Superior had locked all the doors at 11....They decided to climb the ivy on the front of building to an open 1st floor window...."

More silence ...

"One nun says to the other 'I feel like a commando'....
Utter cold silence.

"...and the other says 'So do I...but where do you get one this hour of the night?'"

....

Silence. More silence...then an explosion of laughter—both of them. Despite himself, Ted had fallen into a fit of laughing.

"Ya stupid cunt ..."

This is the only response Ted could manage while gasping for air. He spat all over the windscreen. It was a welcome relief after recent events. He looked over at Tom and couldn't help but admire him for breaking the dark mood....

They pulled into a small cul-de-sac off Marrowbone Lane, Marrowbone Close. Dolphin Motor Repairs was only around the corner, yards from the entrance to the cul-de-sac. The two men fell into an agreeable silence and waited for the call.

Two girls in green uniforms from the local Loreto school passed by, heading to school after their lunch. A dog barked somewhere in the distance. The traffic on Marrowbone Lane hummed in front. They were hidden behind a flat-bed Bedford truck, with no view ahead. The phone rang after 20 minutes. Ted nodded and finished the call quickly.

"We're in. Good to go...." Ted's jaw was firmly set.

They walked the few yards to the main road, turned right, looked through the palisade fence and entered a sizeable premises where a large Nissen Hut type structure stood at the bottom of the yard, dominating everything. They could hear a car running and the sound of metal on metal. It wasn't possible to see inside the building.

In the yard lay two old jeeps, a blue Ford Transit Van, an old two-tone yellow and white VW camper van, a blue vintage Opel Ascona, a Ford Fiesta, a Ford Focus, and a dilapidated Fiat Bambino. Various bits of engines and assorted engine debris were strewn around the yard, some on timber pallets which were in various stages of decay.

They moved quickly to the source of the clanking. As they adjusted their eyes in the gloom of the garage itself, they could see two men in blue overalls carrying what looked like most of an engine towards a heavy wooden bench against the back wall. It was clear one of them was Ulser.

"Hard on that back of yours, Martin? ..." shouted Ted through the petrol fumes of the garage.

"Wha'...?" There was a response from Ulser but his

head didn't turn because he remained focused on what he was at.

"I'll be with ya in a minute...."

Ulser hadn't twigged who had entered the building. There was a heavy thud as the large item hit the bench. There followed two long releases of breath from the mechanics. Martin turned to face the new arrivals—now only feet away. His jaw dropped and his eyes flared.

"I was looking around for somewhere new to get my car serviced....Surprise, surprise...look who I find...."

Ulser didn't say anything. His face hardened.

"I always look around to see that the proprietor operates a very tight safety regime. I can see safety is a priority here alright. Takes care of his employees, you might say....Particular emphasis on manual handling, it seems. Very impressive in that regard! That's a particular pet hate of mine...and yours, as I recall...."

His voice was laced with heavy sarcasm and he could feel his blood boil as the hatred welled.

"I hate poor lighting, oil spills, unnecessary manual handling—I see you always use mechanical devices here, have an extremely tidy yard to avoid slips, trips, and falls....I see you're applying all those principles...." Ted continued with a heavy sardonic tone...caustic even.

"Fuck you! ..." was the best Ulser could muster. Ted knew he was closing the vice on Ulser and was taking great satisfaction from it.

"OOOh...don't think I'm taking any pleasure from this...." There was the deepest scorn and derision imbued in the tone.

"I'd suggest we need to have a talk about your 'accident' and the bouts of acute pain in your back that have rendered you a multiple paraplegic ever since—immobile, I'd dare suggest!...We need to revisit lots of things. You're to report to my Departure Lounge at 4 pm this evening...did I just say Departure Lounge out loud?...I meant My Office this evening at 4 p.m. to discuss your future with Eirtran. What an unfortunate word to use in your case—FUTURE? ..."

Ted harrumphed as he uttered the last word. There was still some sandwich catching in his throat since lunchtime. He laughed and looked at Tom—throwing his eyes to heaven in a "what a silly billy I am" type of way. He even managed to say "tsk" as he did so....

"Future—I meant your current predicament of course... which on reflection could turn into a future one, I suppose. Very, very careless...what a naughty boy!" Ted didn't care at this point that he was releasing some of the pent-up hate he felt towards his adversary. His voice sounded bitter and harsh. The battle was all but won.

Ulser was gathering his thoughts fast. He knew this wasn't the time to be a smart arse, but he was mystified.

"How the hell did you know...where I was? Who grassed? This is my own property, my own business—meaning it's none of yours...." He couldn't help himself. He was panicking but didn't want to show it.

"I'll get who grassed, don't you worry ..." He was saying without thinking—despite himself.

"Worry, my good man? I'm not worrying on your account. Don't you worry your own little head about me either...."

The pithiness was clear. Ulser took two steps forward, raised his arm to land a fist in Ted's smug face. His mate grabbed him in time. Ted looked down his nose at Ulser disdainfully, without as much as registering a flicker. Ulser's eyes were blazing. Ulser sensed the end game.

Ted turned away and beckoned Tom to follow.

"Don't forget...and I know you won't. 4 p.m. —today, my office...."

As the two men passed through the yard, two gulls were fighting over a discarded heel of bread. A larger gull was hovering overhead, squawking loudly. As the pair exited the yard, the third gull dive-bombed, squawking loudly, scattering his feathered friends and triumphantly flew away, stale bread hanging from his beak.

CHAPTER 23

Jimmy was not a happy camper. He'd just got a call from Ulser for a meeting with the management in the afternoon. Stupid twat had got himself caught—working while he was meant to be sick.

Jem was pontificating on the approach to the strike. He'd got wind of what was going to be in the exit package to grease the wheels around a smooth closure. Jem knew that, despite the fact that his colleagues and himself would soon be out of work, he needed to get the best deal possible for them all. His own days were numbered so, it was in his own interests to maximise the deal. He hadn't told anyone that the National office of his own union had approached him regarding a national role—a position he'd be happy to end his career with as a full-time union official. However, he needed to demonstrate his abilities to his new union bosses that he could manage this closure effectively for his colleagues.

As he put down the phone, a thought came to him. He smiled.

-o-o-o-o-o-

It was 4 o'clock. Tom and Ted were feeling good

going into this meeting. They had him. Caught with his hand in the till. The only issue now was the sentence.

On the dot of 4 o'clock, Jem strode confidently in with Martin Cullen in tow. Jem pulled up a seat and Ulser sat in beside. They both look somewhat smug, thought Tom. He knew they had an ace up their sleeve.

'What in God's name is going on?' thought Tom.

Ted opened the discussion.

"We all know why we're here...." Ted proceeded to go over the events earlier in the day. Jem or Ulser didn't interrupt for a full 15 minutes.

"In summary, Mr. Cullen has abused the privilege of sick leave, has disabused us of the notion that he has a bad back, is clearly working in another capacity while he should have been at work in Eirtran—dereliction of duty. There may be other issues, but I think that is enough to be getting on with.

"I intend to deal with Mr. Cullen in line with the procedures laid down. In the interim, it is my intention— as of now—to send Mr Cullen home on full pay. It is also my intention that this will be dealt with quickly. We will all re-assemble here tomorrow at 9 a.m. for the full hearing." Ted sat back the way a man does when he is totally satisfied that he has brought a difficult chess game to its end move.

"Mr. Black, I appreciate the seriousness of the issues you have put before us here. Mr Cullen is aware that he isn't in a very strong position. However, you do realise that Mr. Cullen has a sister who needs his full-time care and devotion? Every penny counts. He needs to work two jobs just to keep up with all the bills and pay for her care. You are also aware that there is a very serious backdrop to this case in that Eirtran is being ear-marked for closure. It is not a situation that bodes well for our futures here—indeed, for any of our staff. Brother Martin is in a position worse than most.

"As you know, the lads are concerned and worried and would view unilateral action against Martin before those talks conclude as precipitous and in bad faith. Brother Martin is one of us and we believe his recent actions need to be considered in the context of the overall future of Eirtran. We look forward to the meeting in the morning and would ask you reflect on any sanctions in light of what I've said. Thanks for your time."

With that, Jem rose and beckoned for Ulser to follow. The door closed and Ted looked at Tom.

"This is fucking war! There is no way he is going to weasel his way out of this one...." Tom noticed that a dribble was running down Ted's chin.

-o-o-o-o-o-

Ted read through Ulser's file that evening, highlighting issues that had gone before. He knew that he was within his rights to sack him. His HR people had confirmed it. He felt confident that he'd got his man, but Jem's calmness made him uneasy. He rung the hospital about Becks the minute he got out of work to see if there had been any change during the day. There hadn't been. He checked in with the in-laws by phone and spoke to the kids before bedtime. They wanted him home that night and missed Mammy.

Ted tossed and turned in bed and didn't sleep. He wanted a clear head to deal with this in the morning.

-o-o-o-o-o-

Ted was at his desk at 8.30 and reading through the points he had in highlighter pen. He constructed a few notes and was clear how the meeting was going to go. Tom arrived at 8.55.

"How do you want to play this Ted?"

"I have it covered Tom....I just need you as a witness...." As he said it, the phone rang with a Westport prefix. He knew it was the hospital.

"I need to take this Tom...when they come in, just say nothing. I'll be back in 5...."

Ted stood in a quiet spot near the stairwell.

"I'd suggest that you need to get back to Westport as quickly as possible, Mr Black....Rebecca deteriorated rapidly last night. We've also just discovered in a scan that she has an aneurysm...but it's where we can't operate. It has burst in the last hour and she is bleeding on the brain. We can't be sure, but we believe she may be in her last few hours...."

Ted went white, and into shock. He leaned against the wall for support.

"What do you mean—you don't think she's going to make it beyond today? ..." The blood was rushing from his head and draining to his feet. He felt weak and cold.

"This can't be right? ..." His head was spinning. "This is all very sudden...."

"I'm afraid that she's always had the weakness....Had she a shock or been highly stressed recently? It can trigger it...."

Ted was trying to take it all in.

"Yes...Yes...she has. Highly stressed...a lot has been going on in our lives...I'll get there in the next few hours." He cut off the call without as much as a polite 'thank you'. His mind started to race.

'...and the cause of all this is sitting the other side of the door....' he thought. He was fuming and incandescent with rage. 'Cool it, cool it....let's bury him.'

They were all in place when he walked back into the room. In his mind, this was going to be a 5-minute job and he was on the road with that bastard sorted. All the carefully prepared script was out the window. This was a revenge mission—retribution on Ulser, who had wreaked havoc on his beloved family and Rebecca.

"Good morning all", he said evenly, without meaning a word of it.

"I've considered all that has happened and have come to my decision. Martin Cullen—you are being sent home immediately on no pay with the likelihood that you will be relieved of your duties by the end of the week. This hasn't been an easy decision...." —it had— "but you have given me no other option...."

"Whoa, whoooo ..." Jem intervened. Tom knew something big was coming.

"Ted, with the greatest respect, I don't think you've considered anything I put forward yesterday evening in mitigation. Like all the staff, Martin is highly stressed by the current situation. An axe hovers over the head of every member of staff in this company. He is prone, as many of us are, to do something rash that he wouldn't consider in the normal course of events. I think Martin has been highly stressed recently—as indicated by the incident in the picker—and felt he wasn't being believed.

He certainly had hurt his back and it has yet to be proven definitively that it did not occur in the course of his work here. This is cart before the horse I believe...."

Ted was totally exasperated.

"Rash! Hasn't been proven beyond reasonable doubt?...doing something out of character—with the size of this personal file?...Are you for real? Are you out of your friggin' mind?"

He picked up the bulging brown file in front of him and flung it from above his head down into the centre of the table. Leaves of A4 paper went flying in every direction as it hit the bench with force. Even Ulser jumped back. For the first time since Ted arrived, Ulser was afraid of this lunatic.

"This IS his character...a complete waster...an arsehole. A delinquent. A shyster. A trouble-maker who has a turd for a brain!" Tom was getting concerned.

"Ted, that's uncalled for and is character assassination in my presence. The fact that you are negotiating the closure of this business, you cannot continue to do so if you are taken to slander fellow brethren in my presence. He is entitled to the rigour of due process and procedure...."

Ulser was sitting side-saddle, now smirking. He was enjoying how this was going. It was own goal after own goal by Ted.

Ted caught a glimpse of him gloating. It was too much. Ted reached across the table and grabbed Ulser by the neck with two hands. He looked at him eye to eye.

"You gloating toe-rag ..." and with that, nutted him straight on the bridge of his nose. There an explosion of blood and snot on Ted's collar.

Ulser fell back on the chair and crashed to the floor, Ted on top of him. Ulser was trying to get his first breath when Ted head-butted him again. There was a crack this time as Ulser's nose broke. Ted was now sitting astride him and hit him with two right-hand punches to the face. At this point, Tom and Jem moved to pull him off. The door from the corridor had opened and two of the girls next door were met with the spectacle of Ted wrestling with everyone on the floor. Ulser's face was black and blue.

"Jaysus—are you out of your mind Ted?" Tom looked astonished.

"Yeah—and it feels good." He stood up, shook himself down, stretched his arms above his head in front of the assembled throng and looked closely to see what damage he had inflicted to the body on the floor. He smiled, pulled back his right foot and landed a full force kick into the nether regions of Ulser's scrotum. Ulser groaned with the pain and threw up on the floor beside him. Ted bowed deeply with a flourish of his arm, as if finishing Act 1 of Hamlet, and left the room without as much as a 'by your leave' to those assembled. Ted's shirt was askew, two buttons missing and his chest showing.

-o-o-o-o-o-

Ted got a further call regarding Beck's deteriorating health 20 minutes into his car journey, when he was somewhere near Kilmainham Castle, heading west. Sometime later, near Longford, he got a second call. This one was from Brussels. His director was on the line.

"Ted, tell me what I just heard is not true? ..."

"What did you hear? ..." Ted wasn't in the humour for humouring his boss.

"That you attacked a member of staff in your office...."

"Attack—nooo, that's not true...." There was a long pause....

"No. I beat the living crap out of that shithead Martin Cullen that I'm hoping will get him hospitalised...." He smiled as he thought about it.

"For fuck's sake, that's totally off the Richter Scale, Ted. I didn't hire you to do that....You're fired."

"No—I'm not....I resign. And do you know what?...Go stick your job up your hole...to the limits of where the sun don't shine...." He found himself shouting at this point. He hung up.

CHAPTER 24

He arrived outside the ward in Westport around 1 o'clock. He was met by a nurse outside the door of Rebecca's room. She put a hand on his shoulder.

"I'm sorry, Mr Black. She's just passed 5 minutes ago...." Ted didn't hear the rest.

He pushed her aside and opened the door. Rebecca looked like she was sleeping. His in-laws were already there, one each side of their daughter's bed. Ted felt dizzy and the whole world went dark.

When he came to, he insisted going back to Rebecca's room. He sat by the bedside—as if expecting Rebecca would come back to life. He couldn't think of anything to say. His mind was numb. He wanted to say she looked beautiful out loud—had always looked beautiful—but the only thing in his thoughts was that that bastard Ulser had just killed the love of his life and was going to pay the price.

The next few days just passed. He had little or no memory of her laid out in the coffin at her mother's place in Clifden, the visitors arriving in droves, filing past, whispering words of comfort which were lost in space. It seemed like a dream. The only abiding memory was the flowers floating down the full six feet and hitting the coffin with a soft thud where she lay. He can remember Jason holding his hand asking him constantly where Mammy was. Jason only floated in his memory, held by the arms of his mother-in-law.

Ted never told his in-laws that he had lost his job. He needed space from them and the kids. He excused himself to go to Dublin to deal with some "issues". They told him to take as long as he needed, and they were happy to mind the kids in the interim. Ted promised to come back each weekend he was going to be away.

-o-o-o-o-o-

Ted was watching a match from a bar stool in the Tenters Bar. United were playing Burnley and it was scoreless. He had no interest, but the TV kept catching his eye in the corner. He had been drinking since 4.30 and already had a "skinful". At various points in the day, he had struck up conversations with some of the regular "all-dayers". One said there'd be a card game after the match—if he was interested.

Ted fancied himself at cards. In his younger days, he could hold his own in most poker schools around building sites in England. At the time, he was earning a few bob for college during the summer months. With 5 or 6 pints on him, he was really looking forward to it—in fact, he couldn't wait to have something to do for a few hours that would keep his brain occupied.

He got the nod from Rasher at the end of the bar, gathered his pint and jacket and made for the snug. Five lads sat around the table. Rasher introduced his new drinking buddy, Ted, to the coterie. Ted sat in with the group. They exchanged names and he gave a handshake to everyone.

Ted was sizing up each one as he gripped their hands. Eddie was built like a tank, about 6' 5" and a bit too eager to be your best buddy. Mouser was wiry and rough, with a scar across his left cheek. Razor was a "ringer" for Razor Ruddock of Liverpool football team—enough said. Minto was the elder lemon—in his seventies, the colour drained from his face—skin like paper—from years on the fags. Rasher had a beard and resembled Ronnie Drew.

"Nice to have a new addition to the group. Yar welcome—Ted? ..." Razor ventured. Ted nodded.

"Our mate, Nicko, decided to up sticks and head northside. His missus came from there. He eventually gave up listening to her rabbiting on about missing her Ma and friends...so he's done the deed and gone to Ballymun. We're glad to have a replacement so quickly....Anyway, the rules are Jacks to open, then Queens, Kings etc. Half the pot to raise. We play standard poker to start and later on, we move to more interesting games—Texas Hold'em, 7 Card Stud, Southern Cross, etc....Ok with that?...Everyone gets their chance to nominate their favourite...."

"Gotcha", said Ted.

"...Oh, and minimum stake is a pound....Elmo at the bar will call the last hand. There'll be a bit of food around 11 just to keep us going...after we've eaten the sambos it gets particularly interesting...."

Ted played conservatively for the first hour or so, never bluffing, just to get a feel of the player styles. They were all "handy" and he deduced Mouser was the most impulsive. If he got into a showdown with him, Ted could win the mind games easily.

By 11, it had gone to Aces and back to Jacks to open. A sizeable pot had built up. Ted had Kings and 10s. He passed on openers in the hope that one of the 3 remaining would open instead. Mouser called half the pot. When it came around to Ted, after a long pause, he raised half the pot again. The two beside looked at him hard before they folded.

Mouser looked steadily at Ted. He raised again. The next two folded...then back to Ted. "I'll see you...." said Ted.

Mouser threw down 2 cards. Ted reckoned he had trips at least. Ted threw down 1. Mouser picked his two new cards up, smiled or smirked—Ted wasn't sure which. Ted drew his own card—King. Full House.

Mouser was still smirking when he called half the pot. Ted drew breath—he's either pulled the fourth card for poker or he's bluffing. He could also have a Full House but unlikely that he's better than Kings. Ted goes with his gut.

"I'll raise—half the pot again...." He could feel the eyes of the poker school on him. Who's this upstart—is he a shark in the pool? Ted didn't blink. He looked Mouser straight in the eye. Mouser sneered as he called another raise. "Half the pot again....Have you the bottle?"

Ted didn't flinch. He had Mouser down as rash—someone who reckoned he had the edge on everyone. Let him believe it. He reckoned Mouser wouldn't back down in front of his mates—for fear of losing face. He'd keep it going and bluff all the way. He gauged Mouser would never fold under pressure. It was the biggest pot of the night by some distance.

"...and again. Half the pot ..." He saw Mouser raise his eyebrows.

"...yer bluffing...half again...and ye passed openers...."

There was an intake of breath from the rest and eyes back to Ted. Ted reasoned he was their guest, the "blow-in", and maybe time to call a halt. He didn't need to crucify the guy on his first night. He was enjoying the buzz and he wanted to be invited back for more. The more the risk, the more he felt alive. It counteracted how dead he felt inside.

"...I'll see you ..."

"Well, what you got?"

"You show me yours then I'll show you mine!" A guffaw from the rest.

Mouser threw down a full house of 9s and 10s and reached to pull the pot towards him.

"Ah...Aaa ..." Ted threw down a full house of Kings and puts a gentle hand over Mouser's, tapping it as a doctor would a bereaved relative. Mouser's smirk quickly disappeared. Rage blazed in his eyes. He looked around for support from his cronies, but none was forthcoming.

"Who the fuck are you when you're at home?...you passed on openers...how the fuck is anyone that lucky?...I'm watching you...."

Ted felt the ice-cold tension as he pulled the pot into him. His instinct was right. He wasn't surprised Mouser was a sore loser either. It sat with the rest of his character.

At that point, the shutter of the bar opened, and Elmo shouted "FOOD!" A platter of cocktail sausages was passed in with a large plate of sandwiches. It was a welcome break from proceedings. The food was eaten without words from either Ted or Mouser. The rest chatted away about football and a 10/1 winner at Chepstow that a mate of Eddie's had laid £100 each way on the previous Saturday.

The cards resumed after 15 minutes. It became clear that the big money was in the second half. Openers were slow to come by and the pots gained size very quickly. Time was flying but everyone was holding their own. No one was running away with it. Elmo called time on the last game; a Southern Cross hand called by Ted.

Openers had gone up and down twice before Razor opened on what was Jacks trips. Ted wasn't sure but he guessed Razor didn't have them. Razor was hoping to pull something in during the game. Only two others stayed—Ted and Mouser. This was THE pot of the night.

Razor raised. Ted and Mouser didn't raise and paid to see. Ted had two aces—nothing else.

First card turned on the Cross was an Ace. Razor raised again. Ted raised half the pot and Mouser raised again. Razor paid to see and so did Ted.

King on the cross with 3 to turn. Razor raised again— the pot was growing exponentially. Ted raised again and Mouser paid to see.

2 of hearts and two cards to go. Mouser raised half the pot and again Razor and Ted paid to see.

King with one card to go. Ted had a tiger in the tank with a card still to turn. Full house of Aces was unlikely to be beaten and still the possibility of a Poker of Aces remained. What's not to like?

Mouser raised straight away. Razor looked despondently at his cards and folded. All eyes now back on Ted. Elmo had opened the shutters of the snug to see what was going on and was joined by the other two barmen. You could feel the tension in the air.

"I could hardly be lucky twice in same night Mouser? ..." he mused. He was playing mind games. Mouser was unamused.

"Ye'll pay for the privilege...."

"You know, I just might do that...how about half the pot...."

"Is that a call?"

"I'd say it is...wouldn't you?"

Ted's Dutch courage was kicking in. What was he at? He wasn't earning after losing his job. 2 weeks wages on the table and he couldn't afford to lose. He hadn't been great sending money to Rebecca before she passed away and he'd been getting stick from the Witch-in-law.

'I can't afford to lose this. I'm in this deep, there is no way I will back out at this point. I have this git....' Ted thought.

"I'll see yours and raise half the pot...." In his head, he could hear Rebecca and others screaming at him not to go again but his dander was up....

"...Half the pot again ..." The words were out before Ted had thought them.

"You've got to be kiddin'...." Mouser was still stinging from the earlier hit.

"You're bluffin' or you're just plain stupid...half the pot again...."

Ted read that as 'I'm not giving in, no matter what....I'm not going to have a *blow-in* bust my credibility with my mates'. Ted knew this could go on and on—he'd have to be the one to call a halt. Ted also knew that however little he could afford it, this guy can probably afford it less.

"You got me....I'll see you—throw them down before we turn the last...and Razor, show us your openers...."

Razor turned his cards on the table. He had the bare three Jacks....Ted thought he saw a smirk from Razor as he turned them. He was lucky to pull in the third Jack. Ted turned to Mouser....

"...Well, let's see them Mouser"

Mouser threw his cards down triumphantly. A poker of Queens which looked unbeatable. A roar from the assembled throng.

"Beat that, Ted Kennedeeee ..." hissed Mouser. He looked around to his mates for approbation. He had a face made for gloating.

Ted threw down his two kings. There was an initial look of shock until they matched them with the cards on 4/5ths exposed cross. House of Aces and Kings.

"Woooo ..." The crowd seemed to draw breath as one. All on the River card.

"Razor—turn the last ..." barked Mouser. Razor reached in to reveal the final card. Ted was expectant while Mouser looked triumphant—it was a done deal in Mouser's head....

The crowd saw Ace of Hearts and an almighty roar raised the roof. Ted could barely believe it. Mouser was dumbstruck....

"Looks like lightning can strike twice Mouser—ouch!" Razor gave Mouser no sympathy. Mouser was incandescent. He reached across and grabbed Ted's collar with two hands....

"You fuckin' bollix! You're either cheatin' or you've sold your soul to the fuckin' devil....There's no way you can do that twice in one night within the rules." Ted expected the reaction and kept eye contact without wincing.

"Don't play the game if you can't take the heat....Are you always that friendly?" Ted's heart was racing but his eyes betrayed none of it. He looked through his opponent.

Mouser tightened his grip and Ted turned his head towards Minto.

"This is the initiation ceremony for all the new guys—right?" There was a smirk from one or two of the group.

Mouser tightened his grip and tried to lift Ted. Ted turned back to Mouser, put his forehead up against his and through gritted teeth said:

"The money on the table wouldn't pay for the dry cleaning of the collar of this shirt. Take your hands away...."

"...or what?"

"...or we'll play another hand and I'll fleece you all over again....I'll play snap to give you a fair chance!!"

The crowd burst into laughter and Mouser was deflated.

"All's fair in love and war....Thanks for the hug." Mouser sat back and let go of Ted. It had been a close shave.

Ted himself knew it was the drink nursing the bravado. However, he had diffused the tension and it was over.

"Barman, a drink for everyone...and PARTICULARLY for my good friend here, Mouser ESQUIRE...."

That night was the beginning of the End of his Old Life as Ted knew it.

The Barman opened up a small room at the back and the card players drank into the early hours. Eventually, Ted called it a night at 3 in the morning and left via a back door onto Mill Street. He was delighted with his winnings—a few hundred quid that he could really do with after all that had happened recently. In addition, he had left as King of the Castle after being able to buy a round or two in the pub and still be well in the black. It felt good.

He crossed the north end of Oscar Square heading for his new temporary home. He passed the gate at the corner of the park. Unusually, it hadn't been locked but it didn't register with Ted. He was crossing the road to the west side of the square when he heard someone running towards him from behind. He was turning his head to see who when something solid caught him on the back of the head. All went black.

-o-o-o-o-o-

Ted woke up in a hospital bed. Where—he had no idea. His head thumped with pain. The brightness of the lights hurt his eyes. He was wired to all sorts of machines and drips. He couldn't remember how he got there. He remembered the card game. He remembered the few pints afterwards. He remembered his winnings. He remembered Mouser being a bad loser. He vaguely remembered leaving the pub but not much after that.

Suddenly a man was towering over him and said:

"You've been in the wars, you know that? ..." It was a rhetorical question, not requiring an answer.

"You got a right crack across the back of your head.

258

Crowbar—or something similar—we reckon. It actually cracked the skull, but it doesn't look like it damaged anything inside. You're a lucky man—unlucky maybe...but it could have been far more serious."

"What hospital am I in...and how long am I here?"

"Tallaght—and this is your second day in. Somebody didn't like the look of you it seems. Were you in a fight?"

"God no...nothing like that. I was coming back after a few pints and someone took me from behind. That's all I know....When will I be allowed to leave?"

"That depends...I need a few details from you first. We had nothing to identify you when they brought you in. Could you give me your name and address for a start? ..."

"What do you mean? I had a wallet on me, car keys, a driving licence....You're kidding me?"

He thought about the 7 ton he had won that night. That was intended to keep him going for a while.

"My wallet was in my jacket. I remember distinctly putting it there. I'd had a good night on the cards, and I had 7 ton in the wallet....Where's my jacket? ..."

"I'm afraid you came here in just your shirt, jeans and shoes—that's it."

He started to think fast. I haven't a bean to my name; they've patched me up and they don't yet know who I am.

"Where are my clothes—I need to check that they didn't take everything from me....Could you get the nurse to bring them to me immediately? I need my phone in any event—to let someone know where I am so I can get picked up. They're probably out of their mind with worry."

He knew that it wasn't the case—but it sounded plausible.

"While you're doing that, you might show me the way to the bog and unhitch some of this paraphernalia to make yourself useful...."

"But I need some details off you first ..."

"First things first. I'm in need of ablutions and fast. Could you unhitch me and lead the way? ..."

The doctor felt he had no option but to comply. Ted pulled himself out of the bed, holding up his arms to allow appropriate disconnection. He pressed on the shoulder of his companion. The doctor assisted him while Ted shuffled slowly to the nearest WC. As soon as he was ensconced on the toilet seat, he told his helper he'd be ok from here. He left after Ted reassured him.

After 7 or 8 minutes, Ted was back at his bed. The curtain had been pulled around and his clothes were on top of the bedclothes. The shirt had a little blood stain at the back. Ted proceeded to dress as quickly as the pain allowed him to. In the course of tying the laces of his second shoe the curtain came back to reveal the face of an elderly, stern nurse.

"...and where do you think you going to, young man?...You're in no fit state to leave this hospital...."

Ted looked at her straight in the eye.

"I have a name you know....And it isn't Young Man ..."

"Well, young man ..." Nurse Diesel proceeded, obviously not used to being challenged, ignoring his interjection, "that's why I'm here—to get your details so I can address you in the proper manner...."

"So—you don't my name, where I live, or who my

next of kin are?"

"Ooh, indeed, not", she replied in a voice not unlike Maggie Smith playing Miss Jean Brodie. "That's what I'm hoping to ascer*tain*." She placed huge emphasis on TAIN.

"That's great. I can bugger off so and you've no idea who to bill...."

He took her face between his two hands, plonked a big kiss on her lips and headed for the door. He turned at the door and with a wave sang "That's the Way I like It" by KC and the Sunshine Band. He disappeared from view into the corridor and was gone in a flash....

CHAPTER 25

Ted was distracted for the next few days, trying to get his affairs back in order. He cancelled all bank cards, got his phone tracked and disconnected, visited his solicitor in relation to forms for the house, talked to the insurance company over the fire, etc. It kept his mind off all that had gone before.

His head hurt, but not to the extent that it prevented him sleeping. When all the activity died down and he was back living in Weaver Square, the deadness of everything hit him. With each passing day, the hole in his life that Rebecca filled grew and grew, and his hate for the person who had caused so much misery intensified rapidly. He wasn't going to drink or gamble again until he had his pound of flesh. A wicked plan began to formulate in his mind, and he mapped out the approach with squiggles and scribbles on an A4 page.

-o-o-o-o-o-

Ted, as he still officially lived in Dalkey, brought his wife's Mazda 626 down to Island Motors to sell it. He met Georgie and feigned surprise. Georgie had a look over it and thought it was in good nick. He told Ted that he wanted to buy it. Ted pointed out that a few things were wrong with it. The heater needed repair. The tracking was off. It needed a service. The boot lid wouldn't open properly—he had a temporary system in where a cord from the back seat pulled the lock on the boot. It needed a completely new locking mechanism, in his view.

They agreed a price. Ted had a conversation with Enda, Georgie's brother, so that the transaction would go officially through the books. Enda reckoned the work on the car would take three days.

Georgie and Ted talked about how things were going in Eirtran. Georgie had heard rumours that he had family problems and had since left. They got around to Ulser. It was clear that Georgie took to Ulser as a lion-tamer takes to tiddlywinks.

That bit of information was important to Ted. They shook on the car deal. Georgie said that he'd fix the car up in the garage before taking it home. He asked Ted to come back the following day with the logbook and he'd have the cheque. Ted finished the deal the following day and banked the cheque.

-o-o-o-o-o-

It was 2 a.m. as Ted quietly walked up the laneway into Island Motors. He was hopeful that the Mazda 626 that formerly belonged to his wife was still there. He knew that because of the restrictions on space, most of the cars were left outside. Ted lied to Georgie saying that he had lost the spare key for the Mazda. Right now, it was tucked in his pocket. Thankfully, things were as he expected. 4 cars were lined up against the wall. One was the Mazda.

He turned the lock and sat in. When he turned the ignition, it started immediately. Ted pulled onto Barnhill Road. He needed to get the car to the lock-up as soon as he could.

In the next week, Ted regularly visited the lock-up at the back of Thomas Street, where he was keeping the Mazda under wraps. Using his skill as a mechanical engineer, he designed a spring-loaded contraption behind the passenger seat, with a release mechanism controlled from the driver's seat. When pulled, the passenger seat shot forward. He had to buy several heavy truck springs from the knacker's yard at the end of Dunsink Lane to ensure one had exactly the right torsion for the job.

After giving the contraption a substantial greasing, the spring mechanism was working to a tee. He tried it out on a crash test dummy, made up of pillow covers and timber. The timber crunched each time the seat hit the dash. He turned off the passenger airbag for fear of setting it off with the impact.

He rooted around in the attic of the house in the Tenters and dug out a size 12 pair of boots owned by his uncle. Perfect. He bought a President Nixon mask in one of the Poundsaver shops in Liffey Street. He now had most of the paraphernalia he needed to carry out his plan...but there was a little further work to be done in preparation.

He had been walking regularly to get his strength back. Donned in a shell tracksuit and a Nike peaked cap, he looked like every other *get fit* nutter on the street. His route for a week took him to the Phoenix Park and through the back streets around Guinnesses. It also brought him past Dolphin Motor Repairs. He took time to observe when Ulser was there.

Sometimes he went for a walk twice a day. He observed Ulser in the yard regularly until 6.30 p.m. It was dark at this time of the year and he could observe Ulser at work in the lights of the yard.

He walked the Coombe and areas around Clogher Road. Some preparatory work was done on railings in the dead of night. His pre-war preparations were nearing completion.

He resurrected some of the syringes Rebecca used. He made up a small container full of a concoction which contained nitric acid and sealed it well. The time for revenge had come.

-o-o-o-o-o-

...How far from God was he now?

The rains stopped as quickly as they began. There was an ungodly silence all around them. Nixon could hear Ulser's heavy breathing and see each warm breath hanging on the cold air.

They walked in silence across an area that was being resurfaced and reseeded. Each step made an imprint on the ground. Two sets of footprints inexorably moving towards the River Styx. Nixon kicked Ulser at the back of the knee and he collapsed to the ground.

"Lie on your back and listen to what I have to say", Nixon said quietly. He stood over Ulser, gun pointed at his temple.

Ulser was startled to hear a Dublin accent. The voice was familiar, but he couldn't place it. He stared at Nixon, confused and frightened....

PENULTIMATE CHAPTER

...“You know who I am, and I know who you are. My life has been destroyed by you. I’m a dead man walking. You, very soon, are going to know what that feels like. Where you are now is where I‘ve been for the last year. Every bit of my life has been destroyed because of knowing you”, began Nixon.

“You haven’t just touched on my life—you’ve destroyed everything around it that I love as well. I’m now a nothing, just like you. I’m at the stage I don’t care, just like you. I have lost all sense of shame and guilt, just like you. I have no inhibitions, just like you. You are going to pay a heavy price for what you’ve done. You’re a self-serving low-life who is prepared to sell his mother to save his skin.”

“What the fuck are you on about, you mad fuck”, Ulser sneered. Even with the odds stacked against him, he managed to be obnoxious. He still couldn’t place the voice, but he knew it was familiar.

“A year ago, I was a happily married man with a wife and two kids, all of whom I loved”, continued Nixon. “We were trying for our third when I was offered the dream job. Company car, bigger salary, percentage bonus—all I ever dreamed of.”

"I'm bloody thrilled for you!" mocked Ulser. It nagged him that he still couldn't fit the voice.

"I took that job as a means of making my life better", he continued unperturbed. He kept the pistol firmly pointed at Ulser's head.

"I was made Distribution manager of a major Warehousing and Distribution outfit that was part of a group servicing Ireland, Britain, and Europe—I was on cloud nine.

"I still remember the excitement of that day. I danced around the kitchen with Rebecca—my two little boys were laughing at us. It was one of the happiest days of my life.

"We got a chance to move to a house we fancied in Dalkey. I would have the chance to fly around Europe. My life was on the up.

"The Warehouse Centre was based in Ringsend...where the old Dublin Glass Bottle Company used to be—I think you know it? Eirtran?"

With that, Nixon reached up and pulled off his mask to stare directly at Ulser.

"Jaysus!" Ulser gasped. "Ted Black."

"Yeah—a name you are always going to remember. Just to make sure you haven't forgotten, here's a reminder."

He unleashed a powerful kick straight at Ulser's temple. There was a dull thud on impact. Ulser groaned. Black then kneeled beside Ulser and put his face next to his.

"Next smart remark and I'll make sure that you'll never father any more bastards—you just listen up to what I have to say," he whispered.

Out of the corner of his eye, Black saw movement at the edge of the hill. A dark figure was coming towards him.

"Hey, wha's goin' on? Ye can't jus' kick the shoite oura someone like da—ye'll have me te answer for."

Somehow John Traynor, who Black had left in a drunken stupor in the *taxi*, had come around. Traynor now had Dutch courage and was rearing for a fight.

"Come on up and say that to me again", Black shouted.

Traynor did the hard-man's twitch of the shoulders on hearing the threat. He stuck his chin in and out in a single movement. He flexed his arms in typical Dublin *hard chaw* fashion. He let his arms hang by his sides and clenched and unclenched his fists as he prepared to go to battle. Black watched him advance. When he was close enough, Black raised the gun in Traynor's direction.

"Wrong guy to pick a fight with, shithead. I'm not in the mood. Sit down beside your mate and play dead."

"I didn't mean it, mate", Traynor bumbled. His slurred speech seemed to disappear instantly. He realised what he had walked into.

"I am having a heart to heart here with my mate—I am just providing him with a few tips on how not to upset people. Why don't you join us?"

John Traynor made his way slowly to the ground, eyes on the unmasked Nixon at all times.

"Now I'll go back where I was before I was so rudely interrupted. I arrived at Eirtran and within hours, I had trouble from you.

"You arrived in my office with your shop steward claiming that you had an accident in the racks. You claimed you were lifting something from the racks and did your back in. Amazingly, no one saw this accident. Not a single witness.

"You wanted me to sign the accident form. I refused. You gave me grief for the next few weeks and took a court case against Eirtran.

"I was determined not to let you crap all over us. You read me like a book. You just sat back, got a smart solicitor who looked for any gap in Safety Training, wrote plenty of smart letters and headed for the courts. You knew that the courts would always favour the small guy. You'd be happy to perjure yourself to get easy money. You were looking for blood money on the steps again— £30k.

"You know—and I know—that the accident never happened...yet you were angling for £30k. There was a lot said in that time. We met a lot. You were in my face— morning, noon, and night...oh, yes...extremely late at night. You remember, don't you?"

"Don't know what you're talking about", Ulser grunted.

Ulser felt a need to explain.

"I did my back in and was out of work...was on basic with no overtime. I needed that money for my sister...she's an invalid and lives with me. She needs help. She's a paraplegic—I'd do anything for her." He hoped that it might curry some favour.

"Oh, I know she's very ill—very well aware of it. But let's get back to the core of it." Ted's words hadn't a hint of sympathy. His tone was dismissive.

"Where's the mask gone—you're Nixon!", exclaimed Traynor. He was coming out of the alcoholic stupor and was experiencing a reality catch-up.

"Yea—and you're John Michael Traynor, gobshite from Templeogue. And if you ever even think about reporting any of this to your local Garda Station, I'll come after you, your wife, and kids. So just keep schtum while I enlighten you about what scum crawls this earth."

"Which of yous do you mean?" blurted Traynor, already regretting what he'd said before the final word. He tried to retrieve the situation by distracting Black.

"How do you know who I am?" he ventured.

"Intuition", replied Black, tapping the side of his head twice.

"You played the hero really well", said Black, turning again to face Ulser.

"You went on sick pay for weeks. You were having a ball while the company kept you on the payroll. But I was wise to you. I got someone to keep an eye on you—oh, a very good eye indeed. While you were out of work, it gave you a chance to work on your schemes.

"Amazin' how you were able—with a bad back—to take from the back of our trucks...even though you couldn't do any work. Oh, yeah, I got wind of some of your schemes.

"I never found out what you had on the drivers, but they were all co-operating. You always had to be on the make. Lets's hear about one of his get-rich-quick schemes", turning to Traynor for an audience.

"You and your gang knew stock-checks weren't as tight as they should be and only occurred at certain times of the year. You took advantage as usual. So long as you didn't take too much. We got it all on camera.

"The big fridges and freezers were full of packing.

Your cohorts stripped out the packing from the top. They replaced it with kettles, radios, anything small they could find. They resealed them so that security would suspect nothing on the loading bay. Worth a small fortune—each load.

"You then met the driver at an agreed rendezvous outside. All the small stuff was unpacked and the boxes re-sealed. We had no clue as there were no customer complaints. Then you met your middleman to sell off the small stuff. The secret was not to take too much.

"You got the lads to regularly place stuff in the wrong places on the racks during put-away. It became the norm. A stock check was always going to show up mismatches. The mismatches could always be explained by assuming an amount of stuff was placed in wrong locations.

"The Clerical staff were never rigorous enough and didn't want to be shown up. They concocted excuses for management instead of investigating further.

"You thrived on people's ineptitude. Everyone was on the make in the stores, but you were making more than most. You were the brains, and, because of that, the lads tolerated you even though they hated your guts."

"You can't prove any of it", Ulser declared.

"Oh, that doesn't worry me anymore—I'll be meting out my own kind of justice from here on", retorted Black.

"And then there was what you did to my family...and for that, you are going to pay the price." His voice sounded somewhat disconnected, a robotic delivery. It was as if he was regurgitating a script. There was no feeling in his words, and his voice was deadpan.

"I started to pursue you when you were on sick leave and out of work. Of course, being green in this area, I looked at what company procedures applied in such cases. Procedures...for the likes of you? What a joke.

"The unions had it sewn up. They defend any jackass, doing whatever he likes, so long as they can find ONE, and only ONE, part of the procedure that management hadn't correctly applied.

"I went by the book. I asked our Human Resources people to visit you and press you to come back to work. What a waste of time that was! You gave them the run-around...oh, fair play to you." Black waved the pistol.

"You played the system to the last. Appointments were made and broken. They, or we, would arrive—you were out. Couple of phone calls later, and you came up with some plausible excuse....'Had to go to hospital for pain-killers as the pain in me back got very bad that morning'...'had to bring my sister for medical attention'...'forgot to buy milk and went out and got caught in a traffic jam'....Jaysus, I have to say the excuses were legion! You're a wasted talent!"

"Must try some of those excuses if I don't surface tomorrow", chipped in the fast-recovering alcoholic, Traynor.

"Weeks passed and no sign of you attempting to return. I was hacked off trying to get you back. The HR people were as pissed with the system as I was. We had our suspicions as to what you were up to. I started to ramp up the pressure a little.

"I arrived on your doorstep one morning after setting a time and date. Same old story. Shithead here had disappeared again", he said, turning to Traynor for emphasis, waggling the pistol at Ulser.

"...but next time I arrived—unannounced, Dickhead

here didn't like it. He's not a pretty sight at any time. Be sure you haven't eaten beforehand when you see him in his Jocks. Here he was, poor soul, standing at the door in his Jocks, pretty pissed off at me. I pressed him on when he would come back to work. I gave him a date and time to see our company doctor.

"He was annoyed that I didn't accept the certs from his own patsy doctor. After two attempts, and multiple union meetings with the associated hassle and stress, I failed miserably to get him back to work. But Ulser's vendetta was never for me alone. He went for my family the day I started after him."

Ulser was silent.

"What happened?" ventured Traynor, who was now becoming engrossed in the eulogy.

"Mysterious, silent calls in the early hours of the morning. Lewd calls at home in the middle of the day to my wife. Rubbish bags strewn around the garden. Scratches on cars. We changed phone number...went ex-directory...but still the calls came. We couldn't pull up the caller ID.

"I had my suspicions when it began. It started to affect my wife's, and my own, health. With two small kids, we were getting precious little sleep. These stealth calls nightly didn't improve the situation. If we switched off the phone, things started happening outside the house. We were being slowly tortured, and I had a good idea by whom. But could I prove it?"

"Y'er wastin' yer time with de Polis", Traynor interjected. "They're bloody useless....I remember a time...."

"When I want a comment from you, I'll ask for it",

warned Black and Traynor duly stopped in full flow.

"My wife became extremely anxious and started to develop a phobia about going out. The calls would die down and just when things were settling, they'd start again. I was feeling stressed myself.

"This little bollix didn't like the idea of being brought back to work—and I use that word in its loosest form. He got at others to stir it up, even when he wasn't there.

"He came up with a notion that the way we operated the vans wasn't safe. He felt that it would be important to inform our Safety Rep through a colleague of this fact.

"This rep, of which Ulser was perfectly aware, was—and still is, unfortunately—a total gobshite. He took his duties as a Safety Rep very seriously...so I end up with a constant barrage of complaints about what this group of workers (I'm using the term loosely ...) would and wouldn't do because of so-called safety issues."

Traynor was now sitting up, hugging his knees, engrossed in the story.

"It resulted in a number of work stoppages. I spent more time trying to resolve disputes than running the business. Our friend here was stirring the pot constantly in the background. On top of it all, our revered international management team decided that they had all the answers on how to *improve productivity* in the middle of all this. They decided that to bring in an automated system and do away with the workers was a wonderful idea. With my experience of these *workers* in the last year, they may well have a case....

"There was war when the plans got out. The odd stoppage became a full-blown strike.

"I was to the pin of my collar to keep the business on

the road. I was working all hours of the day and night to keep our customers happy. I had to explain the stoppages to my own boss constantly. There were endless rounds with shop stewards. My manager in Europe formed his own opinion of my ability to manage.

"Way before this all happened, I had been finding it hard to sleep. My nerves were on edge and my blood pressure was up. I hadn't time to exercise and was putting on weight. I was having arguments at work and at home. My wife wanted me to give up the job. Strange happenings at home continued.

"He provided me with an ideal opportunity to get rid of him once and for all...or so I thought. I had a tipoff that he had stolen goods stashed away in his locker. I took a supervisor with me one day and we burst the locker open. We found a nice little collection—remember, Ulser?"

No reply from the sullen figure.

"Ulser had got careless. We found a nice little packet of coke.

"We called in the fuzz—my friend here didn't like it one little bit. **It was the worst move I ever made.**"

Ulser was beginning to panic as Black's rant started to become hysterical. There had entered a frantic energy into Ted's voice.

"Look, my sister is a paraplegic—I needed the money to help her get medical attention—hospital bills, drugs—I was in dire need of cash." Ulser was expert in trying to deflect. He had been in tight situations before.

"Oh yes, the caring brother", chided Black.

"Jaysus, that's a tough station", chipped in Traynor. "You've yer work cut out there. You can see why he did what he did?" he argued hopefully, turning to Black.

"Oh yeah, let's look at the paraplegic sister and go back a few years. You see, there was only himself and his sister in the family. However, a few years before, his family home was mysteriously burned to the ground. Arson suspected."

"How the fuck do you know that", Ulser demanded. Ignoring him, Ted continued.

"Might be intuition, but funny how my house went up in flames as well. You'd have easy access to petrol in that old garage of yours, Ulser? Anyway, before I was so rudely interrupted" —he buried a kick in Ulser's stomach for emphasis—"arson was suspected but never proven. Both his parents died in the fire. He was nineteen at the time.

"Ulser's da owned very little, but in Ulser's terms, at nineteen years of age, it seemed a lot. He and his sister would inherit whatever was going. But Ulser wanted it all—seemingly had a taste for expensive motors, as well as a few gambling debts. You like the gee-gees, Ulser?" Ulser didn't reply, winded after the kick to the stomach.

"Still have a few gambling debts, I hear—that right, Ulser? But getting back to the story—wasn't enough gravy in it for Ulser.

"His sister was a beautiful girl, by all accounts—not a paraplegic at the time...and she got half the inheritance, however small pittance it was. They were offered a Council house in lieu of the one burnt down...which they accepted.

"After a few weeks, there was dreadful accident to his sister in the new house. Fell down the stairs and was severely injured—*apparently.*

"Someone seemingly broke into the house when Ulser wasn't there, thrashed the place and did his sister in. She was severely beaten, thrown down the stairs and broke her neck. She was wheelchair bound after it. It seemed to the guards a severe attack—just for a few bits of jewellery and a watch. PITY YOU WEREN'T THERE TO DEFEND HER!", he shouted at Ulser. His neck was extended, his arms had gone back, and the veins stood out on his neck. His eyes bulged as he glared down on his adversary.

"And you've been minding her ever since", said Traynor. "That man has a heart of gold", he suggested to Black.

"Well, if you're suggesting that gold is a form of stone, I would agree with you. Where were you the night of that attack, Ulser?"

"I was in the local with a few mates. I had alibis."

"ALIBI—one only is what I hear....Oh yeah, I remember him. I wouldn't exactly call him an independent alibi—he was a bigger gobshite than you—owed you a few hundred quid. I'd say he was a kind of indebted alibi?

"You picked your night for the pub...it's not too far from the house as I remember it...you were in the pub alright, but not necessarily at the time of the attack.

"The pub was hoppin' because the World Cup match against Italy was on that night. Hard to prove whether you were or weren't there because of the crowd. The cops couldn't pin the time of the attack either because the alarm wasn't raised till you got home—maybe thought she might have been dead by then?"

"What are you suggesting?" said Ulser. "That's

bleedin' ridiculous."

"Oh, I know I can't prove it—but that doesn't mean I amn't right. In fact, I know I'm right. You broke into your own house to kill her. You wanted the full inheritance—her share as well. You got it alright—because she wouldn't say a word against you. Her parents were gone, and she needed you to mind her. You became her guardian and effective owner of her share. You got what you wanted. What you didn't bargain for was minding her.

"You couldn't risk getting her bumped off. People were talking about the arson and then the attack. They were putting two and two together....They were watching you. You knew you couldn't step any further out of line. All this bullshit about caring for her—all the medical bills are paid for by the state and home help comes in every day. You do feck-all to help her.

"This is the scum that I had as an employee."

Traynor said nothing. Ulser said nothing.

"...so, when I call in the pigs to investigate the cocaine in this scum-bag's locker, they were delighted, because he had history. They wanted to nail him."

"You can't prove that."

"In the following weeks, someone spray-painted slogans on the side of the house. My wife's health broke down completely and she was hospitalised. Didn't know me...didn't know her own name. She was already a diabetic on top of it all. I had to get the kids minded by their grandparents because I was a wreck. They missed their mam.

"Then Rebecca took seriously ill after a number of different shocks and events related to work and our home. Her parents took her under their wing. But ..." He slowed down at this stage. His eyes were moist. He lifted his head to the blackened skies above.

"I don't have her anymore", he said quietly. "A number of things happened both to her and me around the same time. It led to her being drugged up constantly to keep her calm. Then they discovered she had an inoperable aneurism on her brain. They asked me if she'd been highly stressed in the recent past—it can bring it on. She died soon after. I buried her and can barely remember it. She was my sanity in this world. Now I have no one." The air was still. A zephyr of cold wind blew past the three sodden figures.

"I really started to feel the pressure then, but I now had no one to confide in. I was on every known pill known to man—to keep my blood pressure down, to keep my nerves in check, to regulate my heart. I know my doctor on first name terms at this point; I have met him that many times.

"My performance on the job nosedived. Eventually, I lost it, told my boss to shove his job and resigned. It was the last day I worked.

"...so now I'm here to even up the score." Ted was relieved to have got that all off his chest. He felt drained.

Ulser didn't look up. This annoyed Black. He unleashed a kick straight into Ulser's scrotum once more. Ulser gasped and then puked. Black went down on one knee and put his face over Ulser's ear.

"This is payback time, fucker", he hissed. He lifted the pistol in Traynor's direction.

"I think it's time for you to split. You saw nothing and heard nothing. If I even *think* that you reported this to the police, what this little cunt did to me will be nothing to what I'll do to you. Believe me, I'm mad enough.

"So, what I suggest is that you walk away in that direction ..." —Black pointed in the direction from whence he came—"...and don't turn back or ever think about this night again. I have no argument with you."

Traynor didn't need a second invitation. He jumped to his feet and turned to go. He paused momentarily. He felt the need to say something to his newly made friends.

"Hope you can work things out between you", he ventured.

"Eff off", said Ulser.

"I guarantee I'll have it sorted to my satisfaction very soon", said Black ominously.

The silhouette of Traynor quickly retreated into the night. When he got to the edge of the pitch and down the hill, he broke into a run.

Black silently reached into his trousers and pulled out a long syringe with a needle attached. He had a cover over the needle. He pulled out a small container of liquid. He pulled out the plunger and filled the syringe to the limit with the liquid. He did it out of sight of Ulser's eye line.

"Now, you bastard, time to pay."

He turned around. He looked scornfully down on his hapless victim lying atop the mucky ground. He lifted his leg and brought his boot down on top of Ulser's head. He screamed in pain. Ted kept stomping on his head until the body beneath him passed out. He knelt beside Ulser and checked for a pulse. It was weak—but it was there. He took a small torch from his pocket, searched for the main carotid artery in Ulser's neck and drove the needle into it....

...Traynor was delighted to be free and was running as fast as he could when he heard the piercing scream.

"Oh, Christ—God help him." ...

...Ulser's violent contractions slowly died down and everything was still.

Black left the scene, running across the park towards Sundrive Road. His mind was in autopilot. He climbed over the railing and into the toilet block.

He pulled off the plastic sacking he was wearing, revealing a navy tracksuit underneath. He pulled off the size 12 site boots to reveal a pair of Nike size 8 trainers inside. The size of the imprints on the ground would put the guards off the scent, he reckoned. He pulled a Nike cap from the waistband of his tracksuit. He placed the mask, the plastic bags, the shoes, the tools, the syringe and the container in a plastic Dunnes bag.

He stood in the shadow of the toilet block, checking out Sundrive Road to ensure no one was within 100 yards. When it was clear, Ted Black walked out the entrance gate of the toilets. He put his head down and walked briskly, as if out for exercise.

He took in the warm smell of the "Capri" chipper across the road. It brought back memories of Gaelic football matches in the park as a kid and tucking into a 6d. single of chips afterwards on his way home. He walked on past Superquinn and towards what he always understood was Kimmage village. He had always been wrong—Kimmage is the KCR about a mile away.

The footpaths were wide at this point and cars were parked on the open expanse to avoid the clearway. The familiar smell of stale drink wafted from the Stoneboat

Pub. He had a craving for a pint to settle himself down.

He peered into the large bar and spotted a corner where it was quiet. The barman nodded at him and he ordered a pint of Smithwicks. It was good to be back to normal. Two middle-aged men sat at the bar watching the match on the TV. Arsenal was playing Blackburn in the Premier League on Sky. Thierry Henry had just scored, having skinned three Blackburn defenders. Both men were engrossed.

He placed himself silently in the corner. He could watch the match from where he was. He placed the bag under the table. The first mouthful tasted good. He took two long slugs and put the glass down. The foaming white head clung for its life to the side of the glass—just like a good pint should. Just like how that little bastard was clinging to his life not very far away. He watched the foam slowly slip down the side of the glass, oblivious to what was going on around him.

He finished the pint in three more gulps. He raised his hand to the barman and pointed to the empty glass for the same again. When the barman dropped down the second pint, he pulled the only "tenner" he had from his back pocket and paid for the drinks. It was a habit he always had. Even when he had no wallet, he always liked to have money on him—just in case.

He took his time on the second pint. He found it hard to concentrate on anything. The match was happening in front of him, but it passed him by. He felt cocooned from the world in which he was supposed to be present. He was very much alone.

He finished the second pint. He picked up his bag, checked under the table and left quickly. He strolled towards the traffic lights at the crossroads and onwards towards Mount Argus.

He passed the "Red Rice" Chinese take-away—the familiar smell of hot soya and Chinese cooking made his mouth water. He went inside and looked at the menu. He couldn't take it in and ordered a spring roll and chips out of habit. He ate them as he walked, finding it a bit awkward to eat whilst holding the Dunnes bag.

He couldn't fathom time—he watched the red taillights passing as if hypnotized. He chucked the papers of his finished meal over the railings into one of the gardens. This was something he would never do—his mind was totally distracted.

The orange streetlights reflected on the red-brick houses. He felt comfortable in the darkness. In the distance, he could see the light of the Spire from O'Connell Street...The Stiletto in the Ghetto...The Spire in the Mire...The Needle in Ulser's Neck....He could see Ulser's distorted face when he'd completed the final act of vengeance. For the first time, the realisation of what he had done began to hit him.

He crossed Grand Canal Bridge and felt queasy. He stumbled down the steep stone steps on the other side, turned into the dead-end beside the pub to the gates of the scrapyard. He put his hand to the wall and threw up. He wretched 6 or 7 times and felt weak at the knees. Not a soul passing above could see him below. He managed to prevent the bag being soiled.

He carried on past Leonards's Corner, past the Headline bar and the Asian shops and takeaways of Clanbrassil Street. This a street which had been dilapidated when he was a kid—now it was new, thriving, and bright. It felt alien to him. HE felt alien to him. What he had done was totally alien to him.

He walked blindly for some time. He arrived in Cow Parlour at the back of the Tenters. The familiar hoppy smells of Guinness's Brewery permeated his consciousness and jogged his mind into the present. He felt totally exhausted. He checked he still had the bag.

He wandered in the direction of the flats at the back of Weaver Square. He stopped at the front door of the small 2-up 2-down brick house, one of a group of four. The front door opened directly onto the footpath. The ground floor window had black railings fitted to prevent burglaries.

He slipped his hand through the letter box and found the string with the key attached. He pulled it out and opened the door.

He shared the house with another man who worked night shifts. The house was in darkness. He put on the light—one bare bulb in the hall—and climbed the stairs. He went through the open door of his bedroom and closed it quietly behind him.

He sat on the edge of the bed in total darkness and began to cry. The silent tears dropped from his eyes and hit the Dunnes bag, a little dull thud as each fell. The crying turned to sobbing, the single tears now a torrent. His soul was dying that night—he felt he had entered Hades much earlier than the Good Book indicated. He would carry this burden with him the rest of his life. Ulser would never leave him. They were conjoined at the hip forever more.

Early next morning, Ted Black took the Dunnes bag on his bike and cycled to the old tip at Dunsink Lane.

There was rubbish strewn everywhere—on the road, over the ditches, in the fields. The tip-head was due for closure, but Dubliners still abused their environment, fly-tipping with impunity. Ted threw his bike on the ground and pushed himself through a gap in the hedge.

He took a jam-jar full of petrol from the bag. He opened it and poured it over the contents. He stood back, lit a firelighter, and threw the firelighter on the bundle. It burst instantly into flames...flaming anger, flaming hatred, flames of Dante's Inferno.

The fire licked and spat, the flames rose and fell with the wind. The pungent odour of the burning rubber boots caught his throat. The black plume rose above the bushes. It went unnoticed in Dunsink—from where he stood, he could see three other plumes of acrid black smoke from burning tyres.

It reminded him of the grim pictures of burning oil-wells in Iraq in 1991. He remembered how he felt at that point—as if Armageddon was upon us. He felt that same feeling again. He stood entranced and sickened—he could see Ulser's distorted face in the flames. He could see the Fires of Hell.

-o-o-o-o-o-

The announcement over who exactly was being targeted in the forthcoming redundancies was delivered by Tom Hannigan.

There would be three tranches. Val was in the last tranche. As Safety Representative, he had been given a stay of execution. He was reasonably satisfied with the outcome. To him, it was recognition of his status. No one would make fun of him again. He would be taken seriously. Ulser, that bastard, had given him a hard time when he arrived first in Eirtran.

Val also lived in Kylemore Crescent—near Ulser—in Ballyfermot. He remembered standing watching Ulser's family home burn, liking the smell and knowing the satisfaction of getting his own back. He thought there was no one in the house at the time. There was no car out front. It was unfortunate his parents had died in the fire...but that's life.

And then there was that manager, Ted Black. Val hated him even more. With his fancy suits, his airs and graces, his flash car. And how he had made him feel embarrassed—correcting his English, making little of him. He was an important person. He had an important safety role. Who was Ted Black to make little of him? He knew he spooked Ted with the phone calls from the phone box near Ulser's place. Ted's wife was nice, though. He hadn't intended that she get hurt. Him and his fancy house in Dalkey! He made sure that this time no one was in the house. He had checked that the boss was away. He had checked front and back that there were no lights in the house when he threw the firebomb.

Now there was this new guy from Stockholm, Hans Larsson. He was taking their livelihood away. It was time he learnt the Irish way of doing things....

-o-o-o-o-o-

Ted felt the emptiness of his life—and it was vast. The love of his life was no longer there to help him and soothe him. He had carried out the most hideous atrocity

on another human being. He never thought that he was
capable of such savagery. He was drinking and gambling
again in the Tenters with his new mates. However, his
mind was in a dark space. Drinking helped dull the pain.
He was losing money at poker and Mouser had made
back multiples from him since the first night. The
Tenters was a local pub—but it wasn't open early enough
in the day for Ted to continue to drown his sorrows.

Three weeks after events in the park, Ted found
himself along the docks in the early houses. The
Ferryman on Sir John Rogerson's Quay was a favourite
but within a week he'd been barred after starting a fight.
It started when a docker started swearing at a referee on
TV for not giving a penalty to Liverpool. This guy was a
regular and probably wore what was an XXXL size
replica shirt—the shirt that ends up on the sales rack for
lack of demand. The colossus reminded Ted of a phrase
Terry Wogan was wont to use to describe Demis Roussos,
the supersized Greek singer; "The Singing Tent". Ted
hated Liverpool as a young man and backed the ref out
loud—"fair play, ref" —within earshot of the exceptionally
large docker. He was still arguing when the fist from the
6'4" cube of a docker sent him spinning through the
doors of the Cardiff Street entrance.

Ted wasn't bothering too much with hygiene either.
He already had an unkempt beard and looked like he was
homeless. He was unrecognisable from the man that only
months before was deemed "dapper" by his peers.

In between bouts of drinking, there were short stints
of sobriety. During these intervals, Ted fell into deep
stretches of remorse over the position he now found
himself in. In those intervals, he could be found sitting at

the back of either the Carmelite Church in Whitefriar Street, or its brother St. Joseph's on Berkeley Road, solely dependent on whether he'd been drinking north or south of the Liffey beforehand.

He preferred Whitefriar Street, with its two gold statues of Mary and Jesus (he supposed) at the entrance. Jesus could easy have been St. Valentine, whose relics are held in the vast chamber of the chapel. He wasn't bothered enough to find out—although when he did look at the statue of St. Valentine in the Church shrine once, he couldn't see any similarity with the one at the entrance.

For long periods, he'd quietly sit there as choral music on tape played through the speakers around the building. It was soothing, ethereal, heavenly, and gave him a level of solace. Sometimes a live choir—an obviously incredibly good one—practiced the songs of Thomas Tallis and some Gregorian Chant classics. The sound moved his soul and he thought of those he had loved and lost. Rebecca, his dad, his kids—whom he now couldn't bring himself to visit anymore—and friends he could no longer face.

He loved listening to doors opening and shutting in the background, cleaners banging and clattering on the alter, reverential devotees in the pews whispering prayers as beads were worked through fingers and the sounds intermingling, echoing as one piece of live theatre through the vast, cavernous space.

The flickering banks of candles in red glass soothed his eyes and his mind. He hated this institution of organised religion—religiosity, he called it—and loathed the fact that he was drawn to it at the same time.

Whenever there was a Mass, he'd always leave. The quiet time for reflection was broken by the drone of the familiar invocations of a man-made church. He didn't feel the need to follow a script to relate to the Elysian Fields beyond. It was an intrusion on his introspection. He was perfectly capable of engaging in his own way to do that. He didn't need a prescriptive set of words to invoke The Author of the Heavens supplied by self-satisfied priests with no worldly-wise experience. They had little, if anything, to offer.

At other times, when it was quiet in the church, he sat there reflecting on how he had plunged to the depths from such a height. The only human companionship he had these days were fellow travellers, whose only goal in life was to drink their peers under the table. They talked shite for Ireland and beyond. These inane conversations filled space and time, full of self-pity and "no-one really understands me", before going home to beat their partners senseless and leave the little ones hungry and afraid. He knew they were useless wankers—just like those he had set out to tackle in Eirtran.

Looking at himself now, maybe he should have made some allowance for past histories before taking everything on gung-ho in the job. Maybe those he managed didn't have the height to fall from. They couldn't even imagine those lofty perches—they were destined to be bottom feeders. Come to think of it, Ted was having difficulty seeing how he himself could ever climb out of his present predicament. He was facing despair and despondency and he couldn't envisage ever climbing from the sewers again. Is that how Ulser always felt? Why was Ted being in any way empathetic to the predicament of the person who brought him down to this level?...And yet...and yet...here he was, with nothing, seeing no future, not having income from any source, hand to mouth with no sense of a need to change.

He was under the radar, off all the systems he so cherished. He was underground. Systems meant nothing to him at this point. Was that how Ulser had felt? No! This was namby pamby, sandalista, ways of thinking. Feel sorry for Ulser? No way...and yet...and yet ...

-o-o-o-o-o-

Ted was wandering further afield for drink. He was one evening drinking in Hennessy's on Dorset Street. This was towards the end of a long "bender" of three days. He had stayed over in doss houses some of those nights because he hadn't the wherewithal to find his way back home—south side—to his lodgings.

At 3 a.m. this particular morning, he managed to make his way as far as O'Connell Street. He was staggering side to side as he walked. The few pedestrians who were about were giving him a wide berth. He wasn't 100% sure where he was headed—his homing instinct was bringing him southside.

He wandered off O'Connell Street into Middle Abbey Street so that he could find a suitable place to relieve himself. He knew he couldn't perform such an act on the city's main thoroughfare, no matter how inebriated. There must an alleyway somewhere. He wandered into unlit Bachelors' Way to do the necessary. He felt a bit queasy as well.

He disappeared down the alleyway about 20 yards.

Propped by one hand against the wall, he was in full flow when he heard shuffling behind him. Two drug addicts sharing a needle hadn't appreciated his arrival on their patch. They were as high as kites.

"Hey you!! Gis what money you go' unless you want bleeding Aids...." He had a needle pointing at Ted's back.

"Who d'ya think y'are?...pissing on our patch, ye bleeding nut job...."

"I want your effing money, you git", said Toe Rag 1.

"If ye want to live, put both your hands to the wall", added Toe Rag 2. Both had skin-head haircuts, and looked like they could do with a good steak and a few elocution lessons.

Ted, because he was in full flow and the fact that he wasn't processing their requests very well through an alcoholic haze, continued in flagrante, oblivious.

"Are ye fucking stupi' or wha'?" interceded Moron 1.

"Yeah—you deaf? ..." added Moron 2.

It was only then that Ted turned his head under his supporting arm to see the figures feet from him.

"Can't you see I'm fucking busy or are ye too stoned to notice?"

Not a clever comment in the circumstances and quite unhelpful considering the convivial atmosphere that had been developing. As reward, Moron 2 caught him hard with a punch just under the ribcage and Ted gasped, falling to his knees. He puked and wet himself as he bent double.

Before it registered with Ted what was happening, the toe-rags descended on him. He was on the ground now. Kicks rained in—to his head, his face, his ribs, and he recognised a strangely familiar metal smell. He'd been knifed in the right side of his chest and blood was oozing onto his hand.

He looked up to face his assailants and was rewarded with an almighty stomp on the head. That's the last he remembered.

FINAL CHAPTER

The helpers were bending over the homeless man, trying to revive him. An ambulance was blocking the lane. He was lying on the street in his own blood and vomit. He was cold and his face was the pallor of death. His eyes were open, but they seemed vacant.

"Can you remember what happened?", the nice lady in the red scarf said. The man just gawped with his mouth open.

"What's your name? ..." Still no response, slobber dribbling from his mouth, eyes rolling.

He heard people talking over him, around him, about a man whose head hurt. It was pounding, and he threw up on the nice lady's skirt and shoes.

"He's unresponsive—better get him to hospital", she said hurriedly, looking down disdainfully at her newly coloured shoes and dress.

-o-o-o-o-o-

It took a few weeks in hospital before the staff could get a word from him. He slowly began to regain his speech. The staff were trying to trace his family. They'd put a picture of the bearded homeless man on

"Crimeline" and in the papers in the hope someone might recognise him. No one did.

The man seemed to like cartoons and was fascinated by reruns of the Flintstones. His favourite was Fred Flintstone. When they eventually asked him had he managed to remember his name, he gave them the only one he knew—Fred.

-o-o-o-o-o-

Fred screamed in terror at the flames. His face was melting, and the heat was intense.

"Nurse, nurse ..." someone shouted in the ward. "It's happening again. He's havin' that dream."

"JESUS—Help me!" screamed Fred.

"It's ok, Fred—it's me, Nurse Gemma", a quiet but firm voice said, somewhere out there.

"You're just dreaming again. C'mon, just wake up and we'll do your medication—it always helps, doesn't it?"

She put a wet cloth to Fred's sweating brow. Gently, she tapped his cheek with the other hand.

"You ok, Fred?"

Fred started to come around and looked up at the kindly features of his carer.

"I am really afraid, Nurse—the bad dream was back—I must have done something really bad."

A sliver of spit rolled from the side of his mouth. It dribbled down the rough grey stubble where he hadn't been shaven for two days. He was quivering, as if with a fever—the sheets of his bed were wet with perspiration. He smelt of fear.

Nurse Gemma looked down at what seemed an old, thin man in front of her. His eyes were wild, yet vacant. He lived in a different world to that of the rest. He was on a different planet, poor soul, most of the time.

He had been found half-dead nearly five months ago—lying in a back lane off O'Connell Street having been beaten to a pulp. He was practically dead when someone from the Vincent De Paul on their rounds spotted him. He was rushed to St. Vincent's hospital straight away.

His heart stopped twice on the way to hospital, but the ambulance staff had resuscitated him each time. It was reckoned that the combination of heavy drinking and heart failure had caused brain damage.

When Fred was admitted to care in St. Catherines Nursing Home for the Sick, the only thing that Ted Black remembered was that he was called Fred.

The staff could not trace any relation of his. He was totally alone in the world. Nurse Gemma had seen it so many times. She only had to look around the ward.

"Fred, c'mon, take your pills and I'll bring you down to the Chapel. You can say a few prayers. That always helps."

"Yeah—that'd be nice. Can we sit there for a long while?" he said with childish helplessness.

"Course we can—I'll get the wheelchair."

With the help of a male orderly, Sister Gemma gently lifted the old man from his bed to the wheelchair. His pyjamas were a pale blue, stained. She placed a blanket across his knees. He looked up at Sister Gemma and gave her a big smile. She was always good to him.

She pushed him out past fellow tenants of the long grey ward. The building was old Victorian. The bottom sills of the tall, narrow windows came just above the height of the tubular steel bed frames. The result was that the room seemed gloomy, even on the brightest days. All one could see from a bed was acres of red-brick and sky.

The other inmates had the same scruffy stubble. It was a long time since anyone had a hair cut. The long grey hair of many of them stood wildly on their heads. Nurse Gemma felt she was managing a ward of 20 Father Jacks—"drink, girls, feck!"

Many of the patients were elderly, friendless, and toothless. They had no one to visit them. Many never had a visit—ever. It was easier for the nurses not to bother putting their teeth in each day. They looked like competitors in a face knurling competition.

Nurse Gemma and Fred turned into the old Victorian corridor that extended into the distance. The windows were set high on the walls. The sun cast shadows from the window frames of one side onto the opposite wall of the corridor. The small panes created a patterned shadow, much like a spider's web.

Fred never saw any of it. His head was bowed, as always, looking firmly at the Terrazzo floor that passed him by—that familiar grey and green Terrazzo that covered the floor of every old convent school in the country.

The ceiling was exceedingly high, maybe 20 feet above, from which lamp shades were suspended 10 feet from ceiling level. The whole place looked old and depressing. The dust had settled on the skirting boards and the place was last painted a pale yellow some 10 years previous.

The nurse pushed on through the doors of the large glass partition and reached the lift. You could see the inside of the lift-shaft through steel bars. When the lift arrived, she pulled back the skeletal steel frame—concertina fashion—until it locked against the post. She then pulled back the inner skeletal steel frame for the lift itself. Fred was familiar with the routine and she rolled him in. She closed each of the skeletal gates in turn before activating the lift. Fred's head remained bowed. He was mumbling. Nurse Gemma knew he was reciting the Rosary.

At ground level, she turned left, down past the statues of the Virgin Mary. Stern pictures of Matrons in days of yore stared down from the walls, most—if not all—nuns. Fred mumbled on, oblivious.

She turned into another corridor and opened the double doors at the end. The chapel was nearly full, and a service was taking place. A coffin adorned with two large wreaths and Mass cards was placed at the top of the aisle, sitting on a contraption to roll it in and out.

"Fred, we'll have to be quiet during Mass", she whispered. "We'll sit here near the back."

Fred nodded, understanding. Fred liked the Chapel best when quiet but also liked if Mass was being said.

"Why are there so many people here?" he whispered to Nurse Gemma.

"It's a funeral. A man died in the hospice two days ago."

Generally, it was easier to have deceased patients' Masses in the hospital, as the number of mourners attending was usually quite small.

Fred lifted his head when he finished his Rosary. He

started to observe those around him. He spotted a girl dressed in black who was sitting in a wheelchair at the front of the aisle. Her head was slightly to one side. Her head never moved.

"Who is that?" asked Fred.

"I was talking to one of the other nurses at lunch yesterday about it. She is the sister of the person that died. His name was Martin Cullen and he came from up around Ballyfermot. For some reason, he got the nickname 'Ulser'—I'm not sure where that came from. She was his only living relative—I don't know how she's going to manage without him.

"He brought her everywhere. To the pub, to the park, to matches in Croker—she loved watching Dublin play football. He was a gentleman.

"He worked every hour God gave him. He and his sister were as thick as thieves.

"She had a serious accident when she fell down the stairs at home and it affected her terribly.

"At some stage, Ulser got involved in some shady dealing. He was no angel, but the deal went wrong. It meant some others got stung when they felt they didn't get sufficient cut. These thugs reckoned they were owed money and went to Ulser's house.

"They battered down the door of the house. Then they went to work. She wouldn't tell them where Ulser was and they took it out on her. They eventually got hold of Ulser on his mobile and said that they would hurt his sister unless he got home quick. He arrived home too late.

"Whatever happened that night affected her greatly and left her unable to speak. The story went 'round that the guards couldn't pin the culprits.

"Ulser finally found out who did it. He got a few of his mates to turn the screws on these guys. However, the thugs didn't like Ulser's approach and came after him. They didn't like being threatened. Ulser had bitten off more than he could chew.

"It seems that one evening, one of these guys kidnapped him. I won't sicken you with the details of what the kidnapper did to him...injected him with an acid mixture, I believe...horrible! Suffice to say that Ulser never recovered and was brought in here to die."

There wasn't a flicker on Fred's face.

"However, there is a ray of hope in this entire story. Whatever way Ulser had it sorted, it seems he had a pile of money stashed away for his sister in case of a rainy day. With his death, he bequeathed enough money to her, so the story goes, to ensure she receives the best of treatment for the rest of her days." Nurse Gemma's eyes were moist as she finished.

"That's a very sad story but it has a nice ending. Why are people so bad to each other? She's lucky—she had a nice brother to mind her. What have I got?" asked Fred.

The priest droned on, then climbed to the little pulpit to say a few words. Fred had the feeling that the priest was talking to him.

"Martin was no angel. We all know that. Perhaps he didn't attend church as often as he might. However, to Mel, his sister, who is sitting in front of me, he was a saint.

"Mel and Martin had to deal with a lot in their short lives. They lost their parents in a fire some years ago. Martin, as the eldest, became the provider in the family at an age when most of his friends were out enjoying themselves...."

Fred was losing interest and looked around the small chapel and those in attendance. He was particularly interested in Mel, whom the priest had just mentioned. He could see the back of her head from where he sat. She sat in a wheelchair; her head slightly bowed towards her left shoulder. She wore a black veil on her hair.

The side of her face was visible to him. From where he sat, they were the classic features of a very beautiful girl—high cheekbones, a small pert nose, and a graceful neck. He felt sad for what she was going through. He knew sadness. It is not a nice place to be.

She was lucky because until now she had someone who cared for her. But soon she would have to face the zone he already inhabited. He was alone in the world with no-one to care for him. The past didn't exist. He just was. He didn't know whether he had brothers or sisters. He couldn't remember his parents. Did his parents even love him? Did he ever love anyone? There was just emptiness. The only person that cared for him was Nurse Gemma.

He felt no sorrow for Mel, but he understood that she might be sad. He knew about sadness. He didn't know how to be sorry because he had no relationship with anyone, and he knew of no one belonging to him who had ever died. He reckoned he would be sorry if Nurse Gemma was dead.

A shaft of light came through the window at the side of the church. It fell onto the coffin and seemed to illuminate it. It took everyone's eyes from the priest to the coffin. Fred imagined that God was taking Martin to heaven along the shaft of light. It was God's way of saying to Mel that He was taking care of her brother. God was rewarding Martin for taking care of Mel. Martin must have been a good man, thought Fred.

The smell of incense filled the small chapel. It caught Fred at the back of the throat. It smelt of burning and of fire. The fire at Martin's and Mel's house. He could see faces in the fire. Screams. Panic. He could see the faces melt in front of him. He could feel the heat. He tried to find the shaft of light. God, please send your light to me. But he couldn't see it. Only fire and darkness.

Fred began to gag. Nurse Gemma felt the restlessness beside her. Fred was staring into space, but it was obvious to Nurse Gemma that he was not seeing. Fred seemed to be having extreme difficulty breathing.

"God, where are you? Help me. Stop the flames", screamed Fred.

The crowd, including Mel, turned around to see Nurse Gemma grabbing Fred as he thrashed around in the back seat. Without warning, he collapsed in Nurse Gemma's arms. Nurse Gemma screamed for someone in the congregation to get a doctor to help.

Fred was gasping for breath, unable to utter a sound. Inside, he felt cold as the flames licked all around him. He thought of the shaft of light. All he could see was a tunnel of darkness. Fred knew this was what dying was like. But there was no friendly face coming to see him.

He started to say the Lord's Prayer but could not remember the words. He could see Ulser in the shaft of light close by and knew his face was familiar. The face from his past that he remembered was tough and cruel...but not now. The face he saw now was peaceful and calm.

He remembered now. Ulser—Martin Cullen, the man he left for dead in Sundrive Park. Ulser's hand reached out through the shaft of light into the darkness and flames and Ted reached to grasp it. Ted was moving away from Martin, who was obviously heaven bound. Their hands met. The cold left Fred instantly and light and warmth flooded in.

Hell is black and Heaven white. Only on Earth do shades of grey exist. The blue planet was fast disappearing behind Martin and Fred. Both had endured their Purgatory in life. They were redeemed in forgiveness. The true judgement is that of their Maker.

THE END

ABOUT ATMOSPHERE PRESS

Atmosphere Press is an independent, full-service publisher for excellent books in all genres and for all audiences. Learn more about what we do at atmospherepress.com.

We encourage you to check out some of Atmosphere's latest releases, which are available at Amazon.com and via order from your local bookstore:

This Side of Babylon, a novel by James Stoia
Within the Gray, a novel by Jenna Ashlyn
Where No Man Pursueth, a novel by Micheal E. Jimerson
Here's Waldo, a novel by Nick Olson
Tales of Little Egypt, a historical novel by James Gilbert
For a Better Life, a novel by Julia Reid Galosy
The Hidden Life, a novel by Robert Castle
Big Beasts, a novel by Patrick Scott
Alvarado, a novel by John W. Horton III
Nothing to Get Nostalgic About, a novel by Eddie Brophy
GROW: A Jack and Lake Creek Book, a novel by Chris S McGee
Home is Not This Body, a novel by Karahn Washington
Whose Mary Kate, a novel by Jane Leclere Doyle
Stuck and Drunk in Shadyside, a novel by M. Byerly
These Things Happen, a novel by Chris Caldwell

ABOUT THE AUTHOR

RJ Deeds was born in Dublin. He retired in 2019 after giving 40 years' service. He has accumulated vast experience in a wide range of management positions.

RJ, as a junior and middle manager, upheld the company's policies whilst negotiating with craft trade unions. During the same period, he was himself an elected Trade Union official. He was representing his junior/middle management colleagues on a range of issues in discussions with Senior Management.

Ultimately, he was promoted to the Senior Management cohort. As a Senior Human Resources Partner, he helped forge the strategic direction of Employee Relations in his company. Ulser is RJ's first foray into novel writing.

Lightning Source UK Ltd.
Milton Keynes UK
UKHW010832140121
376915UK00002B/42